ABSAROKA WAR CHIEF

BRYAN NEY

Based on the life of James Beckwourth,
b. 1798 d. 1866

Dedicated to my wife, Lisa, for her unwavering support and affection.

ACKNOWLEDGMENTS

James Beckwourth is considered prominently in the pantheon of his era by historians, but his name is virtually unknown to the general public. This is despite having left a detailed autobiography of his exploits in "The Life and Adventures of James P. Beckwourth." The reason for his relative obscurity can be guessed at, but regardless, I will consider it a great accomplishment if I raise awareness of this amazing man, as well as entertain my readers.

I would like to thank several people who have helped me in this endeavor. First, my long time beta readers, Toni Edwards and Andrew Shaner, for their valuable input reading and rereading progressive drafts. I would like to thank Sam Pisciota and Bill Gwaltney for reviewing an early draft and lending their expertise on Beckwourth and his era, and to Angie Thomas of The Museum of the Mountain Man for putting me in touch with them. Similar input from Glenn Laird helped flesh out aspects of firearms of the time. I would also like to thank my three developmental editors for their very valuable advice and encouragement: Bill Thompson, Sara Anne Fox, and Michael Ray Brown.

Readers who are intrigued by the history that underlies this fiction may want to refer to my notes at the end, which give an overview and chapter-by-chapter account.

"To what race do you belong – the white, black, or Indian?"

— QUESTION PUT TO JAMES P. BECKWOURTH BY THE MILITARY COMMISSION INVESTIGATING THE SAND CREEK MASSACRE OF CHEYENNE BY U.S ARMY TROOPS, MARCH 7, 1865

❧ I ❧

ST. LOUIS, 1824

James Beckwourth chugged uphill toward the master blacksmith's shop. He was late. Late for another day of wielding hammer and tongs, sweat stinging his eyes as it poured from his brow. His head throbbed and his stomach churned; a small price to pay for an evening of revelry with his beloved. He burst into the shop and slapped on his leather apron, glancing at his fellow apprentice.

"I hope she was worth it," said the other.

Beckwourth plucked a pair of tongs off the wall, but as he scanned for a hammer, he sensed a presence behind him.

George Casner thought of himself as a fair master to his apprentices. But with this one, his patience was wearing thin. "Beckwourth," he said, "what excuse do you have for me this time?"

"I think I will finish up these beaver traps today, sir," Beckwourth said, evading the question. Cinders crunched under his boots.

"You lazy bastard," said Casner.

"I am not," said Beckwourth.

"You lazy, half-naggur bastard," growled the smith.

Beckwourth stiffened and turned to face his boss.

"You may call me lazy, though I am not. But I will not stand the rest. Take it back."

"Oh, you won't stand it, eh?"

The other apprentice faded into the wall behind him as best he could.

"Take it back, or I will make you eat those words." Beckwourth tossed the tongs on the floor between them.

"Pick that up," said the smith.

"Take it back," said Beckwourth.

"Pick it up now."

"Go to hell."

Casner grabbed a hammer and threw it at Beckwourth. He ducked, and the hammer hit the wall behind him with thud.

"I'll call you what I want, when I want, boy," said Casner. "And you will do what I say, when I say."

Beckwourth felt his face flush. He scooped up the hammer and in the same motion fired it at Casner with all his might. Casner fell to the floor, and the hammer clattered into a bank of half-finished grappling hooks. He rose with a snarl and charged Beckwourth. Taller and wiry, the master smith grappled the younger man to the ground. Beckwourth twisted this way and that until he was able to free his right arm and land a powerful shot to the master's face. That stunned him and gave Beckwourth the opportunity to land a few more. Casner released him and sprang away.

"Beckwourth, I have tolerated you long enough in the name of your father. But this is it. You are fired," he snarled, wiping blood from his mouth, and cinders from his clothes.

"Suits me just fine," said Beckwourth. "I would sooner burn in hell than work for you another minute." He threw his apron at Casner and walked out of the shop.

A small crowd had gathered to watch the fracas through the gaping door. Beckwourth pushed past the disparaging looks of well-to-do merchants and the jeers of the ragged boatmen and roustabouts. He scooped water from a rain barrel, splashed it on his face, and ran downhill toward the ramshackle grog shops. A cluster of Indians, partially shaved heads protruding from their buffalo robes, regarded him with regal indifference. There was his boarding house, pinched between the grog shops. He burst through the doorway.

"Greetings and salutations, Mrs. LeFevre," Beckwourth said.

"Lord above, James, what happened?"

"Mr. Casner and I had a disagreement," he said. "I am no longer in his employ."

"My word! Your face!"

"Psh. He looks worse."

"That's not good either," the woman said, dabbing at his face with a cloth. "Not for the likes of you."

There was a knock at the door. LeFevre opened it. It was Casner.

"There he is," the smith said. "Evict that scoundrel, Mrs. LeFevre. I will no longer be paying his bills."

"My affairs are no longer of any concern to you, sir," Beckwourth replied. "I will pay my own way."

"Then you owe me for the unfinished time in your contract," said the smith. "You will pay for that."

"You may stuff that contract up your bung, sir, or if you prefer, I will gladly do it for you," said Beckwourth.

3

Casner's eyes widened, and he charged Beckwourth again, but he received such a beating that he retreated outside and stormed down the street, slurring curses through swollen lips.

"It is probably best now that I depart for my father's place, ma'am," said Beckwourth to LeFevre. "I will miss your cooking greatly, and our evenings of speaking French together."

"Go. And quickly," she said.

In his upstairs room, Beckwourth poured black powder into the muzzle of his pistol, then rammed in a wad and a lead ball. His few clothes went into a sack, on top of which he laid the rawhide pouch that held his papers. His precious, despised papers. The pistol went in his belt.

Beckwourth heard loud voices downstairs. It was Casner and another, and he had a notion who the other was. Mixed in with the swearing was that racial epithet. Twice in one day. The last time he had heard that had been a few years ago, from a schoolmate whom he had made swallow those words and spit a couple teeth. He nodded to himself and tossed the sack on his bed. Ear to the door, he drew his pistol.

"Beckwourth, it's Buzby," said the second man.

"Yes, Constable?" said Beckwourth.

"I would like a word with you."

"What about?" Beckwourth asked.

"You know what. Come on down."

Beckwourth kissed the coin that hung on a lanyard around his neck, the one possession he had from his mother, and then opened the door to his room. He pointed his pistol down the stairs at Buzby. "Come any closer and I will shoot you dead."

"Don't be a fool there, son," said a startled Buzby, backing up a step.

"Don't 'son' me."

"Careful, Beckwourth," said Casner. "You would hang for it."

"Just leave then. The both of you."

"All right then, let's cool down, Beckwourth," said Buzby as he backed away. "I'm leaving." He tossed his head towards the door, and the two slunk out.

Beckwourth followed them and watched as they two scurried away, mention of the sheriff wafting in their wake. He hustled upstairs to grab his things, thrust coins into LeFevre's palm, and was soon outside, headed out of town. But first, a hurried goodbye. The grog shop where his love worked was steps away. The bartender gave him a nod and motioned to a back room. There was Eliza, sound asleep. He shook her shoulder.

"My love," she said. "Your face! What happened?"

"I traded blows with Casner."

"Oh, James, why?"

"He called me a name I allow no man to use."

"You are such a hothead sometimes. I am proud of you for standing up for yourself. I am. But now what?"

"Well, I also held Buzby at gunpoint. So, I can't stay."

"You didn't."

"I did. So, I came to say goodbye, for now."

"No. Take me with you."

"Wouldn't be wise. Besides, I have a better plan for us."

"Us? What plan?"

Beckwourth grasped her darker hand in his. She entwined his fingers.

"I will seek my fortune trapping out West. Our fortune."

"Wait. How long would that be?"

"A year. Or so."

"A year or so!" She pulled her hand away.

"I know. I know. But think of it. I can come back wealthy."

"I love you. As you are. I don't want wealth. We could go to New Orleans."

"It will tear at me forever if I don't try."

"I don't know," she said.

The moment was right. He had given it some thought for weeks now.

"Eliza, dearest," he said, falling on a knee. "Marry me."

Eliza dabbed blood from Beckwourth's lip and kissed him gently.

"Go," she said. "I will wait."

"Is that a 'yes'?" he asked.

"Yes," she said. "That is a 'yes'."

2

Jennings Beckwourth winced as he shifted in his chair. "So now you come back home, hounds at your heels," he said.

"I won't be here long, Father."

The elder Beckwourth twisted in his chair again, trying to find a comfortable position. More than forty years ago, when he was barely more than his son's age, Jennings had taken bullets in his knee and his backside from the redcoats. Every movement now reminded him that he still retained those lead souvenirs.

"I paid for four years of schooling, and then got you that apprenticeship," said Jennings. "Now what? It's all going to be wasted?"

"Not wasted. But as you say, Father, the hounds are at my heels."

"So where will you go then? Eh? Downriver and hide in the Louisiana swamps?"

"No, sir. General Ashley…"

"Ashley? Ashley? Is he trying again after last year's disaster? And what makes you think he would take you on anyway?"

James stiffened, then took a breath. He needed

his father's help. "As you say, last year was a disaster, so maybe he can't afford to be too choosy."

"Dangerous work." Jennings shook his head. "Ashley stirred up the Arikara last year, so this year he is headed to Blackfoot country. They're worse. Damned dangerous."

"What about your sweetheart?" asked James' younger sister, Lou, pouring coffee.

"You mean my fiancé?" He gave her a sidelong smirk.

"Ooh," Lou squealed. "A wedding when you get back!"

"My congratulations," Jennings huffed. "Well, my boy is a man."

"I want a real start for us. Ashley is splitting whatever a man traps, 50/50."

"Half what you can trap in a whole season? More than just a good start."

"It is not without danger, I know."

"Well, you do come from a long line of military men."

"Back as far as the battle of Hasting in 1066; as you have told me a thousand times, Father. Two knights in my lineage, and your grandfather was a baronet."

"You have the combativeness, but you don't have the discipline, flying off the handle at every little thing like this."

Beckwourth gritted his teeth. "Nobody at the Battle of Hastings was called a half-naggur bastard."

"Ah, so that's what sparked your fury. That's not something you try to kill a man for. A white man, mind you."

"Didn't try to kill him, really. Otherwise, he would be dead."

"James, your temper," said Mathilda, his older sister.

"Yes, Mother." She had taken on their mother's role after her death, and he looked up to her so.

"You mock me," she said. "But I only want what is best for you."

There was a long pause. Jennings twisted his wedding ring.

"Oh, I know," said the old warrior. "I can't ever know what it is like for my mulatto children. Well, don't you ever forget, I was disowned for marrying your mother. Mind you that."

"You made sacrifices," said the younger Beckwourth.

"Try to imagine what your life would have been like if we had stayed in Virginia." He sighed and looked at the girls. "So, you are going to see Ashley?"

"Can't go back to St. Louis. Not anytime soon."

"Well, let's outfit you like a modern knight then. Take my best horse, my best rifle, and powder and lead enough for a year."

"I am grateful, Father."

"And take your papers, of course. And remember, there is always a copy with my lawyer."

His emancipation papers, the ones he had packed so carefully when he left LeFevre's. Beckwourth bristled at the very thought of them, of the day they had gone to court and had them drawn up. Of the way he was described in them as if he were a horse; enumerating his scars, describing the birthmark above his eye so that if there was a question of his identity, some white man could poke him and prod him to find hidden proofs of his identity.

"I won't need my goddamn papers in the mountains. All the more reason I'm going there."

. . .

Beckwourth swung a leg up onto his father's best horse. He took the reins from Quincy, his father's slave on the one hand, on the other his best playmate growing up.

"I spoke to father," Beckwourth said.

"I appreciate that, James," said Quincy.

"He will free you in his will. He promised me."

"I thank you for that, James. You know I do."

The family gathered outside the rustic but comfortable main house, smoke curling from the chimney. Beckwourth glanced at the slave's quarters attached to the stable and pondered what a huge difference the accident of birth made in a life. He surveyed the sorrowful faces of his sisters and studied the deep lines of his father's face.

"Do you remember the first time I took that old swayback on this trail?" James asked Jennings.

"I do," answered his father. "You were about nine."

"That day will forever be etched into my being. Fare thee well, one and all."

Beckwourth saluted his father and turned his horse to the trail. Coming to the edge of the clearing, to the stumps of trees he had felled as a boy, he turned to take one last look at his father's farm, his family, his home. He waved and set his horse at a trot. That first time on this trail, his heart had sung with pride, for father had entrusted him with a great responsibility for a lad of nine; a sack of corn to take to the mill. Halfway there lay the Jackson place, and he had looked forward to showing off for Amanda, the girl on whom he had a budding crush.

Here it was. The forest had reclaimed the Jackson homestead, but he could see it in his mind's eye as it had been that day. Beckwourth dismounted and picked a bouquet of wildflowers. He walked toward the ruins of the home, remembering the pungent smell of the smoldering log cabin. This was the spot. This was where he had first seen them: the lifeless bodies of eight children, an infant the youngest, the oldest fourteen, and their parents, strewn about where they had fallen, wounds fresh, blood pooling. A few steps now, and he was where he had found Amanda, her face turned toward him. A knot formed in his throat and his vision blurred. Only an inhuman being would kill such an innocent child. And only the most perverse savage would scalp her, would consider her soft blond hair a trophy to be flaunted, an emblem of pride and revenge. Fright and alarm had struck him so hard that day that he had no recollection of how he got home, no recall of what he did with the sack of corn. Mother, still alive then, had comforted him, while Father had quickly gathered men and pursued the Indians. These were backwoodsmen who had adopted many Indian ways. They knew how to track the enemy, and when they found them, they took no prisoners. Theirs was an Old Testament sense of justice. An eye for an eye, a tooth for a tooth. And a scalp for a scalp.

Beckwourth laid the flowers where he had found Amanda's crumpled body.

❈ 3 ❈

"I believe I am just the sort of fellow you are looking for, General, sir." Beckwourth leaned on his rifle, as if to emphasize his familiarity with it.

Mackinaw boats were being loaded for the expedition; open, shallow-drafting boats with a platform on the back. Ashley put his boot on a barrel, rested his elbow on his knee and examined Beckwourth.

"Could be. You look like a sturdy fellow." He had been appointed his rank in the War of 1812, and the title still stuck now after more than a decade of civilian life.

"I am good with a rifle, and a good tracker," said Beckwourth.

"I hear you near finished a blacksmithing apprenticeship. Tell me about that."

"I can shoe a horse or repair a beaver trap, if that is what you mean."

"I mean, how did that come to such an abrupt end?"

"I get along fine with everyone, as long as they don't abuse my good nature."

"Hm. Well, Beckwourth, I can use another pair

of hands on this little expedition. But make no mistake, I maintain military discipline."

"Yes, sir. Thank you, sir."

"Your duties will be hunting, blacksmithing, and chores around camp. Pay is three hundred dollars for the season."

"Pay, sir? I thought the pay was half the pelts we catch."

Ashley frowned. "That's not what I'm offering you."

Beckwourth flinched. The pay was trifling compared to half the take from pelts. "I can do twice the job of any other greenhorn you hire, sir."

"Let me be blunt then, Beckwourth. I know you," said Ashley. "Or I know of you. Pointed a gun at a white man."

Beckwourth was crestfallen but struggled not to show it. He quickly recalibrated his position. Ashley was much like his father; a patrician slave owner from Virginia. Such a man held nothing in higher regard this side of heaven than his own word.

"I can earn your trust, sir. If I sign on for pay, will you give me a chance to earn partnership?"

"You have your own horse?" Ashley asked.

"I have a good horse, sir. My own gun and my own ammunition."

"I make no promises. We leave Monday."

When Monday came, his horse was packed with a blanket and a few blacksmith tools. Across one shoulder was his powder horn, on the other was his 'possibles' kit: a leather case containing an awl for repairing leather clothing, flint, a handle-like steel bar for striking it to spark a fire, a pliers-like bullet mold, and a surgeon's lancet for removing bullets.

Then there was his shooting bag, which contained everything needed to load, fire, and clean his gun, including a hollow antler point that he knew from long practice would measure out just the right amount of gunpowder, and beeswax for wet days. On his saddle pommel hung a hatchet. In his belt was a knife, long enough to reach the heart of a bear, should he ever have the misfortune to need it for that purpose. On the other side of his belt went his pistol. There was little room for non-essentials, but tucked inside the 'possibles' kit was the waterproofed leather envelope that had previously held his papers. Now it held a thin volume from his father's library; a biography of ancient Greeks and Romans.

They followed on horseback as the boats were laboriously poled and roped up the Missouri River. The plan was to continue that way as far as Fort Atkinson, where they would head west along the Platte River for much of its length, ultimately heading north into the foothills and mountains. The territory beyond the headwaters of the Platte were largely unknown, but one of Ashley's men from the 1823 expedition was to meet them at Fort Atkinson after having traversed it from the opposite direction. It was risky, but the Arikara were aroused now and threatened traffic on the upper Missouri. Besides, the American Fur Company already had posts on the lower Missouri where they traded with the tribes. Ashley's plan was to avoid the expense of building a fortified post and instead have his men do the trapping, wandering from stream to stream. And to motivate them, he would split the profits with them. They would also rendezvous with the 1823 men who had remained and obtain their furs. Then, after the rendezvous, each man would decide if he wanted to head back to "the settlements" or continue their adventures, to rendezvous again the following year. Beckwourth planned to return to Eliza, rich or not, but better rich.

He swung up on his steed, rifle cradled in his arm, and kissed the coin that hung around his neck, minted in the year of his birth. Tucking it into his woolen shirt, he was off; one of twenty-nine of Ashley's men, on an exciting journey into the unknown.

At Fort Atkinson they unloaded the boats and enjoyed their last taste of whiskey for as long as they might be out. Bracken, the 1823 man, had arrived before them. All was going according to plan. Then one fair autumn day they pulled out, heading west along the Platte River. The next stop was to be an Osage village a couple weeks upstream, where they would trade iron goods and beads and such for horses.

They headed up the Platte. The river was spread out over hundreds of yards; dozens of interlaced streams separated by shifting sandbars, its brackish water supporting only stunted brush. Ashley had indeed scraped together a rough lot for this expedition. Only three had much experience in the mountains. One, "Black Harris" was a surly fellow of uncertain ethnicity. The second was Bracken, an energetic Irishman, who largely ignored Beckwourth. The third veteran was Caleb Greenwood, an intelligent fellow with a great sense of humor. Nights around the campfire Greenwood taught Beckwourth and the others sign language. He described how tribes that could not understand a word of each other's spoken language would 'listen' to sign for hours in total silence except for gasps of disbelief or laughter at a joke told only with deft hand motions. Beckwourth had a knack for languages, being already fluent in Spanish and French, and he picked up sign quickly.

Greenwood also taught them some words of the Crow tribe's language, and the ways of Indian maidens, for he had a Crow wife. "She took the disagreeable streak right out of me," he liked to say.

A greenhorn named Pappen was friendly. One evening around the fire, he asked Greenwood how he had come by his wife.

"Well, they just sort of come with the trapping business," Greenwood mused. "Just keep this in mind. If you are ever offered a gift by an Indian, take it. You refuse a gift at your own peril. And the bigger the gift, the greater the peril."

Greenwood figured out by Beckwourth's manner of speech that he had some education. When he learned that Beckwourth had packed a book, he inveigled a reading of it. Around the campfire one evening, Beckwourth read them a passage from Caesar's campaign against the Gallic tribes, complete with grand theatrical gestures.

"Tribes like Indians?" asked Bracken.

"They were barbarians, they say," said Beckwourth.

"I never heard of no Gaelic tribes," said Bracken. "Weren't no Irish Injuns."

"No, no, my good man," said Beckwourth, suppressing a smirk. "The Gauls were in France. And *they* were not Indians either."

Bracken looked daggers at Beckwourth. There was a tense silence.

"Anyhow," Greenwood offered, "Indians don't fight nothin' like that, pitched battles and all. Every Injun is out to prove his bravery first and kill you second. If he can touch you in battle with his coup stick while you still got breath in you, well, he will tell about that for the rest of his life."

The next morning, Bracken approached Beckwourth with his horse. "Here. Needs a new shoe," he said.

Beckwourth examined the hoof in question.

"The shoe is fine," he said.

"No, it's not. Change it."

Beckwourth sized up the man. "It's your eyesight needs fixing."

"You refusing?"

"What if I do?"

"I hear you pulled a gun on a white man."

"Your hearing is better than your eyesight."

"You pull a gun on me, Beckwourth, and you had best use it. You won't have any time to just wave it in the air."

"I will remember that."

"So, I want my horse back in half an hour with a new shoe. Right?"

Beckwourth lacked a good option. "Half hour. Sure."

"That's better," said Bracken. He leaned in. "You watch yourself, Beckwourth."

"I will. And you do the same."

They arrived at the Osage village, a collection of a couple hundred oblong huts of reed mats attached to wood frames, each large enough for an extended family of a dozen or so. Greenwood interpreted between Ashley and the chief by sign. Formalities and gift-giving took hours, but when Ashley came down to business, the chief indicated that he had no horses for trade. The Cheyenne had stolen theirs, it seemed, and had left them with barely enough for their own needs. Ashley invoked the name of the Great White Father in Washington, and intimated that producing horses would stand the tribe well in his eyes. The chief listened most intently, but to Ashley's dismay, all his wheedling and gifts produced only a few steeds of inferior quality.

They needed horses to carry pelts on the return trip. That evening, Ashley assembled all and presented his solution to this problem. The main body would proceed on the original route to a trading post run by a fellow named Ely. In the meantime, traveling light, Harris would travel on foot to a friendly Pawnee village to the south and trade for horses. He would then herd the horses to Ely's, but he would need help.

"Who wants to go with Harris?" Ashley asked.

There was a lot of grumbling and mumbling, but no volunteers.

Beckwourth saw his chance. "I'll do it," he said.

Ashley ignored him. "Nobody else?" he asked.

No takers.

"Harris, it's you and Beckwourth," said Ashley. "Pack out in the morning."

The next morning, Beckwourth packed corn, coffee, and sugar on his back; along with a blanket, rifle, and ammunition. He put his horse in the care of Greenwood.

"Bit of a risk you're taking," said Greenwood. "Gotta admire that."

"I have my reasons. Seemed the rest were quite reluctant."

"There's a rumor going around," said Greenwood. "Harris came back without his last partner. He travels fast, and it looks like he abandoned the poor fellow to his fate when he couldn't keep up."

"Thanks. I will not let that happen then."

They headed away from the Platte the next

morning, out into the broad emptiness of the Great Plains. At first, the novelty of it kept Beckwourth's step light as they plowed through the tall grass. But as the day wore on, the silence became numbing; not a bird twittered, nor an insect chirped; there were no leaves to rustle. Conversation was limited to terse commands on the part of Harris. By noon, the great silence of both his partner and the monotonous landscape had worn Beckwourth down.

"Where will we stay tonight?" he asked, mostly just to hear himself talk.

"See that speck?" Harris asked.

Beckwourth could barely make out a dark spot where the hazy sky met the unending plain.

"That there is a spring."

It took them the rest of the day to reach that speck; a small, wooded area that surrounded a spring. Harris went off to hunt turkey and assigned Beckwourth to gather firewood. It was a relief to get away from his surly partner. When he returned, Harris was plucking a bird.

"This should do for breakfast, too," Beckwourth said as he dumped his load.

No response from Harris.

"What do you have against me, anyway?" Beckwourth asked.

"You light-skinned naggur, with your high education. Sit around the fire and read 'bout dead white folk don't know nothin' 'bout Injuns."

Beckwourth restrained his temper. "Fine, you light-skinned...whatever you are. You know what your reputation is?"

"Don't know; care even less."

"They say you leave your partners at the side of the trail to die."

"Them what says so waren't there. As for you, all

you ever do is flap your big lips, and don't never come nothing of it."

"Here is some lip flapping you had best heed," said Beckwourth. "If you leave *me* by the side of the trail, and I have the strength to raise my rifle, I will drop you right then and there."

"Massa's bastard."

Beckwourth seethed. "All right, then," he said, rising to his full height. "Wrestle or fists?"

"Wrassle," said Harris, putting down the turkey.

"Wrestle it is, then," said Beckwourth.

The two stripped to the waist and circled each other, their breath visible still in the fading light. They ducked and feinted in turn, looking for an advantage. Beckwourth made the first move and tackled Harris at his waist, knocking him to the ground, raising dust with the impact. One gained the advantage, then the other as they twisted on the ground. They separated and circled one another again, panting. Harris tackled Beckwourth and knocked him to his knees. Beckwourth gathered his strength for one explosive motion and flipped Harris up, then down on the ground with his full weigh on top of him. Harris cried out in pain.

"I give," he gasped. Beckwourth's throw had landed Harris's flank on a rock. "Stop, stop. I give."

The next morning, Harris moved slowly, hiding his injury as best he could.

"Can you carry a full load?" Beckwourth asked.

Harris nodded.

Beckwourth wrapped some cooked turkey for later on the trail.

"Leave it," said Harris. "We need to travel light, and there's plenty more at the next spring."

They proceeded in silence, but it was a different silence than before. The bully had been challenged and lost. Still, Beckwourth cursed himself silently. So much for proving himself. What would Harris report to Ashley now?

Harris had miscalculated. There was no turkey at the next spring, nor any other game. Buffalo chips were plentiful, but no buffalo were to be seen; this was their spring range. The day following, the two came into a country that had been burned by a grass fire. All was gray as far as the eye could see. Barely was there an undulation to the flatness that far away blended with an empty sky. They rationed their supplies. The next day, again no game. Beckwourth was alarmed. He went to bed hungry, worried. It would have been a difficult journey regardless, but now Harris's injury slowed them down. The next day they came out of the burn area, but again there was no game. Still, there was hope. Harris was sure they would get to the Pawnee village the day following.

Harris was right. But to their great dismay, the village was deserted. The horses they had come for were forgotten. Finding food consumed their thoughts. With hunger gnawing in the pits of their stomachs, they desperately searched the earth for signs of the food caches that the Pawnee must surely have left for their eventual return but could find none. Starvation loomed.

"Them Indians left here only days ago," said Harris. "They was headed in the direction of Ely's post. Good news is, we can catch them in 3-4 days maybe, 'cuz they's travelling with their women and children. Bad news is, if we follow their trail, they will have hunted out all the game along the way."

"What about heading away from their trail for a ways?" Beckwourth asked.

"East is probably burned. West, the tribes ain't so friendly as the Pawnee and Osage." Harris was gaunt, and Beckwourth knew he looked much the same. "Besides," said Harris, "Ashley will meet the Pawnee and see we ain't with them. He will send a party after us. If we go off the trail, search party won't find us."

The next morning, they lightened their loads, discarding their blankets and anything else not essential. Beckwourth saw Harris grimace as he hoisted his load and winced himself in sympathy. They headed out, along the broad swath of the Pawnee trail. Though they held loaded guns at all times, they never saw so much as a sparrow to tempt their aim. That night they brewed coffee and carefully parsed out for use a quarter of their sugar.

They found no game the next day, and Harris slowed further. That afternoon, they came to a small creek, and Beckwourth decided he had to head off trail to hunt while he still was able, or they would die for sure. "You rest," he said to Harris, who had lost the strength to argue.

He headed upwind, so that whatever game he came upon would not scent him, using his rifle as a staff to steady his weakened frame. Fortune smiled on him, for he came upon an elk. Elated, he crept up on the animal, closer than he usually would have, as he did not trust his arm to steady the rifle. If he only wounded it, he would not have the strength to track it. The elk raised its head and looked in his direction. He squeezed the trigger. The elk bounded at the moment he fired, but then ran in a small circle, staggered and dropped to the ground.

Overjoyed, Beckwourth returned to Harris with the good news, and the two moved their camp to the carcass, just as the sun was setting. They built a fire and roasted strips of meat cut off the haunches. Unfortunately, the elk had been as hungry as they were, so its meat was tough, and it had such a rank taste from whatever it had found to subsist upon that they were afraid of getting sick from it. They left camp the next day somewhat invigorated, but they took none of the meat.

They did not find game the next day. Nor the next, nor the next. For five days they survived on just coffee and sugar. Hunger became their third companion, ever-present, gnawing, a weight on their every movement, haunting their every step. Beckwourth fought the intruding thought that death would be a release from his suffering. He concentrated on home and Eliza. He thought of the way she moved, of the taste of her kiss.

Harris began to stumble and his periods of rest between his feeble footsteps became longer and longer, and the distance traveled shorter and shorter. Finally, Harris collapsed.

"You have got to get up," said Beckwourth.

"Can't," said Harris. "You go on."

"How far is Ely's?"

"Too far."

"To rest is to die," said Beckwourth. "Come on! As far as we have come! You can make it!"

"Can't," said Harris. "You go, send help."

"I can't leave you. Listen! I took this trip to prove myself. I want Ashley to make me a partner, like you and the rest. You die and that's the end of that."

"Can't."

"Here, I'll carry you." Beckwourth lifted Harris and half supported him for a few shuffling steps. But Harris again stumbled.

"I been pissing blood since we wrassled," he said, and he started babbling incoherently.

"Stay here, then. I'll send help, just like you said."

He made sure Harris had his rifle and shooting bag in easy reach and pressed on.

Beckwourth forced one step one after another, making his goal a rock to sit on fifty yards distant. Attaining that, he set his next goal another fifty yards on.

"Wait!" came a pitiful cry from behind. "Don't leave me!"

Beckwourth waved, as if he was too far away to hear what Harris said, and continued on the trail.

Not a quarter mile up the trail, Beckwourth heard a rifle shot from ahead. Two Indians approached on horseback. He resigned himself to his fate, too weak to care. He sat down and watched them approach.

"You Harris?" asked one.

They had to be Pawnee sent back by Ashley. He waved toward Harris.

One Pawnee raced in the direction he had come, while the other pulled Beckwourth behind him and trotted to the delirious Harris. The first returned with several others. They fed the starving pair a corn meal gruel in tiny increments spaced over long intervals. Beckwourth took each spoonful gratefully. Backwoods lore taught that to feed a starving man a full meal is to finish him off. At length, Harris regained his senses and they both were strong enough to ride tandem, each clinging weakly to his rescuer. At the Pawnee camp they were again given small amounts of gruel, then forced into vigorous physical activity, running up and back until they were exhausted. They were then fed more gruel, then run some more. This was repeated multiple times, until finally their hosts sat them down in front of a large stew and invited them to eat all they wanted. Nothing on earth could have tasted as sublime.

Harris signed with their hosts as he ate. "Ashley is nearby," he said to Beckwourth. "Traded these Pawnee for horses enough it sounds like. Our new friends will take us there tomorrow."

The next morning, still too weak to ride alone, they rode tandem to Ashley's camp at Ely's. Their party was overjoyed to see them, and Ashley was generous with gifts to the Pawnee. Beckwourth signed thanks and friendship.

Ashley congratulated both men on surviving their ordeal and fed them a big meal. He took report from Harris, who was characteristically terse and spoke only of 'we.' When asked about his injury he made light of it. Ashley seemed to conclude that Harris was the hero of this adventure, and he showered the veteran with praise. Beckwourth was glad Harris hadn't disclosed the wrestling match, but he was angry that his efforts had been ignored. Greenwood saw this.

"At least he didn't leave you to the wolves," Greenwood said.

"I didn't give him the chance," said Beckwourth. "But I tell you, I've a mind to head back to St. Louis on my own."

"Can't blame you, feeling that way. You near died."

"It's not that."

"What then?"

"Doesn't look like I can earn partnership in this venture no matter what I do."

"Mm. All the credit did seem to go to Harris," said Greenwood. "A trek to St. Louis, though, that would be risky, even for an experienced man like me, let alone a tenderfoot like you." He sized up his friend's emaciated frame. "You could winter with your friends the Pawnee, and they could take you back to Fort Atkinson in the spring. Careful, though," he winked. "You spend an idle winter with the Pawnee, and you might end up a squaw man like me."

"Well, can't have that. I guess it's the mountains for me," said Beckwourth.

"Oh, now, don't you go to thinkin' you're better'n me, on account of me being an old squaw man." Greenwood nudged Beckwourth and laughed.

They might have paused longer at Ely's, but snow flurries reminded them of the season. Ashley wanted to get to the high desert before they might be trapped by winter snows at lower elevations. Resupplied and with horses enough, they continued up the Platte River. To their disappointment, though, game was still scarce. Here and there they shot some ducks that had straggled from the great migratory flocks, but if this was all they got, their corn and squash and flour would not get them through to spring. Ashley put them on short rations, though double portions for Harris and Beckwourth while they recovered. Morale was low. Around the fire at night, there were no jokes, no stories, no fun. Mornings were often silent.

One such sober morning, Ashley called the men together and presented a choice. They could butcher one of the horses and press on, dividing that horse's load amongst themselves. Or they could all fan out and hunt, even though there were no signs of game. It was decided to hunt. The men paired up.

"Pair up with me?" Greenwood asked Beckwourth.

"Thanks, but I'll go it alone."

"Aw, too good for an old squaw man?"

"It's not that," said Beckwourth.

Greenwood glanced at Harris. "Ah, of course."

He slapped Beckwourth on the back. "Go earn your reputation, Jim."

They were in foothills now, where the Platte behaves like a proper river and holds to one stream just thirty yards across. Along the wooded edge, Beckwourth picked his way through some underbrush. He came upon a pair of teal ducks paddling energetically. He was far enough from the others that he would be unable to signal anyone by gunshot. One teal paused, and with careful aim Beckwourth felled it. Elated, he set his rifle down and waded after it into the cold water. On return to the river's edge, he heard a low growl. A lean gray wolf bared its teeth not twenty yards away. Beckwourth drew his knife with one hand and with the teal in the other slowly made his way to his rifle, eyes on his adversary all the while. The wolf crouched and growled louder. Beckwourth was of no mind to let this wolf get the better of him. He set his knife and the bird down and reloaded his rifle, eying the wolf all the while. Hunger was forgotten. The moment his rifle was ready, he raised it to his shoulder, whereupon the wolf trotted off into the bush. Beckwourth lowered the rifle. No need to waste lead and powder on something he wasn't going to eat.

Beckwourth looked at the duck and felt his gnawing hunger return. Wet from the waist down, he shivered, and his teeth chattered. He had flint and steel for a fire. Apparently no one of his party had heard his shot or they would have investigated. Was he not in a more starved condition than any other man in the group? If this duck was divided amongst all, there would be hardly a morsel apiece. His stomach wrestled with his conscience, and his stomach won.

Beckwourth was soon sucking the last bits of

meat off the bird's bones. He felt greatly invigorated by the meal and restored by the fire, but where hunger had gnawed, now his conscience nagged. No one else in the entire expedition had a full stomach at this moment. He had to return to camp with larger game or die trying. Time was short, the night would be cold, and his reception would be colder still if the rest came across his fire and figured out what he had done. Pressing onward, he found a narrow deer trail through some rushes, and following that, he soon spotted a small doe. He was upwind of his prey, and for fear of it catching his scent, he quickly took a long shot. The doe fell, hit in the neck. Beckwourth rushed to it as fast as he could, worried that it might be just stunned from a flesh wound and bound off at any moment. Luckily, he had hit the animal in the spine, paralyzing it. His knife finished the job, but before butchering, he reloaded. Sure enough, there was soon a familiar growl behind him. He tensed, calculating from the sound where the wolf would likely be. Wheeling around in an instant, he fired, dropping the wolf. That felt good. He inspected the animal. Its ribs were near like a washboard. Not likely to be more game nearby if even the wolves were starving. No sign of any other wolves, but you never know, so with all the strength he could summon, Beckwourth placed the deer carcass in a tree fork. Exhausted and chilled to the bone, he headed back to camp. He should have been happy, but fatigue clung to him, and his conscience weighed heavily over the duck.

At camp, he was the hero of the day. They had all come up either empty-handed or with small game. That night, while the deer was being cooked, Beckwourth regaled all with his tale of the wolf and the deer, but nothing of the duck. Ashley took care that portions were equal but gave the choicest cuts to Beckwourth.

"Here, my good man," he said. "You deserve it."

Beckwourth fell silent. He took his portion from Ashley but could not take a bite. He hadn't lied to anyone, but he had not been completely honest either.

"I have a confession to make," he said. "Before I shot the deer, I shot a duck. Shot it and ate it," he said.

Bracken scowled. The others deferred to Ashley, who stared into the fire for a moment. "You're young," Ashley said. "But next time, put the duck in your belt and keep hunting."

There was an awkward silence.

"I swear by all that is sacred that for the rest of my life, I would starve to death rather than ever again behave so selfishly," said Beckwourth.

"I don't care what the hell you did to get us this feast," said Pappen. "I ain't had a full stomach like this since we left Fort Atkinson."

They broke camp the next morning and proceeded upriver. Rock outcroppings now hinted at mountains too far away to see. Whenever they stopped to hunt, Beckwourth bagged at least his share, always hunting alone, increasing his reputation day by day. It seemed that the episode with the teal was forgotten.

Bracken determined by landmarks that it was time to head north, so they moved away from the Platte, through hilly terrain dotted with stands of cedar and pine. Still, game was scarce. One day, snow began to fall just as they were about to start a hunt. Beckwourth protected the charge in his rifle with beeswax. Likely he would only be able to get off one shot without getting his powder wet. Harris stopped Beckwourth.

"Be careful out there today, Dan'l Boone." Harris said.

"Why?"

"I see signs of bear."

"Bear is good eating," said Beckwourth, his hand unconsciously going to the knife at his belt.

"You ever kill a bear?"

"No."

"How fast can you climb a tree?"

"Faster than a bear," said Beckwourth.

"Better," said Harris. "We need you."

"Your limp seems to have gone away," observed Beckwourth.

"Not pissing blood no more, either." Harris winked.

Beckwourth headed out, alone as always. The snow fell heavier and began to accumulate on the ground. Soon it would cover all tracks, so Beckwourth climbed a tree to reconnoiter. Some hundred yards off, he saw a huge, slow-moving, black beast. *Good eating*, he reminded himself. As he climbed down, the lowest branch snapped, and he slipped down the wet trunk. He crept closer to the beast. Stories of bear maulings tugged at his consciousness. It would be best to take a long shot. He found a boulder on which to steady his weapon and picked the beeswax out of the mechanism with a pin. He wiped snowmelt from his brow and hurriedly sighted the animal as best he could through the flurries. On exhale he squeezed the trigger. The gun bellowed, smoke billowed, and Beckwourth watched the beast stagger. But it did not fall, and instead it turned toward him. He rose slowly, squinting at the animal and wiped his eyes again. It was coming for him! He turned and ran for all he was worth to the tree. The first branch was now only a stub, and he wasted valuable seconds trying to climb the wet trunk. The crashing beast approached, and he fled. At a stream he slipped on a rock. He dared not waste time looking back; camp was close enough. Someone there might have a loaded gun.

"Bear!" he shouted, as he neared. "Bear! Bear!"

"Halloo there, Beckwourth," hailed General Ashley. "Bear, eh? Don't see one."

"It's wounded and likely dangerous, sir."

Ashley climbed a tree and scanned the horizon with his telescope. "Ah, there it is!" He smiled at the upturned faces of his men. "Dead now. I'm guessing, Beckwourth, that you have never seen a buffalo before."

Beckwourth's face fell. "No, sir. No, sir, I guess not."

The men snickered.

"Well, either you shot a buffalo, or you have felled the only bear in God's creation with horns."

The buffalo made an excellent meal, and the men proceeded in good cheer, ribbing Beckwourth about his eyesight and cautioning him to be careful not to mistake the horses for deer. Beckwourth laughed along and enjoyed the comradery.

Not many days later, Beckwourth's horse stepped in a gopher hole and shattered its leg. It was a hard thing to see such a faithful companion suffer and not be able to help. With great regret, Beckwourth shot his horse. The available replacements were all Indian ponies; smaller than the fine mount his father had given him, and with less stamina.

It was late winter now in the high desert, cold and hostile. Beckwourth was wracked by headaches due to the altitude and the dry air gave him nosebleeds. Buffalo robes they had obtained in trade from the Osage and Pawnee kept him warm on the frozen ground at night, but on horseback the chill penetrated. Beckwourth was not used to such cold. Other men had traded for buckskin clothes with the Osage and the Pawnee, but he had not, and he still wore his woolen clothes. The wind penetrated these, and he was miserable when it blew hard.

In this arid country, game was again scarce, and when the buffalo meat ran out the mood turned sour. This was more privation than the men had expected, especially the greenhorns. To make matters worse, every man now had to take a turn at night on guard duty to see that no horses were stolen, shivering and stomping to keep awake, for they were now in Blackfoot territory. Where they had suffered in silence before, now the men vented their frustration.

"My stomach is for heading back to St. Louis," said Pappen one night around the campfire.

"It would be far worse for us now to turn tail," said Bracken. "Snow's deep where we been."

"Don't really know how bad it is ahead," said another.

Ashley tried to rally them. "Men," he said, "where we are going, I guarantee you, the rivers and woods teem with beaver. The American Fur Company hasn't been within five hundred miles of where we are going, and the Indians don't care for beaver; they leave it alone. Think of it, men! If you return to St. Louis now you do so as paupers, guaranteed, if you even make it that far. But if we press on, later we return as kings."

Beckwourth cast Ashley a sullen glance. He had done more than his share for the expedition. The others might return kings, but not him. Ashley made note of that glance.

The next day, Ashley commanded Beckwourth to re-shoe his horse. This seemed to him an obvious show of power as again, the horse was in no great need of being reshod. He unpacked his tools with an annoyed flair and settled to the task. The horse was a magnificent animal, regal in bearing, like the general himself. Beckwourth reshod the first three hooves, and was working on the last, but he was a bit rough about it. The horse snorted and stamped again and again. Finally, it pulled away and reared up.

Beckwourth cursed under his breath. "So, you think I'm not good enough to shoe you, eh?" He pulled the horse into position again, and used the tactic of last resort in such work; striking the animal's flank with the side of his hammer. A torrent of swearing came from behind when he did. It was Ashley.

"How dare you abuse my horse?"

"Just doin' what you so generously *pay* me to do, sir." Beckwourth snarled.

"You Goddamn mulatto bastard," said Ashley. "This horse is worth ten of your kind."

Beckwourth rose from his task, hammer in hand. He looked at the hammer, felt its weight in his hand.

"My kind, eh? General, sir, I have served you with respect in all instances, and treated you as family. I volunteered for a mission where I nearly starved to death. As a huntsman, I have saved your whole expedition from starvation more than once." He pointed to the last hoof. "There is one more nail to drive, General, to finish this job, which you may drive yourself, or not, for I will see you dead before I will lift another finger to serve you." He threw the hammer at Ashley's feet.

Ashley stiffened. "You will pay for your insolence," he said with tight lips, and walked away.

The next morning, Bracken brought Beckwourth a horse.

"What is this?" asked Beckwourth.

"Ashley told me to tell you that this is your horse," said Bracken.

"I can't use this broken-down wretch," said Beckwourth.

"Sure you can," Bracken grinned.

Beckwourth accepted his punishment without further protest, and hurriedly packed his pathetic mount. This horse would certainly fall behind, and he could not afford a late start. He did what he could to lighten the animal's load by giving Greenwood some of his personal items, but a heavy burden remained, as Ashley had also designated him to carry a lead ingot for rifle balls. Beckwourth started with the rest of the party, but as the morning wore on, he fell more and more behind. Cognizant that he was a straggler in hostile Indian territory, he dismounted and walked alongside the horse, to lighten its load, carrying his rifle always at the ready. He was able to keep within shouting distance of the rest for most of the morning, but approaching noon his horse fell groaning under its burden. Beckwourth unpacked the panting animal and helped him up, then repacked and continued at a slower pace for another half mile. The horse began to froth at the mouth. Ahead, the others paused for a meal. Maybe, somehow after the break, the horse would be rested enough to finish the day. Or maybe Ashley would see Beckwourth's untenable position and relent. Again, the horse fell. Again, Beckwourth unpacked, helped the suffering animal up and repacked. He pulled the horse forward, but it went barely thirty yards this time before it fell again, whinnying pitifully. Swearing mightily, Beckwourth unpacked it again, hurrying as fast as he could. But it was no use. The horse could not even rise unpacked, and only lay panting and frothing on the ground. Beckwourth felt for the poor animal. He pulled his hammer from his pack and with a single blow to the skull killed it.

"Sorry, old boy," he said as he wiped away blood spatter. "I would rather have done that to Ashley."

"What's that you say?" General Ashley had approached unnoticed.

Beckwourth turned. "What I said I meant, whether you heard it or not."

"Damn you, naggur bastard!" Ashley drew his pistol and leveled it at Beckwourth, who grabbed his rifle and sighted the general between the eyes.

"General," Beckwourth said, "you have called me a name which I allow no man to use, and unless you retract that, it looks like one of us is a dead man."

Seconds seemed like minutes.

Ashley lowered his pistol. "I will acknowledge that it was language I should not have used," he said. "But I will make you suffer for this."

"No, you won't," said Beckwourth, lowering his weapon as well. "I am returning to St. Louis. Now. This moment."

"Are you mad? Alone?" the general huffed.

"Sooner that than to follow your white highness another yard." Beckwourth headed to the others.

"You get back here and help haul this load," said Ashley.

"I will do no such thing," said Beckwourth. "I am not your pack animal. Nor am I any longer in your employ."

Beckwourth marched toward the others, rifle in hand, leaving the general to load his own horse with the dead animal's burden. He caught up with the others mid-meal. Harris noted his blood-spattered appearance first.

"What happened, Beckwourth?" he asked.

"I am headed to St. Louis as of this moment, my friend," said Beckwourth.

"Long way to St. Louis."

Beckwourth stomped up to Greenwood.

"I need my things."

"Where is the general?" Greenwood asked in a low voice, gesturing to blood on Beckwourth's sleeve.

"The general is fine," said Beckwourth. "My horse is not."

The general arrived as Beckwourth was packing his belongings on another horse.

"So, you have not come to your senses, eh, Beckwourth?" the general asked.

"I assure you, sir, I am in full possession of my mental faculties."

"You have some of my ammunition. I will need that back," said Ashley.

Beckwourth slowly straightened up and turned to face the general. "Very well," he said. "As I have plenty of my own, you may have yours back. However, if I had none of my own, I would keep yours or die trying. You are a despicable human being, sir, to even think of turning out someone who has been as loyal as myself, out into the wilderness with no means of defending myself or hunting game." Beckwourth returned to packing his belongings.

Ashley called a conference with his veterans: Greenwood, Harris, and Bracken. "What do you boys say?" he asked.

"Let him go," said Bracken. "Don't seem to know his place, no how."

"We can't turn him out," said Greenwood. "Ain't right."

"It ain't right," echoed Harris.

"We ain't turning him out," said Bracken. "Pig-headed bastard prob'ly wouldn't stay no matter what we say."

"Greenwood," said the general, "do what you can to convince him to stay. Convince the pig-headed, thin-skinned bastard. Tell him I am a hothead like him and that I regret my words. Tell him I want him to stay, but that if he insists on going, to take anything he wants."

"Making him a partner would go a long way towards convincing him," said Greenwood.

Ashley screwed up his face for a moment and checked the reaction of the other two. "Fine," he said.

Greenwood approached Beckwourth. "Long way to St. Louis."

"You are the third person in the last ten minutes to point out to me that rather obvious fact."

"If you stay, you are a partner now."

"Ashley said that?"

Greenwood nodded.

Beckwourth paused, then continued to gather his things with renewed vigor.

"Too late," said Beckwourth. "My mind is made up."

The rest of the men had been watching this drama intently. There were some rumblings among them. Finally, Pappen spoke up. "General, sir, may I have a word with you?"

"Yes, man?" the general replied.

"Sir, I represent about half the men. We don't want Beckwourth to go. But if he does, we will go with him."

Ashley bristled, and Beckwourth paused his packing.

"Beckwourth," Pappen continued, "like I said, we want you to stay. If you stay, and anything like this happens again, you say the word and we will be off with you like a shot."

Ashley scanned the faces of his men. He knew that hesitation could be as bad as the wrong decision.

"I agree to those terms," said Ashley. "And since

you have quit my service, I am offering you partnership. What do you say, James?"

Beckwourth regarded Pappen with fresh eyes. "I will press on," he said, "with my partners."

Steaks were cut off the haunches of the poor pack horse, and a tough meal was had of it. They packed some meat and moved on.

Day by day they pressed on. Game was still scarce, and the wind was bone-chilling. Ashley took sick, and a lack of discipline followed. The sentry fell asleep one night, and before they knew what was happening, half their horses were stolen by Indians. Famished men now had to proceed on foot, carrying heavy loads meant for their horses. As they trudged onward, they encountered snow, thick crusted snow, slowing their every step. Beckwourth suffered more than most in his flimsy woolen clothes.

For a weakened Ashley, every step was an act of sheer willpower. As he slowed more and more, so did the entire party. He called the men around and gave an order to make him a shelter of snow and brush. This, he said, was as far as he would go until he had recovered, if indeed recovery was possible.

"You men go on," he said, "and return when you can." The gravity of their situation hung in the frosty air. "That's an order."

An order is an order, except that none of the men considered themselves soldiers. They discussed their predicament and decided instead to spread out for a hunt. If that failed, then yes, they would take that as an order.

As always, Beckwourth hunted alone. Over snow-covered rises flecked with sagebrush he trekked, hour after hour with no sign of game. He sighted a sandstone outcropping and climbed it for a better view. Far in the distance at a lower elevation, spring dawned. And on the green plain was a brown splotch. The splotch seemed to undulate. Elated, he raced back to the others.

"General," he said, "I have found us more of them horned bears."

They all looked at him quizzically.

"Buffalo!" said Beckwourth. "Buffalo, goddammit! A whole herd of 'em."

A cheer went up, and the men packed their horses with as much as they would bear and shouldered the rest. They raced onward. Only Beckwourth stayed with the general, intending to direct stragglers onward.

The snow dampened all sound, amplifying the awkward silence between the two men. At rest, the cold penetrated Beckwourth's very being, and he stamped about to keep warm.

"You have a girl back home?" the General asked.

"Yes," said Beckwourth. "I am engaged, in fact."

"I just got married, before we left," said Ashley.

"What is Mrs. Ashley's given name?"

"Eliza."

"Eliza! Eliza. That is the name of my fiancé as well."

Ashley averted his eyes, put off by Beckwourth's air of familiarity. "Don't mind dying here so much," he said, "but I hate to leave her a widow. Beautiful woman, and kind and sweet as any of her gender."

"We'll bring you a banquet of buffalo right quick and get you in shape to harass us for months to come," said Beckwourth.

Ashley shook his head. "I don't know what dying feels like," he said, "but if this isn't it, then I truly dread the actual thing."

Pappen returned with the last of the stragglers.

Ashley advised them of the good news and ordered them to follow the others.

Beckwourth thought better of their plan. "General, we have nothing to carry but our guns," he said.

"So much the better to catch up with the others," said Ashley.

"Yes, sir," said Beckwourth. "Or we could make a litter and haul you."

"Absolutely not," said Ashley. "The terrain is too rough, and you men are not at full strength yourselves. Come back for me tomorrow and bring me some delicious buffalo hump."

"As you yourself have said, general, there may be no tomorrow for you," said Beckwourth. "And even if that were not true, it will be much better for us all if we do not have to take the extra time to return for you, sir. We can take turns; two of us pulling you on a litter while the third man carries the guns."

"Do not be so pig-headed, Beckwourth."

"Pig-headed or not, sir, my conscience will not allow me to leave you here with our little confrontation so recent in my memory."

"Let your memory be eased by the fact that I have given you an order to leave me here."

"I would have thought that by now you might have come to the realization that I do not take orders well. Sir."

"Do I have to call you names again to get you to do the right thing? Damn it, man! Leave me here."

Beckwourth raised his voice in anger. "Sir, Mrs. Ashley sounds like a fine woman. I have to question her judgment for having married the likes of you, but the thought that my actions might contribute to such a woman becoming a widow dismays me no end. We are taking you with us, if I have to hog-tie you to do it."

The general had no more strength to argue. "Beckwourth," said he, "I am dismayed that you hold my wife's judgment in such contempt. I will consent to this, if only to have a chance to prove myself worthy of such loyalty."

The men constructed a litter from poles strapped together with leather strips cut from their clothing, and gently loaded Ashley on board. It was slow going to catch up with the others, but when they arrived, a hearty meal was ready, and they relished it greatly.

※　5　※

O nce their hunger was sated, the men explored
the area. On the edge of the lush plain was an
area of marshland laced with streams. It was spring-
time in beaver country! Their quarry was everywhere, at work building their huts and dams with the
willow and cottonwood that lined the streams. Beckwourth and the other greenhorns learned how to
trap from the veterans. A steel trap was chained to a
pole, which was driven into the streambed. The pole
was tilted over the trap, and a string tied to that, on
which was fastened a leaf. On the leaf was smeared
the bait; the oily product of the beaver's own castor
gland. It was simple work once one knew how, and
soon, Beckwourth gathered his fair share of pelts. At
day's end the pelts were stretched on willow hoops,
and each man made sure to carve his initials on his
own for later accounting. And beaver tail made a
great meal.

Dreams of riches once again lulled them to sleep.
But one night, Beckwourth fell asleep to such mus-
ings one night. He dreamt he was nine again, and
riding that gentle horse, carrying a sack of corn to
the mill. But next he knew, he came upon a heap of

bodies, mangled and scalped. But this time they were the bodies of his fellow trappers. He felt a hand on his shoulder and awoke with a gasp.

"Shh. I think I see Injuns," the man whispered. It was Pappen.

Beckwourth was instantly awake. "Did you tell the general?"

"He's too near the fire," said Pappen. "If they's Injuns, they'd see me wake him."

"All right, show me." Beckwourth crawled from under his buffalo robe noiselessly and followed Pappen to a boulder near the horses. He peered into the dark where Pappen pointed. He could see nothing but brush-covered terrain at first. Then, in his peripheral vision, movement. Beckwourth thought he could make out a human form, then another, and two more. He held up four fingers to Pappen, and the two stole back to where the others slept. Beckwourth gently roused two others and wordlessly bade them follow with their weapons. Back at the boulder, Beckwourth assigned each man a target by pointing.

"On the word 'now'," he whispered. He waited for each man to steady his muzzle-loader, then took aim himself. "Now!"

The blasts of four flintlocks were nearly simultaneous, and a flash of light momentarily lit up the landscape. The entire camp awoke, and soon all were at their sides, weapons in hand.

"What is it?" asked Ashley.

"Indians tried to steal the horses, sir," Beckwourth said.

"How many were there?"

"We saw four, sir."

"Next time, wake me."

Beckwourth bristled. "General, sir, if we had,

they might have seen us, with you so close to the fire."

"There's only one general on this expedition," said Ashley. "Next time, wake me. You saw four, but there is no telling the size of their main force, nor how far away."

No man slept the rest of that night, and every rifle was at the ready. At morning's first light, they searched the area. They found two bodies, and a blood-stained trail. Ashley called his veterans and Beckwourth over to examine the two bodies.

"We are supposed to be in Blackfoot territory," said Ashley.

"These are Crow, sir," said Greenwood. "See the long hair? It is like a challenge to other tribes, daring them to take their scalps."

"I thought your Crow were friendly," said Beckwourth.

"Even the friendlies will steal your horses," said Bracken. "It's just sport to them."

"Only four, you think?" Ashley asked.

"Don't see no other tracks," said Greenwood.

"If they were a large outfit, they would have dragged off their dead, so's we wouldn't scalp 'em," said Harris.

"Fortunate for us," said Ashley, "Bracken, show these greenhorns how to scalp proper. And Beckwourth, take that Injun's leggings. I am tired of watching you shiver."

Beckwourth was tired of shivering more than the general was tired of watching. He took the leggings off the stiff corpse and put them on. There was no use leaving them to be torn up by the wolves.

Bracken held up a scalp. "Which of you shot this one?" he asked.

"Me," said Beckwourth.

"First scalp for this little expedition," Bracken said as he tossed the bloody trophy to Beckwourth. "You might make a mountaineer yet."

Beckwourth pondered the bloody trophy for a moment with a sourness in the pit of his stomach. He remembered Amanda, lying where he had found her that day. His first impulse was to throw the thing away, but he reconsidered. *This horse thief was the sort that might have scalped her.* He rolled it up and packed it under his saddle. Pappen had the honor of the second scalp. It turned out that the other two men Beckwourth had recruited had had buckshot in their guns and could at worst have only maimed their targets. Now those two Crow were doubtless well on their way back to their people or were there already.

It was time to move on anyway. Ashley had recovered enough, and the beaver were trapped out. The streams they trapped drained south and west, but their rendezvous was north, so they packed up and headed back to the high desert. Hyper-vigilant for signs of Indians, they crossed the edge of that, heading north toward distant, snow-capped mountains. The plain became a broad valley, and they found a stream to follow. Soon they were traipsing through lush meadows fringed with aspen and dotted with lakes. Day by day the snowy peaks grew closer, and the dark rim below the snow was distinguishable as lush pine forests. Game was plentiful, there was grass for their horses, and wildflowers to please the eye. And in these meadows were more beaver. Ashley divided the men into groups of four to spread out and trap. Beckwourth was surprised and flattered that Ashley offered him the lead of one group, but he refused, professing lack of experience. Really though, it was that Bracken was to be in his group, and there was no way that he could see Bracken taking direction from himself. The groups headed out, with an appointed date to return.

They trapped plenty, and Beckwourth took care to avoid conflict with Bracken. When they returned, he counted himself a wealthy man by the number of pelts in his possession. Now it was on to the rendezvous with the 1823 men. From there, home to Eliza and his kin, home to a warm bed and a full stomach all the time, a man of some means.

Beckwourth was cinching a pack load one morning when he heard the cry, "Indians!" Quickly turning in the direction of the shout, he saw a large force of warriors galloping toward them. Weapons in hand, they whooped and yipped. Beckwourth and the rest went for their guns and awaited the word from their general.

"What do you think, Harris?" the general asked. "Is it for show or are they attacking?"

"They snuck up," said Harris. "They's out for scalps."

"This is it, boys," Ashley shouted. "My apologies to you all, but let us sell our lives dearly! Rifles first, then pistols." He took aim with a steady hand. "No one fire until I fire."

The charging Indians showed no sign of letting up. "General, don't fire," Greenwood said. "They are Crow." But the din of the approaching horde drowned him out.

The lead Indians were within rifle range, still at full gallop. Some warriors leapt from their horses to the ground and bounced back up, others clung to the necks of their steeds on the opposite side so that they were barely visible. Beckwourth shouldered his rifle and looked anxiously back and forth between Greenwood and Ashley, not knowing what to think.

"General!" Greenwood shouted again, "Do not

47

shoot! It's for show!" He dropped his gun and stepped forward, raising his hand in friendship.

At the same moment, Ashley pulled the trigger. His rifle clicked. A misfire! He pulled his pistol from his belt, but as he sighted his target, he saw Greenwood moving forward. The Crow split into two lines and circled Ashley's men, then regrouped before them. Greenwood signed friendship again while he called to the General, "Sir, I think you did not hear me. These are Crow, friends of the whites."

"Odd way to show it," said the general.

The Crow chief was evident from his regal demeanor and his long war bonnet. Greenwood signed to him and indicated Ashley as his counterpart.

Beckwourth examined the Crow. They were a fearsome lot, no two alike in their red, black, and white war paint. Their horses were painted as well, though these were of a more whimsical nature — a circle around an eye, stripes, handprints, and so forth. Beckwourth found himself close to Harris.

"What do we do now?" Beckwourth asked.

"Mostly we hope Greenwood knows what he is doing."

Ashley and the chief sat cross-legged across from each other on buffalo robes, Ashley mirroring the chief's steady gaze, his noble manner. Greenwood repeated everything that was said by the chief, loud enough for all the men to hear, and signed Ashley's words to the Crow. The Crow chief inquired as to Ashley's success at hunting and trapping, asking for all sorts of details. He inquired of their starting point and perked up at mention of St. Louis.

"He asks if the great red-haired chief still has his lodge in St. Louis," said Greenwood.

"Ah, yes, Clark of the Lewis and Clark expedition," replied Ashley, "Does he know the red-haired chief?"

"He says, 'Yes, we gave him safe passage through our lands, twenty winters ago'," Greenwood quoted the chief.

"Tell him," Ashley said, "that Chief Clark made his mark on a paper giving us permission for this expedition."

The chief smiled at this and asked through Greenwood, "Do you have this paper with you? I want to see the mark of my friend, the red-haired chief."

"If I had known that I might meet a friend of Chief Clark on this journey, I would have brought this paper," said Ashley, "but no, I do not have it with me."

"That is a shame," said the chief, "for he taught me to make my mark on paper. Come, let us share a smoke." He produced a pipe, and Ashley supplied tobacco.

Greenwood called out the chief's next question. "He asks if we have come upon any Blackfeet. General, I think the Crow we shot must have been his warriors."

Ashley paused. "Tell him that when we were in Blackfoot territory, we shot two Blackfeet."

The chief responded jovially, and Greenwood translated. "'You are still in Blackfoot territory. Where are their scalps?' he asks. 'I wish to bring these scalps to my people so they may dance over the scalps of our enemy'." In the next breath Greenwood said, "I will tell him we did not scalp them."

Greenwood translated the chief's scornful reply. "He thinks that very strange, that we would not take their scalps. Beckwourth, bury those scalps so they don't find them."

"Do as he says," Ashley said evenly, without looking away from the chief. "All you men finish packing, so's to give him cover."

Beckwourth did as directed, slowly, deliberately, while Ashley and the chief parleyed, collecting Pappen's trophy as well. He slunk off to the nearby river and buried both scalps in the sand, and also, reluctantly buried his leggings, the ones from the dead Crow. On his return, the parley was winding down.

"The chief says this is dangerous territory for white men," said Greenwood. "The Blackfeet are nearby always, a tribe with an unquenchable hatred for the white man. He invites his new friend, Chief Ashley, and his warriors to the Crow camp."

"All right," said Ashley. "Mount up, men. This could work to our favor."

But just then a Crow brave confronted his chief, holding two sand-flecked scalps. The chief listened impassively as this brave harangued him. The brave's ear had been recently injured, in a manner one might expect from a buckshot blast.

"Beckwourth," said Ashley, "looks like you didn't bury those deep enough."

"Shredded Ear there must be one of the ones we shot that night," said Beckwourth. "He must have followed me."

'Shredded Ear' held the scalps high and made another impassioned plea to the chief.

The chief spoke to Ashley, and Greenwood called out his words. "So, these were not Blackfeet that you killed but Crow, my own warriors. Do you disagree?"

"It was night. We did not know they were Crow," said Ashley. "Would you not yourself shoot anyone who crept up on your camp at night to steal your horses? Had they come to my camp with open palms in daylight I would have gladly fed them and smoked with them."

The chief rose from the parley and mounted his horse. By sign he demanded they follow. There was a tense moment while Ashley considered his options, but he told the men to comply. On the ride to the Crow camp, Beckwourth sidled up to Harris.

"Now what?" he asked.

"It's a good sign they let us keep our weapons," said Harris.

That evening, at the Crow camp, the chief and Ashley met around the campfire while angry-looking warriors milled about. Beckwourth watched them, weapons in reach. If it came to that, though, given the numbers, all they could do would be to take a few with them. He noted a few women in camp, and boys in their early teens who managed the horses, fetched water, etc. with great alacrity.

"Harris," he said, "half of the men and the women are missing fingers. Why is that?"

"Someone close to them dies, they cut off part of a finger, or a whole one. See though, the warriors never cut the two for drawing an arrow."

Greenwood came for Beckwourth.

"The chief wants to see you and the other shooters," he said.

"Leave the others out of it," said Beckwourth. "They followed my lead."

"Very well," Greenwood agreed. "That might work."

Greenwood led Beckwourth to a circle of Crow warriors sitting cross-legged around the campfire with Ashley. 'Shredded Ear' sat opposite the chief, glaring at Beckwourth. Pretending that he was the guest of honor rather than the object of an inquiry, Beckwourth sat next to Ashley. Silence hung in the air as the chief lit a red stone pipe, then raised it to the night sky, the earth below, and the four corners of the compass. The pipe was then passed to every man in the circle without a word spoken. Beckwourth took a puff in turn and passed it to Ashley. From there it was returned to the chief, who broke the silence with a long speech as he simultaneously signed, and Greenwood translated. The chief explained that they were of the Mountain Crow, that two moons prior they had started on foot on a retaliatory horse-stealing raid against their enemy the Blackfeet. He described in detail the mountain and river crossings of their journey, the weather, the wildlife, and so forth. He explained that 'Shredded Ear' was of the River Crow, a separate band of their tribe, and commanded him to describe their raid on the white man's camp.

'Shredded Ear' complied. He told of his burning desire to prove his bravery, and his hatred of the Blackfeet. He described in detail how, against the chief's orders, he and three other warriors had snuck away one night to steal Ashley's horses. He detailed how they had crept up on the herd that night, and their surprise at the four simultaneous gunshots; how they were momentarily blinded by the gun flash, and how he had felt the sting of shot in his face, and their flight back to their chief.

The chief spoke again. "Chief Ashley, now you know that these warriors acted against my command. The Crow have always been friends to the white man, ever since Clark, the red-haired chief traveled through our lands on his journey to the great salt water where the sun sets."

The chief motioned to 'Shredded Ear'. "This

warrior will not have revenge on the white man while he is in my village, but as I have told you, he is not of my band, but of the River Crow. What can you do to soften his heart, Chief Ashley?"

"As chief of these men, and as an emissary from the red-haired chief in St. Louis," said Ashley, "I tell you, my Crow friend, that it is my honor to smoke the peace pipe with such a great warrior as yourself. You say that these warriors acted against your orders, and they confirm this. I believe your words. It is my wish to repair the feelings brought about by this bad thing. But before I make gifts to this man, I must tell the chief that I see many of my own horses among his herd, horses stolen from us several sleeps before we shot at this warrior and his friends. You say you did not command your warriors to steal our horses. How is it then, that you have our horses?"

"Yes, we stole them from you," Greenwood translated for the chief.

Ashley waited for further explanation, but it was not forthcoming. "If the chief is such a great friend of the white man, ask him why he stole them," said Ashley.

The chief smiled. "I was tired of walking," Greenwood translated. "After I took them, I had a fight with a party of Blackfeet, who were stalking you. They would have rubbed you out given any chance, but I chased them away, because I am a friend of the white man." The chief emphasized the sign for 'rubbing out', rubbing the heel of one palm in the other. "I did you a great favor chasing the Blackfeet from you, but if I had come to your camp and told you that I would protect you from the Blackfeet, you would have only given me tobacco. That is as it is, for you did not have extra horses to give us. But tobacco would not carry me back to our country.

Only horses would do that. So, I took some of your horses, though I could have taken all of them, and I told my warriors to take no more. When I took your horses they were lean and poor. Now they are fat. With your horses, we were able to steal more from the Blackfeet. We have plenty of Blackfoot horses now; you may take back all of the horses that belong to you and choose some among those we have taken from the Blackfeet as well."

"That is all good," said Ashley. "As you are a friend to all white men, now I am friend of all Crow. I wish to soften the heart of this warrior of the River Crow with these gifts."

Ashley laid out iron arrow heads, a rifle, lead, and gunpowder. 'Shredded Ear' sat still, but his eyes were drawn to this wealth.

The chief asked Beckwourth to tell his story of that night. Beckwourth figured to copy the tempo of the chief's story, so he went into every detail of being wakened (without naming Pappen), scouting the enemy, getting two more men, assigning a target to each man and that they shoot on the word 'now', and the flash of light that lit the landscape. He explained that the man who had fired at 'Shredded Ear' had buckshot in his gun, accounting for the nature of his injury.

The chief spoke to his men. "You see, my warriors, how the white man fights. The white man makes a plan. He uses his cunning to determine how to win, not to just prove his bravery. His warriors obey their leader. What does the Indian do instead? The Indian enters battle for himself first. He intends to prove that he is brave, and if he is killed and goes to the Other Side Camp, so be it. The white man follows orders. You," he motioned to 'Shredded Ear', "you will take these generous gifts of Chief Ashley and you will speak of this no more in my presence."

'Shredded Ear' took these items, but with a glance of resentment at Beckwourth.

The chief spoke to Greenwood, who relayed to Beckwourth, "He wants to know if you have an Indian name."

"I have not had that honor," said Beckwourth.

"Then he names you 'Shoots Good in the Dark'," said Greenwood. "He says you are a clever warrior, and Chief Ashley should be proud of you."

Ashley replied, "I am pleased the chief recognizes my Beckwourth for the clever warrior he is. I have many clever and brave warriors. It is my hope to combine forces with the Crow as we head back to meet with others of my men who have been roaming these mountains since last year. Then we will proceed to the Missouri River, where great canoes will take us back to St. Louis. There, we will meet with red-haired Chief Clark, and we will tell him that he still has a steadfast friend among the Mountain Crow, so that he may write a letter to the great chief in Washington and tell him the same."

The chief seemed genuinely satisfied.

Ashley called for Bracken, who described to the chief where the rendezvous was to occur. The chief determined it to be in Crow territory.

"It would please me greatly to guide Chief Ashley through the Blackfoot lands we are in now to where he will meet the rest of his men," Greenwood translated for the chief. "If we meet the Blackfeet on the way, we will show them how the Crow fight, and see for ourselves how the white man fights."

❧ 6 ❧

The Crow led the way, Ashley's men in tow. Crow scouts were out of sight on all four sides as they picked their way through the meadow along the stream that over days combined with others to become a small river. Every man kept his weapons at the ready. For three days they traveled without incident, but on the morning of the fourth, scouts galloped into camp with the news that a large force of Blackfeet was headed their way. Their encampment was at a horse-shoe bend of a river, chosen the night prior for its defensibility. Immediately, they placed the horses in the care of the women and boys, hidden among the willows at river's edge. At the neck of the horseshoe were a few boulders that would make good cover, and to the right, the river embankment was steep, also potential cover. Beyond the neck of the horseshoe was the field of battle; an open meadow backed by dense woods.

A council was held, and Ashley presented his strategy. Despite the enemy's superior numbers, he was confident they could withstand an attack, for days if necessary, due to their excellent defensive position. His men would take cover behind the boulders at the neck of the horseshoe, and the Crow would take positions screened by the willows, to pop out when the enemy was in range. When the Blackfeet charged, the whites' rifles would be fired first, then their pistols, after which the Crow archers would cover Ashley's men for their retreat to the willows. Horses would be saddled and ready for an offensive charge if the opportunity came. Greenwood translated all this to the Crow.

'Shredded Ear' spoke first. "This is not how a Crow should fight," Greenwood translated. "We are not women. Give us the chance to count coup against the Blackfeet. Let the whites stand at the river's edge with the women and shoot their guns at the Blackfoot dogs from there."

The chief spoke to Shredded Ear. "Your words are too strong for my ears," Greenwood translated. "We will follow Chief Ashley's plan."

Ashley dispersed his men as evenly across the neck of land as cover allowed. Beckwourth and Pappen each took opposite sides of a large boulder. Beckwourth gave Pappen a nod just as mounted Blackfeet appeared at the meadow's edge. Whirling on horseback and whooping at the top of their lungs, they gathered their force. Beckwourth felt butterflies in his stomach. Every other time in his life he had faced anything like this, he had had no time to think, but now that he had the time to reflect, his heart raced and his hand trembled. The Blackfeet charged.

"Every man announce his target," said Ashley, "but hold fire until I give the word. Aim for the saddle. That way you get either the man or his horse."

Beckwourth's butterflies disappeared. His hand steadied. He searched for his target. Down the line, each man announced his mark.

"I got 'Two-Feather'," said Beckwourth, sighting down the long barrel of his muzzle-loader.

"I got 'Red Sash'," said Pappen.

'Two Feather' charged with blood in his eyes and a howl in his throat. Now he was inside a hundred yards.

"Fire!" called Ashley.

The sound of two dozen shots filled the air, and more than a dozen Blackfeet fell. The rest stopped, well out of pistol range. They retreated, pulling their wounded up behind them. Beckwourth felt a rush of pride. Not for getting his man, but for having conquered his fear.

"They have never fought whites before," Ashley said. "Surprised them to have so many fall at once. But they won't be surprised twice. They will keep coming the next time."

The next wave came. Sure enough, they did not stop when the simultaneous fire felled more of their number. They kept charging, their horses' hooves pounding the earth.

"Fire pistols at will," Ashley called out. "Retreat after you have fired."

Beckwourth sighted a Blackfoot, but before he could fire, his target was felled. He searched for another through the smoke. Pappen fired and ran.

"Retreat!" called Ashley.

A Blackfoot charged Beckwourth, his war club was raised to strike. Beckwourth fired and missed. Last man out, he ran for all he was worth. 'Shredded Ear' loomed in front of him, seemingly aiming an arrow right at him. Beckwourth dropped to the ground. The warrior's horse thundered past him, riderless. Beckwourth turned just long enough to see the Blackfoot on the ground with an arrow in his abdomen, then rose and ran to the willows. The Crow were firing arrows as fast as they could haft them, and Ashley's men reloaded and got off some shots at the retreating Blackfeet. The Crow ran out to exult over their victims and scalp them.

It was over, for the moment. One of Ashley's men was badly wounded and was removed to the river's edge, where the Crow women attended to him. Ashley directed the rest back to their positions.

"General, sir, I have an idea," said Beckwourth.

The general's skepticism was reflected in his face. "Let's hear it, then."

"Let them attack once more and wear themselves out. Before the smoke clears, I can take a few men and horses to the right along the river, under that bank. On their next advance, we will charge their flank and create confusion."

"They won't expect us to attack when we have such a good defensive position," said Ashley. "It might work. Very good. Greenwood!"

The general reviewed the plan with the Crow chief through Greenwood. The chief smiled and grunted his approval. "The Blackfeet mean to rub us out today," Greenwood translated. "If it were otherwise, they would see our strong position and leave us for another day. We must fight to the last man." He insisted that some of his men be in the flanking maneuver, 'Shredded Ear' among them. Ashley agreed, and the flanking party was assembled.

Beckwourth had Greenwood bring him to 'Shredded Ear'. "Tell him first that I wish to thank him for saving my life," he said.

The warrior only grunted at Greenwood's translation.

"What is his name?" Beckwourth asked.

'Shredded Ear' smiled at the question. His smile

showed how the blast had paralyzed half of his mouth.

"Of late they call him Crooked Smile," Greenwood translated.

"Tell him that we now go into battle against a common enemy. When I was nine winters old. The Blackfeet killed my friends, eight children and their parents. Tell him." It was highly unlikely that it was Blackfeet that killed Amanda and her family, but a little white lie could be forgiven here.

Greenwood translated this, then Crooked Smile's response. "He says that you have shown well how the white man fights. Now he will show you how a Crow fights."

"There was a lot more in there than that," said Beckwourth.

"Ah. Well, if we succeed," said Greenwood. "His insults won't mean so much."

A shout went up from the line at the boulders. The Blackfeet were charging again, screaming like devils possessed as they urged their horses across the field. Again, Ashley's men fired, then made their strategic withdrawal. The Blackfeet proved their bravery at great cost. Before the smoke had cleared the flanking party waded their horses downstream, shielded from Blackfoot view by the dense willows at water's edge, and then by the high embankment. One Crow scouted ahead, crawling on his belly, motioning the rest ahead in twenty-yard increments until he signaled that the enemy was one arrow-shot distance from him. Beckwourth and Greenwood crept to his position and observed a cadre of Blackfeet in the woods, sharing a pipe, resting. The Blackfeet tamped out their pipe and mounted, readying for the next charge. The flanking party mounted as well, lying flat against their horses' necks. On hearing the whoops of another Blackfoot charge, they galloped around the embankment with whoops themselves.

The main body of Blackfeet was thrown into confusion. Some continued their charge, some wheeled to face the new attackers. Seeing the Blackfeet in confusion, Ashley called up horses and mounted a frontal charge. The Blackfoot chief called retreat. They turned their mounts and fled, with the Crow chasing them only far enough to ensure that they kept going.

Ashley's men and the Crow exulted only briefly, for there was no telling where the main Blackfoot camp might be, and whether they would mass a force to avenge their losses. The wounded mountaineer had died, their first casualty since they had left St. Louis. Ashley's men buried him in a shallow grave and rolled boulders over the spot so the wolves would not get to him. Ashley said a few hurried words and they broke camp. A head start would be their only advantage, so it was best taken urgently.

They traveled all day and night, non-stop for two days. Late the next day they crossed a river, and the Crow seemed to relax. Two more days of travel, and they came in sight of smoke from the Crow village. Scouts were sent ahead to tell of their impending arrival, while Crow warriors smeared black grease on their faces and donned feathered war bonnets. They paraded into the village on horseback, scalps held high on their lances, with Ashley's men trailing behind. The entire community turned out, the men chanting to the rhythm of drums, the women sounding a warbling ululation. It was a noisy, triumphal procession, to the accompaniment of the barking and yapping of great numbers of dogs.

After parading through the village with the Crow, there was a feast and a celebration. The enemy scalps had been stretched on willow hoops and were all tied to a tall pole in an open space. Crow warriors formed a circle around it, and their women formed a circle around them, with the rest of the village and Ashley's men surrounding the whole as they danced. The warriors danced in a slow-moving circle; three short hops on one foot, then the other, chanting to the beat of the drums. Their faces were still blackened with grease and charcoal, which Greenwood explained symbolized that the Crow had left with fire in their hearts and returned successful with the fire of revenge quenched. Gradually the pace of the drums picked up and the dancers followed the faster rhythm with ever more exaggerated and individualized movements. Faster and faster they danced, hour after hour, long into the night. Finally, the Chief called an end to the dance. On cue, women raised a great cry of despair. Greenwood explained.

"The raid was a success," he said, "but still the warriors that fell must be mourned."

The chief addressed the assembly with his tale of their expedition, while Greenwood translated for the whites. The chief told of how they had started on foot, described the terrain they crossed, the game they encountered, the care they took to remain undetected, how they came upon Ashley's men and debated whether to steal their horses, deciding that the One Above Person had presented the horses as a gift and took them, but not so many that Ashley's men would perish. They had come upon a Blackfoot camp and stole more horses. He told of their meeting with Ashley's men and how the One Above Person had caused Ashley's gun to misfire, preventing much bloodshed. He told of the encounter with the Blackfeet at the horseshoe bend and praised Ashley's wisdom in battle strategy. Then he invited warriors to tell their individual stories. One by one they came forward and after affirming that all that the chief had said was true, they told their tales, emphasizing each deed by striking the scalp pole with their coup sticks. At his turn, Crooked Smile spared no detail of the raid he had led, of the death of his fellow warriors and his own injury, even as he provoked laughter displaying his crooked smile. He told of his role at the horseshoe bend, and how he had saved Beckwourth. When the last warrior finished his tale, the chief called to Greenwood.

"So, Shoots Good in the Dark," said Greenwood, "The chief wants to hear you tell about your maneuver against the Blackfeet."

Beckwourth picked a stick up off the ground and walked to the pole. *When in Rome...*, he thought. He began his story, adopting the cadence of the other orators, striking the pole as they had. Where he knew the Indian sign for an English word, he used it, and Greenwood translated to the Crow piece by piece the story of that morning at the river horseshoe.

"Chief Ashley had a wise plan, to allow the wicked Blackfeet to come just close enough that we could kill them, knowing that we could repel them from our strong position for days if we had to. Twice the Blackfeet attacked, and I saw that the Blackfeet were tiring. I came to General Ashley and asked if I could lead a party flanking the Blackfeet, to surprise them and throw them into confusion. I was much pleased that my chief thought this a good plan, and more pleased that he gave to me the leadership. I am not wise in the ways of the Indian, so it was good that your chief gave me several of his best warriors, including Crooked Smile, who had saved my life exactly as he described." His audience was enthralled, and grunted approval at intervals. Beckwourth, for his part, loved the attention. The celebration went on for three days, with breaks for feasting and rest. At one of these breaks, Beckwourth saw Crooked Smile speaking to a small group of warriors and noted that the topic of conversation seemed to be himself. Crooked Smile spoke with disdain, but the others seemed quite curious. Beckwourth approached Greenwood.

"Greenwood, my good friend," he said, "These fellows seem to have taken a keen interest in my personage. Do you have any idea why?"

"You made quite a spectacle of yourself at the scalp dance. Could be that."

"This Crooked Smile bears a grudge. I want to know if he is plotting something against me."

"Not likely, but could be."

"I aim to find out. Come with me." Beckwourth headed towards the Crow.

"What the hell are you doing?" asked Greenwood.

"The best defense is a good offense, they say."

"All right. But I'm only doing this to save all of us from the mess you might get us into."

Beckwourth swaggered up to the group. "Ask that fellow what his interest is in me," he commanded Greenwood, pointing to the one who stared the most.

The warrior's gaze pierced Greenwood through as he listened. When Greenwood finished, he replied with word and sign and looked to Beckwourth for his reply.

"He says you are a brave warrior. He asks where you come from." The Crow put his forearm next to Beckwourth's. They were virtually the same skin tone.

"Tell him I come from St. Louis, where the red-haired Chief Clark has his lodge. Tell him my

64

mother was darker than he is, and that my father is white, and a great warrior himself, and from a long line of great warriors."

Greenwood gave him a smirk, then a playful look crossed his face. He spoke to the Crow and they grunted. He elaborated, which excited them further, and the original questioner grasped Beckwourth's arm in a sign of friendship. Crooked Smile glared at both Greenwood and Beckwourth in apparent disbelief.

"That seemed to impress them," said Beckwourth. "What was that all about?"

"So, Beckwourth," said Greenwood, "how are you at keeping a straight face?"

"I can do that."

"Very important to know how to keep a straight face when you live among the tribes."

"Let's hear it then, Mr. Greenwood."

"Good, because they are watching you. So, I didn't exactly tell them your lineage as you so artfully put it."

"What did you tell them then?"

"I asked them if they remembered a particular Crow defeat at the hands of the Cheyenne more than a dozen years ago. Of course they did, as this was when a large village was devastated, and many of the women and children were taken captive. I told them that you were born a Crow Indian and captured in that raid as a little boy. I told them that then the Cheyenne sold you to white people who raised you in St. Louis."

Beckwourth strained to keep the straight face he had promised, then coughed violently.

Greenwood slapped him on the back. "That will teach you to go off half-cocked and try to get us all in trouble." He winked and pushed his friend away.

❈ 7 ❈

A week of rest was plenty for Ashley's men, for they were itching to get on to the rendezvous. Farewell gifts were exchanged between Ashley and the chief, speeches made pledging eternal friendship and loyalty, and Ashley's party was off down the trail, with a contingent of Crow to guide them.

A journey of more than a week was uneventful and without hardship. Game was plentiful and varied, the spring weather pleasant. Beckwourth had to agree with the Crow that their territory was the best anywhere, this land of broad valleys and meandering streams, bordered by towering mountains and forested foothills. The rendezvous was to be at the confluence of two rivers according to Bracken. The Crow guides knew their land well, and soon they came within sight of campfires. A signaling gunshot brought out a contingent of the 1823 men to greet them, firing pistols in the air in celebration. Old friends embraced and introductions were made all around for the newcomers. How had they fared? Who among them had "gone under"?

The 1823 men first sought messages sent by their loved ones back home, and then, around the campfire at night, news of the world. The Seminole Indian war smoldered in Florida. Steamboat traffic was becoming commonplace back home, tying St. Louis to New Orleans to the south and all the way to Ohio to the east. A large, side-wheel steamboat was under construction that would be a wonder to behold. Ashley impressed on all the men that President Monroe himself would thank them for keeping British traders out of the fur business in these parts, and he welcomed those trappers who had defected from the America Fur Company for the better pay.

The 1823 men reported of the Army's pathetic attempt to punish the Arikara for their attack on them the preceding year. The Army had been led on a fruitless chase by the wily Arikara and ultimately had taken the rather cowardly tactic of burning the Arikara village.

"I hear you have a tale to tell, Jed," Ashley said to one of the 1823 men.

"I did have a bit of a disagreement with a grizzly," Jed offered, "if that is what you mean." Thoughtful and devoutly religious, Jedediah Smith was cut from different cloth than most of these profane men dredged from the St. Louis grog shops. "I grow my hair long now, so's not to scare women and children."

"Come along now, Jed, show 'em," said a fellow named Clyman. "Show 'em your ear. He made me sew it back on," he said to the rest.

"Y'all can take a gander if you want." Smith pulled back his long hair and showed his ragged scalp, with a swollen, oozing, discolored lump of tissue in the middle.

"The bear near clawed your head off, I see," said Ashley.

"No, no," said Smith, "don't know if that would

67

have been better or worse, but what you see is from the varmint trying to *bite* my head off."

"He had a white streak in his skull four inches long from the bear's teeth," said Clyman, "'fore I stitched him up."

"Damn fine handiwork, I must say, Clyman," said Ashley. "If you wish to take up tailoring back in the settlements, I would be pleased to give you a recommendation."

"I think you would look a damn sight better if your ear fell off there, Jed," said Greenwood, "which it looks like it might any day now."

"Well, at least I hear my bear left me better looking than old Hugh Glass's bear left him."

"Glass came to pay me a visit in St. Louis," said Ashley. "I would say that compared to him, your bear went easy on you."

"There's one tough buzzard," said Greenwood.

"Where is old Hugh these days, anyhow?" asked Jed.

"Taos," said Ashley. "I think he heard the bears are smaller there."

They all laughed.

Over the following weeks, the surrounding tribes brought furs and horses to trade for copper pots, sheet-iron arrowheads, blankets, and beads. Even the Blackfeet came, inveterate enemies of the whites, and all kept their animosity to themselves while in camp. The rendezvous came off as well as could be expected, or better. There was one episode of stolen horses, but they were recovered quickly and soon it was forgotten. They had plenty of horses now.

There was an abundance of idle time, which the men, red and white, filled with various contests. They raced horses and raced on foot. They competed at target practice with rifles, bow and arrow, hatchets, knives, and any other weapon that struck their fancy. The warriors had a favorite contest where they would see how many arrows one man could get in the air before the first one hit the ground. Beckwourth marveled at their skill at this: winners could get as many as eight arrows in the air at a time. The whites played cards while the Indians watched, and the whites watched while the Indians played a game called hands; a game of sleight of hand like the shell game they knew. Teams of braves would pass an object between themselves, then have the bettor choose which fist held it. No contest was undertaken without betting. A boast would be met with a challenge, and the challenge mocked. Bets would then be bandied about and the stakes raised until someone felt either that he could win, or that he would lose face by not accepting the challenge. The whites bet wildly, but nothing compared to the warriors. They won and lost whole herds of horses in these games and contests, and when a warrior lost all his horses and all his other possessions of value, he might bet his wife, or even sell himself into servitude. And no matter what the stakes were, he showed not a trace of regret if he lost. Beckwourth marveled at their recklessness, but even more at their impassivity at losing. He asked Greenwood about this.

"That Injun was taught from infancy to seek all opportunities to show that he could endure any pain without showing it," he explained. "The pain of losing at gambling is to be endured like any other. In fact, it's a chance to show that he can endure more pain than anyone else."

One day, the 1823 men bet that their boy Davis could out-wrestle whomever the 1824 men chose as their champion. The 1824 men wanted Harris.

"Naw," said Harris. "Beckwourth's your man. I peed blood for a month after I wrassled him."

So Beckwourth and Davis stripped, surrounded by a ring of cheering whites and silently attentive warriors. It was all in fun until Davis tossed a racial slur at Beckwourth. The men fell silent.

"Oh, now," said Greenwood, "let's see if your boy can be the first to call Beckwourth that and live to tell."

The men roared. Beckwourth held out his arms in mock conciliation. "Very well then, Mr. Davis," he said. "If you think you are so much my better, I will wrestle you blindfolded and still put you to shame."

The men roared louder still, and the odds were adjusted. The contestants slathered themselves in bear grease and glared at each other. Beckwourth tied on a blindfold, and they faced off. Davis whirled around him a few times, slapped him on his leg as a feint, and then tackled him from the other side. Beckwourth grabbed Davis around the waist, negating the disadvantage of the blindfold. Wiry, muscular, Beckwourth twisted and threw Davis to the ground. They rolled around in the dust as the rest cheered and cursed. It looked like Beckwourth might have a quick win. Desperate, Davis bit him on the arm.

"Oh! Davey boy!" Beckwourth released him and adjusted the blindfold. "Did you put a squaw in your place? Give me another kiss, honey, but not so rough this time. Come on now, girl, let's go at it again. Give me a big hug."

With a stream of profanity peppered with more racial epithets, Davis charged. Beckwourth made short and brutal work of the man. Broken, panting, Davis limped away, the butt of jeers. He took it with gritted teeth and a forced smile.

After some weeks, Ashley ran out of goods to

trade, and the tribes left, one by one. It was decision time for the trappers: would it be home to "the settlements," or another season in the mountains? Most of the 1824 men who had come out with Beckwourth chose to remain in the mountains. Davis and a number of the 1823 men chose to return, though Ashley was surprised at how few. Still, there were enough returning that they would not be easy prey to roaming bands. Beckwourth had had the thrill of his life in the mountains, and gave staying a passing thought, but the memory of Eliza's soft touch beckoned him home.

On the day of departure, Ashley settled accounts: beaver pelts against trade goods taken, with any balance to be paid the next year in goods for those that remained, or in cash in St. Louis. Beckwourth was pleased with his balance; he had accomplished what he had set out to do. Ashley gave a stirring speech, thanking all and bidding them "a thousand times welcome" to come visit him in St. Louis. Staid goodbyes were said with the full knowledge that for any one of them, this might be the last time they would meet. Ashley led the returning men home over the range of pine-covered hills to the east and down into the plain beyond, the Powder River valley, heading toward the Missouri. There was no reason to hurry, so every few days they paused to trap, then moved on. After several days, they crossed a river that marked Crow territory, and their Crow scouts returned home.

One morning, Beckwourth could not find a trap he had placed the day prior, though he knew he had driven the anchor pole deep into the riverbed. Had Indians stolen it? There had been no sign of any. The river at this spot was shallow and frequently forded by buffalo. Beckwourth climbed the riverbank and gazed out into the broad valley. Quite distant, he spotted what appeared to be a badger by its awkward, waddling gait. As he approached, however, it became apparent that this was a beaver, caught in his trap, far from the river. There was no way that the beaver could have uprooted the anchor pole, much less dragged it that far. How had this happened? Beckwourth surmised that the trap had been torn from its mooring by a buffalo, the chain getting tangled in its horns, who then had carried the beaver to where it was now. Quite an extraordinary thing.

That evening, around the campfire, the men relaxed and swapped tales of their adventures. Jim Bridger, one of the 1823 men, entertained everyone with a tall tale of a glass mountain that magnified a deer such that it fooled him into firing at it when the deer was twenty miles off.

"Aw, ain't no such thing as no glass mountain," said Davis.

The men snickered at his gullibility. "You sure, there, Davis?" asked one. Beckwourth decided to tease his wrestling opponent further.

"One of my traps was stolen today, Davis." Beckwourth said.

"Stolen!" the man replied.

"Yes, it was stolen by a buffalo."

"Damn you, Beckwourth," said Davis. "You are the fool to think I would be taken in by such a lie."

"Only a fool would call me a liar," Beckwourth replied.

"Goddamn duck poacher," said Davis. "Yeah, I heard about that. Goddamn naggur."

Instantly Beckwourth was on Davis with his fists. Davis rolled away and went for his pistol, and Beckwourth went for his. Before either had the chance to take aim at the other, though, the rest restrained and disarmed them, shouting for them to come to their senses.

"Come at me again, Davis, and believe me, one of us will be buried that day," said Beckwourth.

"Y'all going to let him talk to me like that?" spat Davis.

"Come now, Davis," said Ashley. "It was a story, a joke, a jest."

Davis scanned faces and did not see support.

"So that's how it is, then," he said. "Then I will see y'all in St. Louis, if I make it, or in hell if I don't." He shook himself loose and packed his horse, not responding a word to those who tried to convince him of the folly of setting out on his own. They gave him back his gun and ammunition, and Davis was swallowed by the night.

An accusatory silence surrounded Beckwourth, a silence that spoke volumes. Davis was not really liked by anyone, but these were mostly 1823 men who had faced death with him on more than one occasion. And now he was a man alone in hostile country. Beckwourth knew that in their eyes he was just the naggur who had eaten duck while the rest were near starvation.

The next morning, there was no sign of Davis, and the silent accusations continued. Beckwourth went about his business, hoping this would pass. But Ashley took him aside.

"It's best that you strike out and trap on your own for a day or two," Ashley said. "We will camp here for a couple days in case Davis comes back."

"I am a member of your party, General. A man loyal like none other. Loyal to you and loyal to the group."

"I do not question your loyalty, Beckwourth. This is not about that. I like you. But you seem to be a magnet for conflict. Combine that with a hair-trigger temper, and you are a veritable human powder keg."

"I am a pretty easy-going fellow until someone brings the color of my skin into the mix."

"As well I know," said Ashley. "And I apologize again for my words. I can be a bit volatile myself at times. Well, anyway, I think it best for you to make yourself scarce for a bit. Go out and trap for a couple days and then come back. If we are not here, just follow the Powder on to the Missouri."

"I still feel guilty about that duck," said Beckwourth.

"Don't worry about that," said Ashley. "You have acquitted yourself quite well on this expedition."

They shook hands, but Beckwourth was not so sure from Ashley's manner that he was going to be 'a thousand times welcome' in the general's home.

Beckwourth mounted up and headed out into the Powder River valley with the silence of his comrades wafting in his wake. He followed Indian trails cautiously, watchful for fresh signs. At night he camped away from the trails without a fire, eating pemmican from the Crow. His rifle and pistol were at all times loaded, and he slept lightly with them both in immediate reach. The next day he relaxed some. Why not? He had no responsibility for anyone but himself, and total freedom in a pristine, inspiring wilderness. Here he walked where, as the saying goes, 'no white man ever trod before.' *That's ironic*, he thought as he rode along. *Now that I have been here, would they still say that?* But no matter. Free as any man had ever been, he wandered among God's handiwork, and pondered life's mysteries. And he thought of Eliza and how he would soon enough sink blissfully into her embrace.

The muted thunder of hoof beats interrupted his reverie. A herd of horses crested a rise behind him.

Indian horses, and a large herd, though no Indians were in sight. The herd surrounded him, and he resigned himself to his fate. Indians had obviously spotted him first and used the herd to prevent his escape. That was better than an arrow in the back as first indication of their presence, but his odds of living to see the next dawn had diminished considerably. He dropped the reins and allowed his horse to join the herd, acutely aware of being driven in the opposite direction from his party. There was nothing he could do. Through the dust, he caught a glimpse of two young Indians who drove the herd, probably sixteen years old or less, calling to each other at intervals. So, not likely a raiding party, just tenders, grazing the herd, and therefore probably close to home. But which tribe? It made all the difference in the world. The dusty ride seemed interminable. A village came into sight through the dust, and one of the boys rode ahead. Beckwourth touched the stock of his rifle, fingered the pistol at his waist. To use them would be certain torture and death, regardless of the tribe. He pulled out the coin that hung around his neck and kissed it.

"Mother, save me," he muttered.

❧ 8 ❧

Mounted warriors rode out to meet
Beckwourth and by signs demanded his arms,
which he gave up, knife and all. In the village, a
crowd of all ages scowled and gawked as he was es-
corted to a large tipi. At its entrance were several
scalps, twisting ominously in the breeze on their
willow frames. He was thrust past them and into the
darkness. Once his eyes had adjusted, his greatest
fear was allayed. There, seated next to what was obviously the chief, glared Crooked Smile. These were
River Crow, likely friendly, or at least so disposed in
the right circumstance. The chief wore an elabo-
rately decorated leather shirt, made frightful by its
fringe of human hair. He wore a large silver medal
around his neck, which Beckwourth also took to be a
good sign. These were presented to chiefs who vowed
friendship with the whites. The chief sent a messenger out. While they waited, the chief and
Crooked Smile smoked a pipe, without offering it to
Beckwourth.

The messenger returned and ushered in a trio of
older women. The chief spoke to them. With wide
eyes and bated breath, one by one they approached

Beckwourth, and with no regard to his privacy, stripped him. They peered and prodded his person, for Beckwourth's taste, altogether too reminiscent of a slave auction back home. Each woman, when satisfied that she had adequately examined the captive, addressed the chief with a disappointed sigh and left.

So that's it, thought Beckwourth. *Crooked Smile wants to test Greenwood's Cheyenne captive fable.* Another, and another cadre of women examined their specimen. He expected that soon the last of them would heave her disappointed sigh and leave him to the chief's whim. But it was not to be. A very dignified older woman was led in. She peered at his face from inches away, and without further ado pulled down his eyelids. Beckwourth had almost forgotten about the birthmark noted on his emancipation papers, but there it was. Astonished, the woman cried out. She hugged and kissed Beckwourth and shouted her joy. There was no mistaking to her she had found her long lost son. He pushed her away and signed to Crooked Smile his dire need to rejoin his party but received an icy glare in return.

The women dragged Beckwourth outside, and among excited chatter he was taken from tipi to tipi and shown off. Finally, after having been hugged and kissed by so many new female relations that he thought his face would blister, they stopped. An older man exited a tipi and addressed all in a stirring manner, with the old woman at his side. The crowd dispersed, all but a few dogs that sniffed and growled at him, and small children who stared and chattered. His new father introduced himself by pantomime as Big Bowl. His new mother indicated that Beckwourth should call her Ishkali and introduced him to his two new sisters. They told him his childhood name, but Big Bowl corrected them with the Crow words for Shoots Good in the Dark. Ishkali beckoned him inside the tipi and cleared a place of honor for him; an elevated platform for sleep, under which he could store his only belongings the Crow had not confiscated; his book, his saddle, and his traps. Ishkali scooped steaming stew from a kettle on a tripod at the tipi center and served it to him in a horn bowl. He was ravenous and slurped it down without ceremony, signing his appreciation when finished. He tried to communicate to Big Bowl his urgent need to return to his party. Big Bowl seemed to understand him after some time but indicated that he would have none of that. The old man was not about to disappoint his wife.

That night, as he lay in his place of honor and contemplated the coals in the fire, Beckwourth contemplated escape. He turned over various plans in his mind, but with no weapon, no horse, and a narrow window of time to figure out how to steal them, he decided it was hopeless. His best hope was that Ashley would come and negotiate his rescue, dim though that hope was.

Beckwourth was awakened the next morning by a voice calling the same short phrase out over and over again. Big Bowl rose and beckoned him to follow. The voice was that of a mounted herald, awakening the camp. Beckwourth trudged behind Big Bowl to the river, low as ever he had felt. There the long-haired warriors stripped and bathed, then slathered themselves in grease. This finished, they held hands to the sky and prayed fervently. A meal was waiting for them on their return to the tipi, and Beckwourth's new sisters tried to cheer him up. Lamenting his greasy clothes, blackened from months of wiping his hands and his knife on them, they gave him a new buckskin shirt and leggings to match, resplendent in bead work and porcupine quill embroidery. Again, that night, Beckwourth slept fitfully.

Ashley did not come.

Over the following days Ishkali taught Beckwourth Crow, word by word, with the signs to go with it. His facility with languages made him an apt pupil. The first time he strung a short sentence together, Ishkali was delighted. The attention of this kind woman warmed Beckwourth's heart and reminded him of his own mother. From time to time, she touched his face with her calloused hands, hands that were missing several fingertips. One time when she touched him so, he held her hand firmly between his. She touched his chest and motioned as if to replace one of the fingertips.

Beckwourth explored the village every day after his ablutions, followed by a gaggle of children, all agog at this strange newcomer, the youngest among the boys wearing nothing but an amulet around their neck, but all the girls dressed modestly. He spoke English to them, to which they would giggle and speak excitedly among themselves. He invited them in sign language to follow him as he wandered about, and he learned from them the names of many objects. After a time, though, the novelty of a stranger wore off, and Beckwourth wandered the village without this entourage. The scattering of tipis was quite random to his eyes. Each had its back to the wind, smoke wafting from the peak, where triangular flaps on long poles stood ready to be closed in case of rain. On the leeward side there was an oval opening and a flap to close it, with pegs to secure the flap. The tipis varied in size, the largest he estimated at thirty feet across. Some were decorated with the most elaborate drawings of war scenes, others with wavy lines and circles; perhaps just decorative.

Beckwourth learned the rhythms of a Crow day. After breakfast, the herald again rode through the village, beating a tambourine-like drum, repeating an announcement from one end of the village to the other. Women fell to their work. Some would gather firewood, perhaps carrying an infant in a cradle-board, or trailed by a little girl with a doll who mimicked her, picking up twigs. Older girls helped with working hides and sewing. When released from their chores they would go to the play village; a group of miniature tipis on the edge of the village. Here the girls mimicked their mothers at their chores, often bringing toddlers along to be their living dolls. The boys played at being their husbands and staged mock hunts and sham battles and brought home toy trophies.

The boys who were too old for this spent much of their day with a teacher. A warrior passed among the tipis mid mornings, calling these boys to follow him. Beckwourth tagged along some days, and watched the teacher instruct them how to set traps for rabbits or to shoot arrows at targets of rolled buffalo chips or willow hoops. The lessons were always framed as a contest, and the winner was given some reward, such as a feather or just words of praise. One day Beckwourth watched the boys crawl on their bellies, sneaking up on racks of buffalo meat drying in the sun. On a signal they rushed the racks and stole strips of meat, running away as the women laughed and scolded them. It seemed an idyllic childhood. Beckwourth never saw a temper tantrum, nor did an adult ever have a sharp word for a child, let alone a hand raised. Babies never cried, save once that he saw. That one time he observed a crying infant's mother calmly prop the child some distance away where it fussed for a time in its cradleboard without any attention. When it stopped the mother promptly returned.

Ishkali was constantly active. She did the heaviest work while directing her daughters at scraping hides on upright frames or pegged to the ground. Elk or deer brain was pounded into them to make them supple, then chalk was pounded in to make them smooth. The women collected fuel for fire, gathered water, pulled up the skirts of the tipi when it needed airing, put them down when it was too windy or cold, mended clothing, and cooked all the meals. They pounded berries into buffalo meat strips, hung them on racks to dry, and chased away the magpies that tried to steal the fruit of their labor. It was hard, physical labor, and the older women looked the worse for a lifetime of this. But to Beckwourth they seemed happy as they went about their work, singing and talking and laughing among themselves, all the while instructing their daughters in these many tasks.

The idleness of the warriors was striking in comparison. After bathing in the river, they spent hours visiting each other to smoke and talk or to play hands and other games. When they worked, it was to fashion weapons. Now and then a group of men went out on a hunt, but even when they did, it was the women who would go out to butcher the animal where it had fallen and haul the meat back to camp.

And the dogs. As numerous as the people; four to six for each family, if one included the puppies that were the children's playthings. Yipping and yapping, snarling and barking, here licking the face of a child, there fighting for a tossed scrap of food; dogs were everywhere. A cross look sent them scampering, though, for misbehaving resulted in a cudgeling.

Thus, the days went. And every evening the war horses, designated by their notched ears and trimmed tails, were separated from the grazing herd and tethered at their warriors' tipis for safekeeping. Cook fires caused the skins of the tipis to become heavily oiled, and in the evening they glowed like lanterns from the fires inside.

One day, one of Beckwourth's sisters, whose name was Jumps to the Sky, packed all of her few belongings and was seen in Big Bowl's tipi no more. His other sister was named something like Never Wavers, as best he could gather with his understanding of the language. Beckwourth asked her what had happened by pointing to Jumps to the Sky's former place in the tipi and shrugging. With a big smile and a laugh, Never Wavers went into a long explanation, none of which he understood, so she took him by the hand to another tipi. There Jumps to the Sky was, and she greeted him joyfully. It seemed she was now married. As far Beckwourth could see, there had been no ceremony of any sort. But clearly, she was happy.

Every ten days or so, grass for the horses would become scarce, and the carcasses game animals began to stink. On some signal unknown to him, the village would then wake one morning and start packing. The women would strike the tipis after breakfast and with the poles make travois for the horses to drag. Everything was loaded on these travois, even toddlers, around whom willow cages were fashioned. Children gleefully struck their play tipis and packed them on travois to be dragged by dogs. Those as young as four were strapped to colts, or they would be sandwiched between older children on a gentle pack horse. Barely an hour after the process had started, one of the lesser chiefs gave the word, and off they all went, warriors in the lead, and in a huge cloud of dust behind them their families followed.

Beckwourth had been among the Crow for three such moves when Crooked Smile found him and beckoned him to follow. He knew enough sign to ask why but felt it better to just obey. They proceeded to a tipi where inside sat several warriors cross-legged on the ground. Crooked Smile sat and indicated a place for Beckwourth. He produced a beautifully embroidered pouch from which he took a wooden shaft and a red stone pipe bowl. Fastening them together, he lit tobacco in the bowl, held it aloft, then to the ground, and to the four points of the compass. He took a pensive drag and passed it to the next man, who did the same, as did Beckwourth's when it was his turn. It was not tobacco, but something milder, with a sort of spicy taste. He passed it on. When the pipe came back to Crooked Smile, still not a word had been spoken. Crooked Smile broke the silence and simultaneously signed. He indicated that Beckwourth had been in the village for many sleeps, after a long journey from far away, which words brought grunts of agreement from the warriors in the circle. Crooked Smile pantomimed that he had half a face that never smiled, but all of Beckwourth's face never smiled. The Crow all shared a laugh at that one. He indicated that Beckwourth was a brave warrior with some details that Beckwourth did not catch. He told that the white trapper who was married to a Mountain Crow had told them that he was taken captive from them when a boy, and Ishkali had confirmed this. "Let him join us on a war party," Crooked Smile signed. Then there were words and signs Beckwourth could not make out. Crooked Smile paused to ask if he understood.

Beckwourth indicated that he understood all but

83

the last. By pantomime, Crooked Smile made him understand that the raid would be against those who had stolen him when young, which he knew of course were supposed to be the Cheyenne. Crooked Smile resumed his discourse, some of which Beckwourth caught, some he didn't, but at any rate, in his mind, this was his chance to prove himself worthy in the eyes of his captors. And that couldn't hurt his chances of escaping this tender captivity.

"I will go with you," he signed.

I t was a pleasant late-summer day when the war party sauntered out. Each warrior was mounted on a travel horse and led behind him his war horse, painted and fitted with a fine, beaded bridle and saddle. Beckwourth surmised that their tails were cut shot so that an enemy could not grab them. Most of the warriors carried guns called fusees; short-barreled, smooth-bore weapons that came by way of the Hudson Bay Company traders. Mountaineers regarded these inaccurate weapons with disdain. All warriors carried quivers of arrows and bows along with their shields slung over their backs. Some carried lances and war clubs to round out their armament. Beckwourth's pistol, knife, and rifle had been restored to him, and Big Bowl had presented him with a stone war club. Might be closer combat than he had seen before, he mused. Trotting along with the war party came their wolf-like dogs, carrying on their backs packs of extra moccasins. Scouts camouflaged with gray mud and wolf headdresses proceeded, and the main party followed.

A warrior named Hunts Alone took him under

his wing; a welcome relief from Crooked Smile's withering gaze. This fellow had been hanging around Big Bowl's tipi for some time, discreetly making eyes at Never Wavers.

After several days they crossed a shallow river that apparently marked the boundary of Crow territory, for they proceeded more cautiously and paused frequently for the go-ahead from the scouts. A day's ride further and they came upon a herd of buffalo. The Crow watched it for a few minutes, but rather than heading in for the hunt, they headed away. Beckwourth signed Hunts Alone to determine what was afoot. He gathered from the reply that the way the buffalo milled about indicated that they had been chased recently, and an enemy was near. Scouts returned with news that indeed, an enemy was just over the next hill. The Crow dismounted their travel horses, and crept, then crawled to the hilltop, with Beckwourth imitating their every move. From the crest he spied Indians butchering a buffalo; a smaller party than their own. The Crow crept back to their horses and discussed the situation, then eagerly mounted their war horses. Beckwourth, however, felt uneasy. He was to go into battle now with warriors he hardly knew, and with whom he could barely communicate. Hunts Alone saw his hesitation and did what he could to encourage with a nudge and a smile. He signed, but when Beckwourth did not seem to understand, he indicated to just follow him. The Crow gathered and galloped to the crest of the hill, where Crooked Smile let out a blood-curdling scream and led the charge. Beckwourth followed.

The enemy had no time to coordinate; only time to go for their horses. The Crow had the element of surprise, a downhill run, and outnumbered their foe, so Beckwourth thought they would make short work of it. He spurred his horse forward. Suddenly, he became aware that he was all by himself and nearly upon the enemy. The rest had all curved away at the last moment. An enemy warrior readied his gun. Panic gripped him. His hands trembled. Was it best now to flee and risk being shot in the back, or to battle all these enemy by himself? The choice paralyzed him for only a moment, until he was gripped by his usual animus: he must prove himself, at any and all costs. Beckwourth swallowed his fear and with a mighty yell and club upraised, charged the warrior who was loading. Unpracticed in this mode of warfare, he managed only a glancing blow, and soon found himself fighting two of the enemy on horseback, with more on their way. The Crow, for their part, overcame their initial surprise that Beckwourth had not veered away with them, and galloped to his aid. Beckwourth wrestled the gunman to the ground, and pulled his fusee from his hands, clubbing him with it. Now the battle was fought in earnest. Their outnumbered foe fought valiantly, but soon the battle was over.

The moans of the dying were drowned out by the victorious cries of the Crow. Beckwourth still panted from exertion when Hunts Alone came to his side and motioned him to scalp his victim. *When in Rome…*he thought, and with a flourish, he did so.

The Crow banter on the way home was lighthearted, though he could understand little of it. It was obvious that he had gained their respect; though from Crooked Smile it was of a grudging sort. Upon coming within sight of the village, they dismounted and produced clamshells that contained grease blackened with charcoal. Hunts Alone gave some to Beckwourth, and he smeared it on his face. They paraded forward with scalps held high on their lances, singing songs, and the village rushed out to meet them. After winding through the village, warriors presented their families with the spoils of their raid — scalps and weapons. Beckwourth followed suit and gave Big Bowl the gun he had taken from the fallen enemy. Big Bowl took the weapon with the greatest of pride. Beckwourth was unsure of what to do with the scalp, but Big Bowl directed that he give it to Ishkali, who was equally proud.

That night, there were two separate victory dances. Greenwood had told him of the Crow societies, which competed with each other for war honors in every way they could, and it seemed that now they celebrated separately. Big Bowl belonged to one society, so it seemed that Beckwourth was automatically a member of that one, and a guest of the other. Crooked Smile, who seemed to now disdain Beckwourth even more than before, was a member of the other. Everywhere Beckwourth was celebrated as the greatest of the warriors in this foray against the Cheyenne. Hunts Alone told him by sign and word that he had earned the two highest coups of the raid: for having struck the first blow, and for wresting his enemy's weapon from his hands. For this he earned two eagle feathers, which Never Wavers lovingly wove into his hair, now nearly down to his shoulders. Beckwourth had to admit, he enjoyed all the attention. He was a hero!

Beckwourth slept late the next morning and was the last of his new family to rise. The interior of Big Bowl's tipi was oddly empty. The flat-bottomed copper kettle that usually would have held breakfast was missing, so was the pile of buffalo robes that Big Bowl slept on. Beckwourth pushed open the door flap and squinted at a beautiful blue sky. His gaze returned to Earth to find Big Bowl giving away a buffalo robe. As the day progressed, he watched Big Bowl give away horses, more robes, beautifully beaded clothing; all sorts of valuables. He was curious at first, then somewhat alarmed as his father gave away more and more of his belongings, until it seemed he might have nothing left. Beckwourth finally, through sign and pantomime asked Big Bowl why he was doing this. It took some back and forth with his poor grasp of the Crow language, but he came to understand that it was his own great success that caused Big Bowl to give away his valuables. It seemed that Beckwourth had made his father feel so rich that in order to reset the balance in his life, he had to give away much of his wealth. Beckwourth was dismayed. Here, in an effort to prove himself worthy to Crooked Smile and the rest of the Crow, he had managed to impoverish the one person among them that he owed the most.

Beckwourth resolved to replace his father's wealth, and the best way he knew how was to get beaver pelts. Those could be traded for such items as the cooking pot, but not the horses. When Hunts Alone came around to chat up Never Wavers, Beckwourth asked him by signs and drawing in the dirt to show where to find beaver. Hunts Alone was eager to help his new friend, so the two set about trapping in the nearby streams. Beckwourth used their time together to learn as much of the language as he could, and he became able to converse fairly well over some weeks, combining sign with words. Most days they came up with a goodly number of pelts, which Never Wavers and Ishkali scraped and stretched on willow hoops. One day, all Beckwourth's traps came up empty. Hunts Alone took notice of his disappointment.

"My friend," said Hunts Alone, "my heart is heavy when yours is heavy."

"It is nothing," said Beckwourth. "Tomorrow we will catch many beaver."

"It is not just for the beaver that your heart is heavy," said Hunts Alone. "You are far from the people who raised you."

"This is so," Beckwourth admitted.

"I am married to a good woman," said Hunts Alone. "Other than her, I am alone in the world as well: all my kindred have gone to the Other Side Camp."

"What happened to them?" asked Beckwourth. He seemed to have an unlimited number of relations himself as part of Big Bowl's family and thought that all Crow similarly had huge families.

"My father was a poor man who one day did a foolish thing. He wanted to show me the power of gunpowder. He threw some in the fire and burned himself. After several days he died. Not long after came the Spotted Death. How my people suffered from the Spotted Death! Of every five Crow, three died a hideous death, their faces rotting away so that even the wolves shrunk from them. And we who survived despaired that we had not gone on to the Other Side Camp with them. My mother, my sisters, and my brother all died."

Hunts Alone continued, "I now want one friend — a good friend — who will be my brother. I am a warrior, and so are you. You have been far away to the villages of the white man. Your eyes have seen much, and you have now returned to your people.

Will you be my friend and brother? Will you be as one man with me as long as you live?"

Beckwourth was touched deeply. Never had he seen such a sincere plea. "It would be the greatest honor of my life to be your brother," Beckwourth said in English, then translated into Crow. They grasped each other's forearms and pledged their lifelong fidelity.

Beckwourth thought that it was done, but they were only starting.

"It is good," said Hunts Alone. "Now we must exchange our belongings." He held out his fusee to trade. Beckwourth hesitated to trade his father's best rifle for this inferior weapon. But there was no turning back now. Next, they exchanged horses. It was a good thing that he had already lost his father's horse, he thought. That he would have hesitated to trade for an Indian pony. This went on, item by item, until they had exchanged everything they owned: clothing, war clubs, knives, bows; down to their very moccasins. As the exchange progressed, though he was coming out something of the loser, Beckwourth felt enveloped by a glow, a sense of affiliation deeper than any he had ever before felt.

"Now," said Hunts Alone, "in the tradition of my people, we are one while we live. What I know, you shall know. There must be no secret between us."

Well, at least no secrets going forward, thought Beckwourth.

"Come now, we must go to my father's lodge," said Hunts Alone.

"I thought you said you had no kin," said Beckwourth.

Hunts Alone smiled broadly. "Big Bowl is now my father," he said.

Of course, thought Beckwourth, *my father is now his*

father. They found Big Bowl, who received the news that he had a new son with great pleasure. Ishkali was similarly pleased and made a meal for her new adopted son.

Soon after, Hunts Alone came to Beckwourth. "There is to be a raid against the Assiniboine, and you should go."

Beckwourth saw a chance to restore his father's wealth. "Will we capture horses?" he asked.

"Yes. It is a raid for horses."

"If my brother says I should go, then I will," said Beckwourth. "Who leads this raid?"

"Crooked Smile."

Beckwourth paused. "Why is Crooked Smile's heart is hardened against me more since we went against the Cheyenne?"

"You know that Crooked Smile carried the pipe that time, do you not?"

"Yes, I know this," said Beckwourth. To 'carry the pipe' on a raid was the designation of leadership.

"The pipe is sacred," said Hunts Alone. "It was for him to make the first coup on the enemy, but you did that instead."

"Ah," said Beckwourth. "He meant to touch a Cheyenne before blood was spilled. And I spoiled it for him."

"That is so," said Hunts Alone.

"This arouses his anger more than me wounding him?"

"A warrior wears his scars with pride, but this is a different thing."

"I wish to have no enemies among the Crow," said Beckwourth. "What can I do to soften his heart?"

"If there is a way, it will become known."

Beckwourth shrugged and shook his head. Going

on this raid might only make things worse between him and Crooked Smile. "Why do we go against the Assiniboine?"

"They are not such an enemy as the Sioux or the Blackfeet. But in the Green Grass season they stole our horses."

"If this is what it takes for me to restore Big Bowl's horses, then it is good," Beckwourth said. "I will go with you."

"No," said Hunts Alone. "You may go, but if you do, I must not. We are brothers now. We must never go on the same raid together, for if both of us were killed, who would mourn faithfully for the other?"

"But I do not know Crow ways. You must come with me. I will defend your scalp the same as mine," he said.

"That is not our way," said Hunts Alone. "But I will be with you when you depart the village."

"Then that must be enough," Beckwourth said reluctantly. "I have another question. You no longer make eyes at Never Wavers. Does she no longer please you?"

Hunts Alone laughed, stopped to look at his friend to see if he was serious, and laughed again. "Do you not believe me when I say that I am your brother?" he asked. "She is now my sister just as much as you are my brother. Do whites marry their sisters?"

The Crow are a strange and wondrous people, thought Beckwourth.

"Have you done anything that would exert your manhood since the last raid?" Hunts Alone asked Beckwourth.

"I do not hear your meaning."

"Have you lain with any women?"

"No, no," said Beckwourth. "I have a woman in St. Louis, and I am faithful to her."

"That is good. Can you swear to that?"

"Certainly," said Beckwourth. "Why do you ask this?"

"You will see," said Hunts Alone.

❧ 10 ❧

This was a raid, not warfare, so they travelled each on a favorite horse, with a minimum of weapons. Beckwourth was dressed the same as the rest, in breechcloth and leggings, an elk-skin shirt to his mid-thigh, and a buffalo robe over his shoulder. The only reminder of his prior life was the coin around his neck. They trotted north by moonlight, away from the village and into a great open stillness. In time they reached the Missouri River. Smaller streams to the south could be forded at this time of year, but this great river had to be swum. They wrapped their guns and powder inside buffalo hides with a ballast of rocks at the bottom and a leather drawstring at the top and pushed that along as they swam to the far shore. Beckwourth came out wet and shivering, but their guns and powder were bone dry.

Around noon the next day they came upon a small herd of buffalo. Once satisfied that it grazed undisturbed, Crooked Smile spurred his horse onward and separated out a fat cow. He let the reins go as he readied bow and arrow, his horse keeping pace with the cow as it wove about, then deftly sent an arrow straight through the animal's paunch and into the ground. The moment that the bowstring twanged, the horse veered away. The Crow sent the youngest members of the party, mere boys in their early teens, to collect buffalo chips, and waited patiently for the buffalo to collapse. When it finally did, steaks were cut and roasted over the chips, and all ate their fill. Then, it seemed there was to be some sort of ceremony. Roasted intestine was cut up and distributed to small groups. In Beckwourth's circle, each man held the intestine between his thumb and finger and looked to their leader. Beckwourth followed suit. The leader commanded them to never tell any woman what they were about to hear, on pain of banishment. All that followed, they were told, would be related to the village medicine men. One by one, each was commanded to confess any sexual misdeeds since the last time they had gone on a raid and to name their lover and the date that this occurred. Each man did so, and all had something to confess regarding a woman to whom he was not betrothed. It seemed that fidelity was a scarce commodity among the Crow. The men were not bragging, nor did they express any remorse; they were just relating the facts. After doing this, the declarant proclaimed to the earth, and to the sun, swearing by his gun, his knife, and his sacred pipe that this was the full extent of his recent failings. When it came Beckwourth's turn, he felt bad, in a way, in that he had nothing to report. The group was skeptical.

"Do you swear before your God?" one finally asked.

Beckwourth affirmed this in Crow, then added in English, "I swear by God in Heaven, by earth below, my knife, my gun, and by these grisly buffalo guts that it is so," pointing to each.

That seemed to satisfy them, and they moved on to the next man.

When all this was completed, the leader kicked over the buffalo chips, and they let out war whoops. The raid was on. The scouts donned their wolf skins and fanned out, while the rest of the group proceeded little by little at their direction. They traveled in this manner uneventfully for another day, but the day following that, scouts returned with news that they had come upon a large village of Assiniboine ahead. There were those who wanted to stage a daytime raid as soon as possible before they might be discovered, and others argued for a night raid which would give them the best chance of escape. The latter would also allow the stealing of the best horses, which would be picketed at the tipis. Crooked Smile decided on a nighttime raid.

The scouts had identified an approach to the village though a ravine. At dusk, the Crow crept up the ravine and reconnoitered at its rim. The grazing herd was between them and the village, unguarded and easy prey. Crooked Smile appointed less-experienced men to stampede the herd on signal, while he and the best warriors would steal picketed steeds. A bird whistle was the signal for all to act at once. Crooked Smile appointed Beckwourth to the stampeders.

If the leader had been anyone else, Beckwourth might have acquiesced. But the way that Crooked Smile relegated him to the inexperienced men struck a nerve. "I am a warrior like these others, if not greater. I have proven myself in battle, and you must allow me to prove my worth here," he demanded.

Crooked Smile examined him coldly. "You will make a noise, and the enemy will be aroused and kill us all."

"I will not do this," said Beckwourth. "I am going to steal a picketed horse."

"I will allow this, only if you agree to my words: if you alert the enemy, and they take the scalp of any one of us, or even count coup on any one of us, if they do not kill you first, then I will kill you," said Crooked Smile.

"Fair enough," said Beckwourth, lapsing into English. But he already regretted his brashness.

While they waited for the village to go to sleep, a warrior came to Beckwourth.

"Do you know me?" he asked.

"I do not," said Beckwourth.

"I am the husband of your sister, Jumps to the Sky. I do not wish for her to mourn your death. You must follow me. I will pick out a horse for you near mine. When I creep forward, you creep forward. When I flatten to the ground, you flatten to the ground. Can you do this?"

"I will be glad to do this. What is your name?"

"I am Bird That Runs."

When the stars became bright in the sky and the Assinboine camp quieted, and even the dogs slept, Crooked Smile gave the signal. Beckwourth crept toward the enemy, one eye always on Bird that Runs. He crept a few feet at a time, then paused, watching, all the while listening for the bird call that was to signal the final rush. Bird That Runs indicated to him his target, a horse tethered a scant ten yards from its owner's tipi. Beckwourth crept forward and paused, then again. A leaf crunched under his moccasin. He froze and looked to Bird That Runs, who also froze. They watched the tipis for a moment, but the soft snores were uninterrupted. Bird That Runs held a stick up in the air for Beckwourth to see, then poked it at the ground. It took Beckwourth a moment to understand, but he was being told to move such leaves out of his path with a stick. But he did not have a stick. He searched the ground for leaves. There were few enough that he could avoid them, though it would slow his progress. He proceeded on a more zig-zagging route towards his target, every few feet pausing to listen for signs that he might have been detected. A stirring inside a nearby tipi stopped him mid-step. Bird That Runs had only the Assiniboine to fear. Beckwourth had that, and death at the hands of Crooked Smile if he caused them to wake, for he had no doubt that the man meant what he said. A minute passed with no further noise from the tipi, and they both crept forward again. Closer and closer, Beckwourth inched toward his horse. It was a handsome beast; small like most Indian ponies, and alert now, aware of his approach. The horse snorted. Beckwourth paused again. No sound from the tipi. He moved forward. The horse nickered. He paused again. He reached for the horse's picket and heard a leaf crunch underfoot.

A dog barked, then another, and then a great howling from them all. They had been discovered! If the bird call was sounded, it was drowned out to his ears. Beckwourth snatched the picket line and cut it with his knife. He grabbed the horse's mane and swung onto its back. Gunshots sounded near and far, and arrows whizzed through the air. Beckwourth dug his heels into the horse's flanks, and he was away, hoping and praying that none of those missiles would find a target in his party. The Crow thundered away before any of the Assiniboine were mounted. The enemy gave chase for some distance, but a night chase is never wise, and they soon stopped. For the Assiniboine it was only horses; they had not lost a man. But had the Crow lost any?

They rode hard all night, driving the herd before them. Early the next morning they reached a stream and stopped to water the horses. Crooked Smile took stock of his men. It was good. Two with minor wounds, all accounted for. He spoke to Bird That Runs and gave Beckwourth a haughty look. Beckwourth dared not ask. Had coup been scored on any of the Crow?

For the rest of the journey home, the Crow bantered with one another, boasting of their deeds, but Beckwourth did not share their enthusiasm. When they reached the village, Crooked Smile approached Beckwourth.

"You woke the Assinboine dogs."

"If Bird That Runs says it is so, it is so," said Beckwourth.

"All returned safe," said Crooked Smile. "You are fortunate in this. You may choose as many captured horses as the others." He rode away.

He was off the hook!

❧ 11 ❧

One day, not long after the raid on the Assiniboine, Beckwourth watched a group of boys as they played the bow and arrow game, one boy rolling a willow hoop that others shot at with their arrows; just shafts really, with no tip or feathers. It was a pleasure to watch children play, so carefree and joyful, boasting to one another of their prowess. Also nearby, a teenaged boy was being instructed by a woman. Or what seemed at first to be a woman. But the shoulders were too broad, the voice too deep. Beckwourth had heard of *berdache* among the Indians of the plains; men who chose at a young age to dress as women, and who in every way took up the life of a woman. He watched, fascinated and repulsed at the same time. He was not close enough to hear what was said, but could see that the teen paid rapt attention to the advice. When the lesson was over, the boy left. The *berdache* turned to Beckwourth, and returned his stare with a challenge, then an inviting smile. Flustered, Beckwourth hastened away, and in his haste, he ran into Crooked Smile, who had been watching, unobserved while he worked on an arrow. Crooked

Smile looked at the *berdache*, then at Beckwourth with disdain. He drew the arrow shaft through a hole in a stone, then inspected it for straightness. Beckwourth recovered his composure and approached.

"Crooked Smile, you are a great warrior. And a great hunter. I saw you send an arrow like that through a buffalo when we went against the Assiniboine. You have a powerful bow and a powerful arm."

Crooked Smile glanced again in the direction of the *berdache*, and then at Beckwourth. For a moment, the only sound was the squeals of the boys playing the arrow and hoop game nearby. Crooked Smile tossed his bow to Beckwourth. It was a beautiful thing, fashioned in layers from the horns of a ram. Beckwourth fondled it and pulled back the string, arms shaking slightly as he did so. Crooked Smile took the bow back and nocked an arrow. He turned to the playing boys, drew smoothly, and in the same instant sailed an arrow through the boys' hoop. The youngsters squealed in delight and returned the arrow with eager smiles. Crooked Smile praised them and watched as they scampered away.

"You are not a Crow," he said.

"One does not learn to avoid leaves underfoot when living with the whites," said Beckwourth.

"You never were a Crow," said Crooked Smile. "I watched your friend's face, the one with the Mountain Crow woman, I watched his face when he said you were stolen by the Cheyenne."

"You should tell the others, if you think this," said Beckwourth.

"The others are fools," said Crooked Smile. "They have it in their heads that the white man has such great *maxpe* with his guns and other metal objects that because of this they should believe everything he says. I am not so foolish."

"The Crow need allies," said Beckwourth. "You are a small tribe surrounded by more numerous enemies. You need the white man as an ally."

"This might be. But you are not a Crow." He turned his back on Beckwourth and resumed fashioning arrows.

Weeks passed. Beckwourth was resigned to spending the winter with the Crow, but he often thought of Eliza and his family, and when he did, his heart ached. He trapped with Hunts Alone to keep his mind off them, and his friend took him around the village. On these tours, Hunts Alone introduced him to the men as they played hands and their other gambling games. Mostly, the men gathered in their societies. Big Bowl's society, which Beckwourth and Hunts Alone belonged to, was the Dog Soldiers. Their main rival was the Fox society, which Crooked Smile belonged to. Beckwourth was proficient in the language now, and he listened to men of the Dog Soldiers swap stories of bravery and boasts of future conquests; conquests of war and conquests of women.

One day Big Bowl called Beckwourth into his tipi, where sat his brother-in-law, Bird That Runs, and seven youngsters that Big Bowl introduced as his sons. None of these youngsters shared Big Bowl's tipi, and Beckwourth recognized only one, that being the teen who had been engrossed in conversation with the *berdache*. Big Bowl introduced each by name, and that one was named Stands Again. From what he knew of Crow custom, Beckwourth figured that these were probably nephews of Big Bowl. Be that as it may, here they were, all solemn and cross-legged before him, seven boys ranging in age from ten to eighteen perhaps, and Bird That Runs.

"What is the meaning of this, father?" asked Beckwourth. "Have I wronged you in any way?"

"No, my son," Big Bowl replied. "You are only a gift in my old age. The One Above Person has rewarded me with your presence, and I am grateful. But I must speak to you. I see in you strong *maxpe*, but you do not use it as a warrior should."

Maxpe was a term tossed around constantly among the Crow, the full meaning of which eluded Beckwourth. It was both the strength of a man's will, and his sixth sense, it seemed; his connection to the One Above Person. In any case, Big Bowl was questioning his manhood, if he were to frame the challenge in the white man's terms. "My *maxpe* is indeed strong," Beckwourth said. "But I am content, my father. If I were not content with being a member of your family, would I not be ungrateful?"

"There can be room in one's heart to be grateful, and for fire."

"The only fire that is in the heart of a Crow is to be a warrior," said Beckwourth. "I was raised by whites, and it is not so for me. I wish for myself wealth, and wealth for you as well, and for all the Crow."

"But you are brave and cunning in battle. This is your Crow birth showing itself."

"Very well," Beckwourth lapsed into English, then continued in Crow, "my ears are open. Tell me why you have called me here."

"I am a chief, and I wish to see my sons set their feet upon the path of becoming chiefs, as well. Do you know the four deeds a man must perform to become a chief?"

"No, father."

"It is a coup to touch a man in battle. But to be first to touch an enemy in battle, that is a deed on the path to becoming chief."

"I have accomplished that one" said Beckwourth. "Crooked Smile is still angry with me for taking that honor from him."

"That one has a hard heart for you, my son. Second, you must take an enemy's weapon while he still lives."

"I have done that as well," said Beckwourth.

"And for that they sang your virtues. Third, you must steal an enemy's picketed horse."

"I have done that as well," said Beckwourth.

"And in doing so you caused my heart to swell with pride," said Big Bowl. "Your feet have been set on the path to being a chief."

Entirely by accident, thought Beckwourth. "But I cannot be a chief," he protested. "I know none of the Crow ways except the simple things I see with my own eyes."

"You do not need to know Crow ways to be a chief. Leave the storytelling and legends to the medicine men. We have enough of them. We are surrounded by enemies. What we need are brave warriors."

"That is three deeds," Beckwourth said. "What is the fourth?"

"You must carry the pipe for a successful war party."

"What Crow would follow me?" Beckwourth asked. "Who would put their life in my hands?"

Big Bowl grunted. "They sit before you," he said, indicating his 'sons' and Bird That Runs, who stiffened at Beckwourth's question.

"Father," said Beckwourth, "I could not bear to

be the cause of your grief if one of your sons were killed in battle."

"If they all get killed, so be it; I will gladly submit to an old age without them and die alone."

"Yes, but these are so young." He indicated the youngest. "This one is just a boy."

"I am not just a boy!" piped the youngster.

"He may carry the water and firewood, for this, his first chance at battle," said Bird That Runs. "He tires of the games of boys."

"Whom do you wish we attack then, father?" asked Beckwourth.

"The Arapaho have been stealing our horses," said Bird That Runs. "They must be punished."

Again, thought Beckwourth, *no shortage of enemies. And always the Crow think themselves to be the aggrieved party.*

Beckwourth considered. His debt to Big Bowl had been paid. But there was an exhilaration to the Crow manner of war, and the recognition that came from success at it was flattering.

"The days are becoming shorter and colder now," he said. "It is best that we go now if we are to go at all."

Because this was a small raiding party, Bird That Runs advised that they not leave the village in a body in case an enemy was scouting the village. Instead, they would leave one by one at night, and meet at an appointed spot some miles away. Beckwourth arrived first and waited, brooding in the silence of a moonlit landscape. His initial enthusiasm had been dampened by more sober afterthought. He had consulted Hunts Alone and found out that a successful war party hinged on two things. All members had to return alive. That was his intent from the start. But second, they had to return with a scalp; at least one. He had thought that stealing horses would be sufficient, but no. Bird That Runs arrived and interrupted his thoughts. There were few words between them as the youngsters trickled in. The last arrived, and they headed out into the night. As Beckwourth rode, he mused at the path that had brought him here. Among the whites, he had to claw for every scrap of respect. Among the Crow, equality was automatic, and respect came solely from one's deeds. But now, having taken on a task out of a sense of duty, he held in his hands eager young lives. He resolved to use caution at every turn. If they brought back no scalps and he was then not a chief, it was of no matter to him.

They proceeded south on horseback, buffalo robes on their shoulders, all but one trailing a war horse behind. The exception was the youngest, the ten-year old who they called Water Carrier. This was evidently to be a long trip, or perhaps Bird That Runs felt they could not rely on finding enough game, for they carried loops of a sort of sausage over their shoulders. Across broad valleys they went, towards the mountains, fording streams and small rivers on the way. Into sparsely wooded foothills they journeyed, then through mountain passes of piney woods. Nights were below freezing at the higher elevations, but they sheltered comfortably in debris huts made from fallen branches. Once through the mountain passes, they were in the bleak terrain of the high desert that Beckwourth had traversed the prior winter with Ashley. Here is where the buffalo sausage was needed to sustain them, for there was no game. Some days later they descended into a lush valley, where flowed a clear mountain stream, its banks lined with willows and cottonwood trees. Songbirds chirped and hawks soared. Wisps of smoke indicated the Arapaho village.

Beckwourth had had the entire journey to plot how he might thread the needle of this mission. "We will sleep here," he said to his charges. "But I must tell you that I had a dream last night. An Arapaho horse came to me in this dream, one with his ears notched to mark him as a war horse. He said to me that he wished to come with the Crow, to be ridden by the bravest of all the tribes into battle."

"Tell us," said Stands Again. "Did he say more?"

"Yes," said Beckwourth, "but it will disappoint you, for I know you came here to prove yourselves. This war horse said that we must not shed Arapaho blood, for they had treated him well, even traveling far that he might have grass to eat, and not have to subsist on the bark of the cottonwood tree."

Spirits sagged. "We cannot have come so far to only steal horses," said Stands Again.

Beckwourth was ready with another white lie for this. "I also saw that the enemy sleeps lightly, for they have seen another enemy lurking recently. It will be a great victory just to elude their guards and stampede the herd."

His charges reluctantly accepted this, and soon slept.

Beckwourth posted Bird That Runs as first watch, and when his brother-in-law woke him, took the next watch himself. When the predawn light was just sufficient to see the creases in his hand, he roused the others, and after a quick meal, he formed them all in a line on horseback. He gave the signal, and they swooped in between the herd and the village, waving their robes in the air, driving the horses away from the awakening Arapaho with as much noise as they could muster. Thundering hooves drowned out the call of alarm in the village as the triumphant raiders quickly put distance between themselves and an aroused foe.

By the time the first Arapaho riders were in pursuit, the Crow were well out of range of bullet or arrow. They rode hard, switching to Arapaho mounts when theirs became jaded, and gained further when the Arapaho paused to round up those horses. The Crow rode at a gallop from dawn to dusk. Beckwourth exulted; his simple plan had been a complete success, with not even a scratch among Big Bowl's kin. They rode all night, and through the next day, crossing a cold, cold river chest deep. They camped on the other side and lit their first fire since the raid. It was time to warm up, eat, and rest their aching butts. Exhausted, they posted a guard and fell soundly asleep.

The next morning, Bird That Runs cautioned that they were now in territory that no tribe owned, where any of a half-dozen tribes might be encountered, and all were their enemies. But his warnings could not dampen the ebullient mood of the youngsters. They bantered amongst themselves, each recounting details of his role in the raid. When one told his tale, another would chime in a confirmation of the deed. And each glowed with anticipation of the praise they would receive on arrival home. Beckwourth found all this a bit tiresome after a while, and he could not help but tease them.

"I will become the most honored of all the Crow someday," said Water Carrier.

"Yes, youngster," said Beckwourth, "You are indeed destined to become the most feared water carrier the Crow have ever known."

"You mock me, big brother," said the boy. "Do

not speak so. I will be a great chief someday, because I will learn from you the white man's ways, as well as the ways of the Crow. I wish to die in battle, and have my deeds sung for generations."

"If you wish to learn from the white man, listen to me," said Beckwourth. "The greater glory goes to the warrior who wins the battle than the one who dies in it."

"You do not understand Crow ways," said Stands Again.

"This is true," said Beckwourth.

"I wish to marry," said Stands Again.

"And so you should," said Beckwourth. Stands Again looked to him to be sixteen or so.

"But only one who has shown bravery in battle is allowed to marry," said Stands Again. "And I have still never seen battle."

"You will never marry that girl," said Water Carrier. "Even if you slay a hundred enemy. You are too frightened of her."

Stands Again pulled himself up to his full height. "I know one who will give me a potion. He knows the ways of women."

Just then, Bird That Runs, who had been scouting ahead, came tearing towards them at top speed with the news that three Indians drove a small herd of horses directly toward them, two in front, one in the rear. He could not tell of what tribe, but he was certain they were not Crow. Beckwourth surveyed the terrain.

"Water Carrier, Stands Again," he said.

"Yes, big brother."

"Take all the horses over that hill, out of sight."

Their faces betrayed disappointment that they would not see battle, but they obeyed. Beckwourth instructed the rest to lie flat on the ground just short of the crest of the hill they had been climbing. When the oncoming herd came into view, they jumped up with their war-whoops at full volume. The two who led the herd were slain immediately, and the third fled.

"I will catch him!" called Bird That Runs as he started for the third enemy.

"Stop!" Beckwourth commanded. "He is too far."

Bird That Runs' shoulders sagged. "You carry the pipe," he said. "It is for you to say."

After scalping the two fallen warriors, whom they were delighted to find to be Sioux, the Crow resumed their path home. Caution was the rule until they crossed waters that marked Crow territory. The boys fell into even greater bragging, anticipating their reception at home, now that they returned with scalps as well as horses. Every detail of who had done what, and what the enemy did, and what weapons they had captured, how magnificent these horses were, and so forth was gone over and over and over again. In their youthful minds they were all of the same fiber as the greatest heroes of the Crow nation. Beckwourth found it tiresome after a while but held his tongue. Bird That Runs encouraged them, reflecting their pride as his as well, and when they came near the village, he solemnly helped them paint their faces black for the first time in their young lives. The whole village came out to greet the heroes. Their joy was all the greater because the horses recovered from the Sioux had just been stolen from the village. Those were returned to their owners, which still left a wealth of Arapaho horses for Beckwourth to distribute. "Great is Shoots Good in the Dark," chanted the crowd, to the accompaniment of the women's ululations.

That night there was a victory dance among the Dog Soldiers, for all of this party were now initiates of that society. The previous dances Beckwourth had attended seemed only a savage frenzy to his eyes, but now he noticed nuances he had not before noted. The dance was really a ritual flirtation between the warriors at the center and their wives and sweethearts encircling them. Round and round they danced to the rhythm of the drums and the tweeting of eagle-bone whistles. And lo and behold, directing the dance was the *berdache* who had counseled Stands Again. The *berdache* stopped the drums and bade Beckwourth to recount details of the raid.

Beckwourth borrowed a coup stick and approached the scalp pole. He called out the details of the raid to the rhythm of drums, striking the pole after every phrase. He emphasized the caution he had taken at first, and extolled the virtues of each of the youngsters, saying that each would someday be among the greatest of the Crow tribe. When finished, he danced, bathing in the praise of the Dog Soldiers.

The next morning, the herald proclaimed, "The lost son of Big Bowl has accomplished the four deeds. His *maxpe* is strong, and he brings honor and wealth to his father."

So now he was a chief.

The next morning, Beckwourth awoke to the bustling sounds of Ishkali as she made breakfast. She seemed more animated than usual, and when she saw that he was stirring, she began to sing.

"It pleases me to see you so happy," said Beckwourth.

"Look," she smiled, gesturing outside.

Beckwourth poked his head out of the door flap and squinted. The landscape was a brilliant white.

"Ah, first snow," he said to himself in English. His first thought was relief that they were not still out on the trail just now. He ate breakfast with Ishkali, Big Bowl, and Never Wavers, each of whom was in an unusually cheerful mood.

"It is good that it has snowed," Beckwourth offered.

Big Bowl beamed. "Yes, it is good."

But Beckwourth did not share their enthusiasm for the onset of winter, and at first, he could not put his finger on why. When in a contemplative mood, Beckwourth often read and reread his book. In the midst of doing this, while Ishkali and Never Wavers cheerfully fashioned moccasins from old tipis, the reason for his discontent occurred to him. Deep in the recesses of his mind, he had harbored a thought to get back to hearth, home, and his sweetheart before winter. Now he would be with the Crow until spring. His real family would gradually lose hope that he might be alive, and Eliza, thinking him dead, would move on with her life.

Big Bowl finally commented. "Your heart is heavy, my son."

Beckwourth shrugged. "I am happy that snow makes my family happy," he said.

"When the snow first falls, it is the end of the war season. The enemy does not attack because it is too hard to travel through the snow, and too easy to track them if they did. The warriors who pledged to stake themselves to the ground in battle so that others may flee are released from their vows. It is the season now for the sweat lodge. You must come with me to the sweat lodge."

Beckwourth complied. Inside a great lodge the chiefs and medicine men sat around heated rocks onto which water was ladled. At the margins of the hut sat the young men and boys, who breathed in the steam and listened to the history, legends, and myths of the Absaroka people. There was a hypnotic rhythm to the chanted tales. At the end of every phrase there was a drumbeat, and at every pause, the audience grunted, "e" as an affirmation, and then the speaker resumed, "ikye" — "attention." Over the days and weeks, Beckwourth learned much about his adopted people.

Many generations ago, before there were horses, they were of the Hidatsa, an agricultural tribe that still lived along the Missouri River, and whom they still visited every year. The Hidatsa hunted with bone-tipped arrows, and they were clad in the furs of small game stitched together. There was an argument between two Hidatsa clans that came to a head over a trivial matter; that being that a woman was offended when she did not get the portion of a drowned buffalo that she felt she deserved. The clan that became the Crow split and left the sedentary ways of the others, taking up the nomadic life of the tribes of the plains. They called themselves the Absaroka after a bird that now, so many generations later, was not to be found. They wandered on foot in search of a home for generations, following the buffalo herds over the vast plains and mountain foothills. They stampeded buffalo over cliffs, or stalked elk and mountain sheep. They travelled as far south as a great salt water that could not be seen across, and far to the north where summers were pleasant enough, but winters were unbearable, where the wind blew fierce over endless desolation. They pushed west as well, past the tallest mountains, but there they found no buffalo, and they disdained the diet of fish that the local tribes subsisted upon.

Wandering south, the Absaroka met a band of Indians with horses to trade. Unfamiliar with such exotic beasts, a chief got too close to the hindquarters of one. He survived the horse's kick, but ever after his clan was known as the 'Kicked in the Bellies'. The Absaroka rapidly became adept horsemen. Trade brought them metal goods. Buffalo were easy prey on horseback, and the tribe ate well, and were able to make larger tipis from the many hides they now obtained. With greater mobility came more contact with other tribes, and war became part of the fabric of life. Other tribes were larger, and to survive, the Absaroka honed themselves into awesome warriors, labelled by others as the lowly Crow, but feared nonetheless. Their wanderings finally brought them to the headwaters of the Yellowstone River, where they settled. Here it was not too hot in the summer, nor too cold in the winter. The grass for the horses was sweet, there were plenty of buffalo, and streams flowed year-round with clean water, not like the muddy water of the Missouri. They settled here and ever after defended this place as their own.

Beckwourth shook off his melancholy after a time. He was in appearance like any other member of the Crow. Clad in his long buckskin shirt, breechclout, and leggings, he strode about the village with the same athleticism as the rest, as if ready to leap on the back of a horse at a moment's notice. His bronze face was framed by hair that fell on his shoulders, into which Never Wavers had woven blue beads and fluttering feathers. Moccasins had replaced his worn-out boots; in this season made of buffalo hide with fur on the inside for warmth, so even if trailed, his footprints were that of a Crow. He spoke the language well, though occasionally a child might giggle at verbal missteps, such as calling a woman's father by the name for a man's father.

But he still measured his days by the white man's calendar. On this his second Christmas away from family and friends, a longing for home again descended over him. He missed his sisters, his older half-brother who had left home before him to become a riverboat captain, and his father. And of course, Eliza.

Not wishing to explain himself to anyone, Beckwourth spent most of Christmas day alone, singing carols to the birds down by the frozen river. His Crow family and friends recognized his desire for solitude and respected it. But the next day, Big Bowl came to him with a look of concern.

"My son," Big Bowl said, "I see that you still have

within your heart, an empty spot."

"It is hard being separated from…," Beckwourth stopped himself from saying 'my people', "…from being so far from the people who raised me."

"Come with me," said Big Bowl. "Rotten Belly wishes to speak to you."

Rotten Belly was the great chief Beckwourth had been brought to his first day, when his capture had been turned into an adoption by virtue of a tiny birthmark. Something was afoot. Big Bowl led Beckwourth across the camp, such a hive of activity in the summer months, now quieted by its snowy blanket. Even the dogs knew him now and just sniffed him and gave only a yap or two as he passed. Big Bowl lifted the flap to Rotten Belly's tipi, and Beckwourth stepped inside. The great chief's piercing gaze was all that was visible in the flickering light at first. As Beckwourth's eyes adjusted to the dark, Rotten Belly came into full view, scalp-lock trimmed shirt and all, seated in a circle with his lesser chiefs. Beckwourth was motioned to sit. Rotten Belly silently lit his pipe and lifted it to the sky, to the earth, then to the four points of the compass before smoking and passing it on. Each chief wordlessly did the same, and Beckwourth as well. When the pipe returned to Rotten Belly, he broke the silence.

"Shoots Good in the Dark, it warms my heart to see how you have become one of us again. You have proven your bravery, and the village sings your praise. Every day, mothers say loudly to their boys as you pass, 'look my son, look at this great warrior. You should be like him when you grow up.' Tell us, Shoots Good in the Dark; tell us of your deeds."

Beckwourth had come to enjoy every such chance he was given, and he obliged. He told of how he had first touched a live enemy and taken his weapon, thereby completing two deeds at once without even knowing that there was such a thing as a path to become a chief. He told of the raid on the Assiniboine and how Bird That Runs had shown him to avoid stepping on leaves, how when the camp awoke he cut the tether and jumped on the horse. Crooked Smile was in the circle, and Beckwourth took care to praise him, judiciously leaving out the part that he had promised to kill him if he woke the enemy. Lastly, he recounted the war party of Big Bowl's kin, praising Bird That Runs for guiding them over such a great distance and opining that the youngsters on that raid would one day become great Crow leaders. He ended in Crow manner, saying, "I have finished."

"It is good," said Rotten Belly. "You now may sit among the chiefs as one of us. But still, you long for something. Yesterday you spent the day singing by the frozen river, as if you wished to melt it with your song."

"I have only been with the Crow for a short time, Great Chief. At times I miss those who raised me."

"It is natural, I agree," said Rotten Belly. "But you are such a solitary one."

"I have a good friend in Hunts Alone."

"Yes," said Rotten Belly, "but you do not lie with women."

So, the word from the buffalo intestine ceremony had got around. "I have a woman in St. Louis," he said.

"But she is far away, and you are here where the nights are cold." Rotten Belly paused. "There are men among us who are like women. They cook, they work hides, they make the moccasins that we wear when we go to war, they take down the tipis when we move; they do all things that women do."

Beckwourth saw the unasked question. "I have seen such men among the Crow," he said. "I wish you to know that such men among the whites are hated and live in hiding. I have no interest in such men, great chief."

Rotten Belly's face betrayed surprise. "Why do the whites hate such men?" he asked.

Beckwourth had never considered that things should be otherwise. "The whites believe that such men are hated by the One Above Person," he said, "and they believe that therefore they must hate them as well."

"The One Above Person made these men as he made you and me. Why would he hate them?" asked Rotten Belly.

"They have turned from the path the One Above Person set for them," said Beckwourth.

Rotten Belly took another smoke. "Your thoughts on this are curious, but not of the matter before us. You have set your feet on the path of becoming a great warrior. A great warrior must have a wife. You must choose a wife."

"Great Chief, I do not desire a wife," said Beckwourth. He had been aware of the eyes of many women upon him of late, and he enjoyed that, but he spoke the truth.

"A warrior must have a wife," Rotten Belly repeated. "I have three daughters from which you may choose. Tomorrow you will come here to choose."

Beckwourth hearkened back to Greenwood's dictum, that one should never refuse such a gift. As well as that, not everyone among the tribe was his friend. It wouldn't hurt to have the great chief as his father-in-law.

"I would be honored to marry one of your daughters, oh, Great Chief," he said.

The next morning, Beckwourth put on his finest shirt and leggings, wrapped himself in his buffalo robe, on which his sisters had drawn his four deeds, and proceeded to Rotten Belly's tipi.

"These are my daughters; Still Water, Black Fish, and Three Roads," said Rotten Belly. "They are each fine women. Which do you choose?"

Beckwourth gazed at the three young maidens, each eager to become the wife of such an accomplished warrior, one who would as well have access to all manner of items in trade from the whites.

"They each one rival the others for their beauty," said Beckwourth, mindful that the two rejected sisters would become his sisters-in-law. One seemed the more reserved of the three. If he was to have a wife, a quiet one would do best. "I choose Still Water," he said. She gave him a shy smile, and all three sisters departed.

"Now you will be happy," said Rotten Belly.

It sounded more like a command than prophesy.

As he had seen when his sister Jumps to the Sky married Bird That Runs, there was no particular ceremony to becoming married, or more specifically, he had just completed it. Still Water required a couple days of preparation as she separated from her family. During that time, friends and family showered the new couple with gifts, and thus Beckwourth became the owner of another twenty fine war horses. On the third day, he was led to a tipi. Inside, his new wife waited for him, seated on her heels as all modest women sat. The cooking fire in the center of his new abode had a kettle over it. A familiar aroma struck his nostrils. Coffee!

"I made for you the white man's soup," she said.

Still Water was as attentive to Beckwourth as any new bride could be. She made his meals and sewed his clothes. Every day she combed his long hair with bear grease, fascinated by its curls, so different from her own straight hair. She told him what a great warrior he was while she combed and asked him about the ways of the white man. Beckwourth quite enjoyed her tender touch, and it was with some effort that he kept a stoic aloofness. After his hair had been attended to, he proceeded through the snowy village to the sweat lodge and spent the day with men. At night, Still Water made her bed a respectful distance from Beckwourth, as his aloofness told her to do.

His dour mood lifted. Beckwourth told himself that he could still head home in the spring, modestly wealthy from the pelts he could acquire over the winter. When conditions allowed, he donned snowshoes and headed out with Hunts Alone to trap beaver. As he had been taught, he carved his initials in a corner of each and every one of his pelts. Hunts Alone asked him the meaning of this.

"See here?" Beckwourth asked. He cleared some

snow and scratched his full name in the frozen ground. "This is my name. My white man's name." He circled the initials. "I carve the first part of my name in my hides so they are known to all as mine. Let me show you your name in my language." He wrote his friend's name and circled the "H" and "A". "These are your *initials*," he said, using the English words.

"I will not carve like this in beaver pelts," said Hunts Alone, after some thought. "It is not our way. These marks looks like 'Burial Scaffold, Tipi'. To do this would hurt my *maxpe*."

"Does your *maxpe* come from your medicine bundle?" he asked, referring to the bundles suspended on tripods at the back of every warrior's tipi.

"The medicine bundle is my connection to my spirit animal," said Hunts Alone. "My spirit animal is my protector throughout my life. My spirit animal is my ally, and from this I draw my *maxpe*."

"How does a Crow acquire a spirit animal?" asked Beckwourth.

"One is born with one. Then, when I became a young man, I went into the mountains on a vison quest, so that I might come to know him. I starved myself for days and cut myself until I was near death. Not every warrior has a vision when they do this, but I did. I told my vision to the medicine men when I returned, and they told to me its meaning. They told me of my protecting spirit animal. My medicine bundle is of that animal."

"All Crow do this?"

"All Crow do this."

"Can I be a Crow if I do not have a medicine bundle?"

"There are those who go to the mountain and cut themselves and starve themselves for days nearly to the point of death who still do not have a vision. For them, they trade something of value with a great warrior for a part of his bundle. You should do this."

"I do not think this would be good for me."

"Someday, you may carry the pipe for a war party of men, not boys. You have great *maxpe*, so this may happen. But if you do not have protection from a spirit animal, the hearts of those who might follow you will not be strong, and you might fail."

Beckwourth believed all this to all be silly superstition. "If this comes to pass as you say," he said, "I will find another way."

Winter dragged on. One day, a fierce snowstorm blew across the plain. Conditions outside were too miserable to even make a trip to the sweat lodge, but inside Beckwourth's tipi was it was warm and snug. Tipis were protected from the wind by fences of brush staked to the ground, which trapped the snow. They had an inside wall attached to the poles, and grass insulation was stuffed in the space between for just such days. So Beckwourth and Still Water wiled away the hours in pleasant conversation and relative comfort. Still Water asked many questions of Beckwourth's life among the whites, and he regaled her with tales of the larger world that he had not himself seen, his head in her lap as she combed his hair. The gentleness of her touch was soothing.

"May I see the mark that told Ishkali that you were her son?" she asked.

Beckwourth for a moment debated whether to tell her the truth; that this mark was just some giant coincidence. But he did not, and only closed his eyes and pointed. Still Water bowed her head to examine it closely. He felt her warm breath. She kissed him gently on the forehead, then gently on the lips. He responded with a vigorous kiss, and turned onto his knees and kissed her harder, deeper, and felt the softness of her breast with his hand. She responded with a gentler kiss and placed her hand gently against his chest.

Beckwourth broke away and cast his gaze downward.

"I am you wife," said Still Water.

"I know this," said Beckwourth. "I am sorry."

He grabbed his buffalo robe, put on his moccasins.

"Where are you going, my husband?"

"To see Hunts Alone."

The wind blew his robe open, exposing his bare legs. He squinted against the blowing snow, into a whiteness where he could only see as far as his nearest neighbor. Hunts alone lived on the far side of the village. He considered for a moment going back for his leggings but pressed on instead. From tipi to tipi he trudged, intermittently pulling his robe over his head like a hood so he could see ahead, which exposed his legs to the biting wind. He slipped on an icy patch and fell. Hands now scraped and stiff, he rose and continued, from one tipi to the next, shivering and wet. He came to what must have been the edge of the village, for he saw no tipis beyond. His fall had caused snow to get in his moccasins, and now his feet were wet and cold and numb. He headed back. One after another he went, tipi to tipi, none of which he recognized. Finally, he stood at the door of one and swallowed his pride.

"I come visiting," he said. "Is your door open?" It was a custom among the Crow to ask so.

"You are welcome," came the standard reply.

Beckwourth opened the flap and entered the

smoky interior. It took a while for his eyes to adjust to the darkness.

"Hmph. It is you." It was Crooked Smile.

"None other," said Beckwourth. "I am grateful for your hospitality."

"Come share our food," said Crooked Smile. He motioned to his wife and returned to working at a device in his lap.

Though Beckwourth saw the offer of food as just a veneer of grace over Crooked Smile's contempt, he could not refuse. Crooked Smile's wife served him stew in a horn bowl. A small boy hid in the shadows.

"Perhaps they did not have snow where you were raised," said Crooked Smile.

"I have never before had the wind drive snow at me like a thousand arrows."

There was an awkward silence. Beckwourth motioned to the device his host worked. "What is this?"

"Soon the wind will stop, and tomorrow the sun will shine. I make this for tomorrow." Crooked smile motioned the boy over.

"I thank you for your hospitality," said Beckwourth.

"It is nothing."

Beckwourth watched as Crooked Smile lashed.

"It is something for sliding on the snow," said Crooked Smile.

"What burden do you have to pull on the snow?"

Crooked Smile grinned, and for only the second time Beckwourth saw the half-paralysis of his face, the twisted smile that gave him his name. "It is no burden. Go to the ravine tomorrow, and you will see."

. . .

The next day the sky was a cloudless crisp blue, and the air was still. Beckwourth followed the sounds of happy children and their dogs to the ravine. A dozen youngsters cheered and laughed as they took turns sliding down the ravine in pairs on Crooked Smile's sled. Beckwourth approached Crooked Smile.

"Sometimes I wish I could have grown up among the Crow," said Beckwourth.

"It is not your fault that you didn't. Only that you pretend that you once were among us."

"I have never told anyone that I was born a Crow. It is the Crow that decided that I am one of them."

Crooked Smile let this pass. "You enjoy watching children."

"Yes, I do. The whites could learn much from the Crow about children." Amanda came to his mind once again. "I can see that the Crow love their own children. What I do not understand is how an Indian can scalp a child. How can a child's scalp give a warrior pride in his heart?"

"The Crow do not scalp children," said Crooked Smile. "If there is war against an enemy village, the Crow take the women and children with them, and raise them as Crow. Among these children here are some, and you can see they are happy. Also, the women, they are treated well and soon are happier among the Crow than they were with their own tribe."

"Then even if I was not born a Crow, here I am as well. Why do you not accept me?"

"You are such a prideful one, always keen to teach of the white man's ways, so seldom to adopt ours. This, and if you really wished to be a Crow, you would make a baby with Still Water. I have heard why it was that you came to my tipi yesterday. Women talk."

"I am not ready for the burden of being a father."

"The mother will raise the child. And if it is a boy, when he is older, he will follow the call of the teacher, who beckons boys every day to their games. A warrior hunts and wages war. He can be gone for months and may never return. The women raise the children."

Weeks passed, and boredom settled over the village. The warriors became restless. Every legend had been told at least twice in the sweat lodge, and every deed worth telling had been heard by all. One day, Hunts Alone came to Beckwourth.

"I grow weary of winter," he said. "We are many of us going on a ride. Come with us. Let us ride out together and feel the blood in our veins again."

"Where will we go?" asked Beckwourth.

"Let us go to the white traders," said Hunts Alone.

"White traders?" This was news to Beckwourth. "Where are there white traders?"

"Five sleeps travel to the great muddy river. Did you not know of them?"

The 'great muddy river' could only be the Missouri. "You might think that all whites know each other, but it is not true," said Beckwourth. These traders were probably Ashley's rivals, the American Fur Company, and might not be so friendly to him. But rivals or not, they could be his portal home, come spring.

"Who will carry the pipe?" asked Beckwourth.

"Crooked Smile."

Beckwourth soured on the idea. "I will stay," he said. "Take my beaver pelts to trade, and bring me back powder and lead. Also, beads for Still Water."

"If you stay, you will have for company only old men and women. Come with us."

"Some must stay to hunt. I will be one of those."

So, the greater part of the village's warriors left without Beckwourth. And hunt he did, day after day, trudging about on snowshoes. Little did he suspect that there were unseen eyes upon him. For though it was winter, spies did lurk, and returned home to their people with word that the Crow village was vulnerable.

A woman's scream awoke Beckwourth one morning. Dazed, he rubbed his eyes and staggered out of his tipi. Enemy warriors on horseback thundered through camp, sending arrows to flight in all directions. Fear gripped Beckwourth. He was confused, overcome by the feeling that this should not be happening. His father's tipi was his nearest neighbor, and Big Bowl had his war club in hand. "Sioux dogs, come taste the anger of Big Bowl!" the old man called.

Beckwourth dashed inside his tipi, where Still Water handed him his own war club. Outside again, he barely dodged a horseman, who wheeled around for a second approach. The Sioux warrior galloped at him, steel-tipped lance pointed at his midsection. Beckwourth twisted and grabbed at the lance but missed. The Sioux flipped the lance and struck him with the blunt end as he passed and with a look of scorn rode away. The enemy had scored coup on him. That cleared the butterflies for Beckwourth, that look of scorn.

The Sioux stampeded the Crow horses and

pulled back, gathering outside of arrow range. Mothers gathered toddlers and youngsters to the far side of the village. Beckwourth cursed himself for not having kept his rifle and pistol loaded, as now they lay useless in his tipi. He gathered his lance, his bow, and quiver, and ran to where the men gathered. They called out to Rotten Belly for instructions and were sent to each find a horse. Several Crow had fallen already, and in going for their mounts they lost more to Sioux arrows. Beckwourth gathered with the others to meet the enemy. The Sioux charged again, zigzagging to dodge Crow arrows. At close quarters, the Crow met them, fighting with the fierce resolve of men protecting their families. The Sioux again retreated. Rotten Belly called a quick council while the Sioux regrouped. There were voices for one maneuver or another, voices steeped in decades of warfare. Rotten Belly decided to attack, reasoning that the Sioux would least expect that. Live or die, they had a plan.

Beckwourth looked for the Sioux who had taken coup on him.

On word from Rotten Belly, the Crow charged at a weak point in the Sioux line, penetrating it and dividing their enemy. The Sioux had indeed not expected an offensive attack from a force of old men, and so few. Beckwourth picked a foe and charged, swinging his war club. The Sioux parried the blow with his shield and managed to knock Beckwourth off balance. Desperately, he grabbed at his horse's mane. The Sioux raised his war club with a throaty howl, but the howl was cut short, as the bloody tip of a lance protruded from his chest. The lance was in the hands of the *berdache*. Before he could pull it out, a Sioux attacked from behind, and he had to defend himself with his knife. Beckwourth would have helped, but a Sioux rushed him. Brute strength and anger won that fight for Beckwourth.

The Sioux could have pressed the fight and rubbed the Crow out, but at a signal, they withdrew. With whoops of victory they retreated, driving Crow horses before them, back toward the sunrise in triumph. It was over as suddenly as it had started. As the enemy cries faded, the low moans of the dying were joined by the shrieks of mourning women and the whimpers of children. Still panting clouds of breath into the freezing cold, Beckwourth dispatched the dying Sioux that the *berdache* had saved him from with a blow that spattered blood and brains over his bare legs. His chest heaved with effort and anger. He took his knife out and grabbed the hair of the Sioux, incised a circle around the top of the skull and with one fierce pull yanked the scalp free. "Easier to skin vermin when they're still warm," he said in English. The *berdache* a stepped on the chest of the corpse and pulled the lance out.

"I am Red Blanket," said he, meeting Beckwourth's gaze evenly.

"This is yours, Red Blanket." Beckwourth handed him the scalp.

"Sioux dogs," said Red Blanket with a flash of a smile.

A familiar voice, trembling with pain, drew Beckwourth's attention. One of the Crow wounded was Water Carrier, whose mother now cradled his bloodied head. Big Bowl came to her side. His eyes met hers for a fleeting moment.

"I saw you in battle, my son," he said to the dying boy. "You were very brave. I have been proud to be called 'father' by you." He laid his hand on the boy's chest until he had breathed his last. Big Bowl turned to the boy's mother. "My heart is on the ground, my sister. I will not rest until I have avenged your son's death."

Then it hit him. Beckwourth knew the man who had taken coup on him. It was the one who had escaped, one of the horse thieves they had encountered on their return from the raid on the Arapaho. He must have scouted them and returned to his village, inciting revenge on the Crow. *If I had let Bird That Runs chase him, this boy might still be alive*, he thought. He felt a heaviness in his chest, and knew what Big Bowl meant, to have one's heart on the ground.

The dead were wrapped in hides and laid to rest in an area not far from the village, on scaffolding too high for scavenging animals to reach. Their grieving kin cut themselves and amputated fingertips, the men silently and with no visible pain, the women while wailing and screeching and tearing at their hair. It was a sickening scene that only increased Beckwourth's remorse. He came upon Still Water with a knife in her hand, searching for something.

"What do you seek, my wife?"

"I must find a pole, so that I may cut off my finger," she said.

"Do not do this," he said.

"I wish to grieve for Water Carrier."

"I forbid that you mar your beauty so," he said.

"You do not care for my beauty," she said. "Why should I obey you?"

"Because I am your husband."

She threw the knife at his feet. He picked it up in case she changed her mind.

That night the wails of the mourning woke him over and over, and again the night after. The men returned from the traders. The women ran to them, pleading for revenge, running their bloodied fingers on the chests of their men. Grim promises of revenge were made. But mere promises of retribution did nothing to stop the mourning. Day and night Beckwourth's guilty mind was plagued by the wails of the grieving, and by the specter of bloody mourners.

To escape this oppressive atmosphere, Beckwourth convinced Hunts Alone to go trapping with him. On the trail he asked his friend, "How long must we listen to this mournful wailing?"

"Any scalp of an enemy, any enemy, and even just one, will end this mourning," said Hunts Alone. "But until there is a scalp, the mourning will not end."

"Why must the Crow grieve so that they cut themselves?" asked Beckwourth.

"All the tribes do this," said Hunts Alone. Seeing his friend so perplexed, he added, "sometimes it comes from the heart, sometimes it is done because it is expected."

Beckwourth did not ask which it was for the finger his friend was missing.

"My brother," Hunts Alone said, "I told the traders of you. They saw your marks on the pelts."

Beckwourth straightened. "What did you tell them?"

"I told them that you were a Crow Indian who had lived among the whites. They were very curious about this. The chief of the traders, whose name is Kipp, invites you to visit him."

"I will go to them when the snow melts," Beckwourth said. Already the snow had a crust from melting midday and freezing at night. *And from there head home!* he thought.

Still Water did not cut herself, and this was some small consolation for Beckwourth. But she was solemn and avoided him. One day he spoke to her.

"Still Water, my heart is heavy that you avoid me."

"You have forbidden my grieving. As you wish, I have not cut myself, instead preserving my beauty as you command. But my heart is all the more heavy for not being able to grieve with the others. It is different for me than you."

"As you grieve, my wife, so I grieve just as much."

"A warrior may snuff out his grief in an act of vengeance. For a woman, she must wait for her man to act."

"And I will act," he said. "But your father has said that vengeance must wait until Green Grass." Rotten Belly had decreed this shortly after the Sioux attack.

"Green Grass time is near. You should convince Rotten Belly to let you lead the party to punish the Sioux when the time is right."

"No one would follow me, my dear wife. Why should they?"

"The Dog Soldiers would follow you. All the wives say so."

"I see that revenge burns in your heart as much as it does in that of any warrior," said Beckwourth. "But your family suffered no loss from the Sioux."

"I am the daughter of a great chief. As he mourns for the whole village, so do I."

The snow began to melt. One day, Bird That Runs and Crooked Smile came to Beckwourth. "Brother," Bird That Runs said, "The Fox are going out in search of the Sioux. We come to you because many Dog Soldiers would follow you. Come with us, and we will come back with our faces blackened."

"Rotten Belly has spoken," said Beckwourth.

"And he has even posted guards so that you cannot sneak out of camp to do this. I wait for his word."

"Rotten Belly is old," said Crooked Smile. "Old age is a curse that makes the heart timid. Come with us now."

"I cannot," said Beckwourth.

"I said to you he is not a Crow," Crooked Smile said to Bird That Runs. "He does not mourn the loss of Water Carrier. He would not even mourn you if you were killed in battle."

"My knife hungers for the heart of an enemy, not for my own fingers," said Beckwourth.

"Come," said Crooked Smile. "Let this one stay with the women. We, the Society of the Foxes, will avenge our losses while Shoots Good in the Dark and the Dog Soldiers laze at home."

So Crooked Smile, Bird That Runs, and others of the Fox snuck out past Rotten Belly's guards and went out in search of an enemy. One morning after they had left, horses were discovered stolen, and Beckwourth went with the men who gave chase. They pursued the thieves, who were a party of Assiniboine, recovered all their horses, and returned with four scalps as well.

Beckwourth was surprised at how quickly the mourning gave way to celebration, even though the scalps were not from Sioux. But the celebration was cut short by a shriek from Jumps to the Sky. Crooked Smile returned. But he carried over the back of his horse the body of Bird That Runs. The drums of celebration stopped, and the mourning resumed anew.

Rotten Belly confronted Crooked Smile.

"You have disobeyed me," he said. "For this you will suffer." He had men cut Crooked Smile's tipi to shreds, forcing his wife to return to her family with her son, and Crooked Smile to his.

Beckwourth's heart was again on the ground. Bird That Runs had been an admired friend. And he dreaded the mourning to come. When the time came, he followed Jumps to the Sky and family to the burial ground. With bloodied hand and face, his sister trailed the horse that carried her husband, wailing a song all the while. He watched solemnly as his brother-in-law was placed high in a scaffold, wrapped in his warrior's robe. He sat with Big Bowl for days, helping him endure his daughter's grieving, averting his eyes at her bloodied appearance. Finally, he could take it no longer and retreated to his own tipi.

The days warmed, and snow was only to be found in patches where the wind had blown deep drifts. The river was swollen, and birds returned to the meadows. But the grieving continued. While in his tipi one day, Beckwourth heard a rustling and suddenly found himself in the open air. Both of his sisters, his wife, and other women had lifted the tipi off the ground and laid it aside, exposing him. They showered him with gifts — leggings, moccasins, and other handiwork — until they had nearly covered him, all the while chanting praise of his bravery, recounting how he had never been defeated in battle.

"Enough!" he called out. "What do you want of me?"

"Husband, soon it will be Green Grass. Will you not lead men to seek revenge on the Sioux?" asked his Still Water.

"It is for Rotten Belly to choose the pipe carrier. I am the leader of little horse raiding parties, not a war party."

"What sort of a man are you?" asked his sister,

"that you shrink from an enemy that has killed my husband? And of the son of this one, and of this one," she said, pointing to the other women. "Come, now is the time to prove yourself. Are you the son of Big Bowl? Are you a Crow?"

Beckwourth met her gaze. "I will fight to the death to avenge the death of Bird That Runs and Water Carrier. I accept these gifts you bring to me today with the promise that when Rotten Belly says it is time, no warrior will fight as bravely as I against the Sioux. If I am chosen, I will lead, but only then. Now be gone."

The women left, but Still Water was not content with his words. She approached her father, Rotten Belly. Who she asked, would exact revenge against the hated Sioux, now that Green Grass approached?

"He will be chosen, whose *maxpe* is strongest," came the reply.

"My husband has strong *maxpe*. And he has never been defeated in battle, nor lost a man."

"He has never been defeated in battle because he has fought so few," said Rotten Belly. "And tell me this. Will I soon have a grandson?"

Still Water lowered her eyes. "He still does not come to me at night," she said.

"Why is this?" he asked.

"The whites are different from us," said Still Water. "In ways I do not understand. But I know this: my husband can defeat the Sioux."

"How does a woman who has never fought a battle, know this about a man who himself has never faced the Sioux? Perhaps it is you who burns for glory, without regard for the lives of others."

"I see in my husband a sort different from your other warriors, my father. When aroused, there is none braver. But he is not blinded by revenge. I have heard the tales of his deeds, though few those deeds are as you say."

"There will be a council. If it is decided that he should lead, it will be so."

"But I am afraid that he will not speak for himself."

"Then you must find one who will, my daughter," said, the chief. "Be gone, then, and attend to the affairs of women. Before me are the affairs of men."

The days lengthened, the rivers receded from their banks, and the meadows turned green and lush. One morning, a herald announced the long-awaited council. Lesser chiefs gathered and listened patiently as Rotten Belly recounted the history of the Crow tribe, back to the time of the split from the Hidatsa farmers, forming a new tribe that would follow the buffalo, becoming the finest horsemen known, and the most feared warriors. He spoke of how their wanderings brought them to this land that the One Above Person had intended for them, here where game was plentiful, the streams flowed clear, and it was not too cold in the winter, nor too hot in the summer, this perfect land. But their enemies were all jealous of their land and their horses and harassed them constantly; the Assiniboine, the Arapahoe, the Cheyenne, the Arikara, the Blackfeet; but none so hated as the Sioux. If this latest incursion was not punished, the Sioux would be emboldened, and they would ally with other tribes and rub the Crow out as a people, death for many and enslavement for the rest. The gathered chiefs grunted their agreement at intervals during this long speech. When Rotten Belly had finished, they gave their answers, one by one. Each confirmed everything that had been said and spoke of their readiness to act. When the last had spoken, Rotten Belly asked the burning question: Who would lead them into battle?

"There is none here who longs for revenge more than I," said Crooked Smile. "And I wish to atone for disobeying Rotten Belly. I wish to have the honor of leading."

"Crooked Smile is a great warrior," said another. "But my *maxpe* is stronger, and I lost a son; he has lost no one. I wish to lead."

One by one, each chief took his turn, and either presented himself as the best leader, or threw his support to another. Exchanges became heated between the Dog Soldiers and the Foxes. Finally, it was Big Bowl's turn to speak.

"I come to council with a heavy heart," he said. "For I have suffered more from the hated Sioux than others, having lost two of my family to them during the last winter. First, I lost in the Sioux raid a boy who burned to be a leader among us, but it was not to be, for he was cut down at an age before even his voice cracked. Then I lost the husband of my daughter, Bird That Runs, who was known to all of you as a brave warrior. I too want revenge. But I am an old man. My bones creak when I rise in the morning, and my wind fails when I swing my war club. I would lead even so if you chose me, but there is one other of my family whom I put forward in my place. My family will follow whomever this council chooses, but they would best follow Shoots Good in the Dark, whose *maxpe* is strong, and who is cunning in battle, and has never lost a warrior. I have finished."

"Bring him," Rotten Belly said. "Let him speak for himself."

. . .

Beckwourth sat outside his tipi, wearing his best leggings and shirt, for he knew that Big Bowl was to put his name forward. Still Water bustled about, avoiding him, for her part in this had been done in secret. After she had spoken to her father, she had next gone to Big Bowl with her supplications. Big Bowl resisted at first, for he wished to lead himself. But he saw that Still Water was right; his son was the better choice. Beckwourth had agreed to let his father put his name forward just to please him, reasoning that the council was unlikely to accept his nomination.

He passed the time by reading his book of biographies. Crow ceremonies were long and tedious compared to how the whites might decide such a thing. He finished a chapter and put the book back in its leather case. There are three roads to greatness, per the author. Royalty are born to it. Some have it thrust upon them. Others aspire to it.

Beckwourth recalled that day on the journey with Ashley when he had held the general at gunpoint. He had decided then that he would rather die heading back to St. Louis than to be regarded as an inferior. But a friend had spoken up.

"If he goes," Pappen had said to Ashley, "we go with him."

He had aspired to be an equal. But he did not have to be just an equal, he could be a leader.

A messenger came to his door.

"Come," he said.

"Shoots Good in the Dark," said Rotten Belly, "we are to go to war against the Sioux. It is decided. They must be punished. Big Bowl has put forth your name to carry the pipe as we go against them. Your *maxpe* is strong, and you have never lost a warrior in battle. Tell us, do you wish to lead?"

Beckwourth scanned the faces of the River Crow chiefs. "Oh, Great Chief," he said, "It would be an honor above all others to lead the valiant Crow against their enemy the Sioux. As you say, my *maxpe* is strong, and I have never lost a man in battle. I have proven my bravery many times. Others are as brave, but none as cunning. When I was with the white man, I studied war. I read the stories of one named Alexander, a chief of deeds so great that men speak of them more than twenty times one hundred winters later. Through his cunning and daring, he defeated forces many times more powerful than his.

"The warriors of the Crow burn for revenge on their enemy, the Sioux. I also burn for revenge. Greater than that, however, I wish to reward the Crow for how they have treated me, for I have never had such a place under the sun before, a home where all treat me as their brother. But I come to you today naked. If I am to lead your warriors, if I am to carry the pipe for this battle, you must know one thing: I am a Crow in my heart, but my mother was not a Crow. My respect for Big Bowl is greater than ever a son had for his father, but he is not my father. My mother was a woman whose skin was as brown as that of a buffalo, and whose soul was as pure as the winter snow. My father was a white man, a warrior who fought the chief across the great salt water where the sun rises. Greenwood, the trapper with a Mountain Crow wife, is a man who loves to tell stories, and it is on his head that I stand before you a Crow, for it was a joke he told that I am a Crow. I am grateful to him for this, for if you today say to me, 'get out, you are not a Crow,' still, I will have been one for these many moons, and I am proud of it. I have learned Crow ways, taken a Crow wife, played with Crow children, and made my arm red with the blood of Crow enemies. I have come to love the Crow people and their ways. I now ask that you let me earn the right to call myself a Crow, to be a part of your proud people. Let me lead you in battle against the Sioux."

There was a profound silence. Rotten Belly read the faces of his lesser chiefs. "I say then, go," he said, "lead us against the Sioux, and earn your Crow name."

A spring breeze wafted over the rolling hills, the cool air a tonic to Beckwourth and his hundred warriors, and to those women who carried their shields and the boys who accompanied them. The grim cavalcade passed over the land like the shadow of a lone cloud on a sunny day, swiftly, relentlessly, scouts on all sides, moccasin dogs trotting along faithfully. They were now five days out. At least now, mused Beckwourth, he did not have to worry about Crooked Smile agitating others that he was not a Crow; all knew this now. Ishkali had taken it hard, avoiding his gaze ever after the council. Perhaps she would be reconciled by a victory.

Every day of this journey, the men pestered Beckwourth for his tactics. "We wish to know the white man's ways in battle," they would say. He refused, reasoning that if he did so, it would create expectations that would limit his options when the time came for battle. Tiring of their questions, he approached Crooked Smile.

"My friend," he said, "I see in your face that you are as ready for this battle as I am."

"I am not your friend," said Crooked Smile, "but I am listening."

"I wish to strengthen the *maxpe* of the men who, like you, would rather that another lead us."

"You are a white man," said Crooked Smile. "I cannot help you."

"Call me what you wish," said Beckwourth, "but judge me by my deeds."

"You wish to earn a Crow name," said Crooked Smile. "Soon you will have your chance. But you will never be a Crow in my eyes."

"What is in your medicine bundle, Cooked Smile, great warrior of the River Crow?" asked Beckwourth, pointing to Crooked Smile's carefully wrapped bundle.

"I do not wish to tell you," said Crooked Smile.

"You think that the Crow are better than the white man because they have such things?"

"Perhaps it is so."

Beckwourth had an insight. "I have a medicine bundle," he said.

"It must be invisible then, like the wind. Or perhaps your spirit animal is the mosquito, and you have wrapped it in a leaf."

"Mock me all you wish, and smile your crooked smile of scorn. But I have a medicine bundle," Beckwourth said. "It is under my bed. It contains within it many of the stories of my people." It felt odd to call the whites 'my people.' But on the other hand, as his father had told him, the blood of English noblemen coursed through his veins. And he was now on to his own battle of Hastings.

"If this is your medicine bundle, how can it help you when it is there, and you are here?" asked Crooked Smile.

"Oh, but it will," said Beckwourth, lapsing into English for a moment. "I have heard that last yellow grass, a buffalo was stampeded through the village by some young men."

"I know of this," said Crooked Smile.

"The buffalo destroyed a medicine bundle, I am told."

"That happened. For this, those who stampeded the buffalo were banished for some time."

"What happened to the warrior whose bundle was destroyed?"

"He went from medicine man to medicine man searching for the meaning of this. His distress was great over this omen. It was not long before he gave up his scalp to an enemy." Crooked Smile said. "All the Crow you see here have their medicine bundles with them. All but you."

"My medicine bundle is not just under my bed, though. It is here, in my heart," said Beckwourth. "And here, in my head. If the papers under my bed were destroyed, I would not have to run to a medicine man in a panic."

Beckwourth saw that Crooked Smile was unconvinced. He turned his horse away and called in the scouts. Others would harbor Crooked Smile's misgivings, and he had in mind a ploy that would align with the Crow view of the spiritual world. When all were assembled, he spoke.

"If I had been born a Crow, my spirit guide would have been the fox. Bring me a live fox, and I know that we will then have a great victory."

No sooner said than the men scattered to create a surround: a giant circle of hunters that, once formed, contracted inward. As the circle drew smaller and smaller, prairie animals were forced to the center. Tighter and tighter it went, and soon rabbits, a raccoon, and a coyote passed Beckwourth in nervous flight. A cry went up that a fox was spotted. Beckwourth smiled. He had seen fresh scat of the animal when he had called for its capture. The warriors converged on the fox and brought it squirming to Beckwourth. He praised them and ordered the animal choked bloodlessly and skinned. He then took the supple fur and tied it to his lance.

"Warriors of the Crow nation, I thank you for bringing me this fox, the symbol of cunning to the Indian, to the white man, and to men across the great salt water for countless generations past. I say to all of you that I will be as wily as the fox in battle, and that also I will match the bravery of any one of you. We have had an easy time approaching our enemy. Now, let us proceed with stealth and pounce upon them, like a fox pounces on a rabbit."

Grunts of approval told him that this speech had had its intended effect. The men's confidence in him shone in their faces. He was one of them.

The next day, scouts returned with news of a village ahead: not Sioux, but Cheyenne. Disappointment was palpable among the Crow. Beckwourth was inclined to travel on to find the Sioux. But he had been among the Crow long enough to know that a chief only led the willing, so he called a council. There were voices for attack, and those for heading to the east in search of the Sioux.

"There cannot be a Sioux village within a week's ride of a Cheyenne village this large," said Crooked Smile. "I say we attack."

That was the opinion that carried the day. Beckwourth scouted the village and returned with a plan. He would lead a small force of hand-picked warriors to steal horses, making sure to arouse the entire village in the process. The others would be divided into two forces. His men would lead the Cheyenne between them, to be surprised and crushed. He appointed Crooked Smile as leader of one of the forces and sent the women and boys to the rear with the extra horses.

Beckwourth proceeded cautiously with his Dog Soldiers, but before they came near the village, they came upon two unsuspecting Cheyenne, out hunting. They killed them, but not before their cries had alerted the rest of the village. The Cheyenne quickly rounded up their horses, and Beckwourth knew he was foiled. His men taunted the Cheyenne with the bloody scalps they had taken, but the enemy declined to take the bait and instead hurled insults and taunts of their own. He would have taken severe losses had he attacked, so he turned tail, hoping the Cheyenne would follow. They did not, so he held another council to decide their next course of action.

"We should wait until night and attack," said Crooked Smile.

"The Cheyenne know we are here, and they will send out scouts who will see that we have not left," said Beckwourth. "I am not willing to risk lives, even though we might gain a victory."

"Then *I* will lead any who will follow," said Crooked Smile. "Who is with me?" Many voiced their support.

"We have two scalps and have lost no men," said Beckwourth. "I forbid you to attack. You may guard our retreat, Crooked Smile," said Beckwourth. "Should the Cheyenne pursue us, the glory will be yours."

Crooked Smile flicked a crooked snarl and gathered his men for the rear-guard action. Beckwourth led a contingent in retreat, but the Cheyenne followed only to see that they were leaving. Crooked Smile did not get his chance at glory. On return to the village, the Crow were met with cheers and the women's ululations. Though it was no great victory, two scalps and no losses were good enough, and that night the whole village danced enthusiastically; the men around the scalp pole and the women around them with their men's shield and medicine bundles. Still Water danced gracefully, touching Beckwourth gently on the chest with one hand as she held his shield in the other. He was the great warrior she had wanted, and it had never mattered to her if he had been born a Crow. After the dance, she followed him into their tipi and slipped in front of him in the dark.

"Husband," she said, "I must tell you something. Do not be angry with me."

"Why would I be angry with you, my cherished one?"

"It was I who went to Big Bowl. It was I who asked him to put your name before the council."

"How good this is now, that we have no secrets," he said. He pulled her closer and kissed her.

She touched his cheek as she responded to his kiss. He stopped. He found her left hand and held each intact finger to his lips. She grasped his hand tightly and kissed him again. His hand ran up and down her thigh, and they fell into each other's passion.

"I had a dream, husband," she said after.

"I wish to hear it," he said.

"I dreamt that you grabbed an enemy chief's gun in battle as he fired it."

"Am I hurt in your dream?"

"If this thing comes to pass, you must act without hesitation, or I will lose you."

"Whites do not believe in dreams, my wife."

"I saw this as real as if I was there, my husband. Act without hesitation. Dreams can mean many things, but it is not wise to ignore them."

"If you say it, this must be so, my wife."

❧ 16 ❧

Beckwourth was now held in such esteem that he was appointed the leader of the Dog Soldiers. His men of that society daily invited him to smoke and talk, and many were the damsel or wife of another who gave him a flirting look or a small gift as he went about his business. One in particular was persistent; a pretty thing, but a mere girl.

"Be gone, child," he finally told her one day. "I tire of your attention."

"I wish to marry you, Shoots Good in the Dark," she said.

"Marry me!" he said. "I already have a wife. And look at you, not more than fifteen winters old."

"You are a great warrior," she said. "I wish only to be the wife of a great warrior. A great warrior must have many wives."

"You are as pretty as a flower," he told her. "You will someday deserve a great warrior for a husband. But until then, play in the children's village, and let the boys bring you a coyote skin and pretend it is a scalp. Spend your days there until you are old enough."

"I know I am young, but I care not to roll hoops

and play with puppies. I wish only to have my face painted by you when you return from battle, and then I can rejoice with the other women and dance the victory dance with their warriors' shields and their medicine bundles. You will also give me fine things from the white traders; beads and scarlet cloth. And I will make you pretty leggings and moccasins and take care of your war horses."

"When I look upon you, in my heart I see a little sister, not a wife."

"That is good, for I do not wish to come to you in the night."

"Little one. Go back to your father and honor him until you are older."

"I have no father," she said. "My people are the Piegan. I was taken from them when I was young."

Piegan? He thought. *So many enemies.* "What is your name, little one?" he asked.

"I want you to call me Little Wife," she said.

So Beckwourth took her to Jumps to the Sky, the widow of Bird That Runs, who now lived in Big Bowl's tipi again. "Humor this one," he said. "Let her believe she is my little wife, and let her help you with your work." His sister was pleased to have another pair of hands to help with her work, and happily took the Piegan girl into Big Bowl's household.

Beckwourth spent Green Grass hunting and trapping beaver with Hunts Alone, carefully carving his initials in all of the pelts and hides that were his. Soon he would take them to Kipp's trading post, and from there he would head down the Missouri, leaving his adventure with the Crow behind. His trove of beaver pelts would be worth thousands of dollars in St. Louis.

Beckwourth spotted antelope on one of these trapping forays, and decided he wanted to test his skill with bow and arrow. So, one spring day, he headed out with Hunts Alone to do so. Soon, Hunts Alone alerted Beckwourth that they were being followed. Enemies preyed upon small hunting parties all the time, and theirs was as small as they came. They ducked into a ravine and drew their weapons, ready to sell their lives dearly if there came no choice. But only one approached. Slight of build, mounted on a horse as nimble as herself, it was Little Wife! Hunts Alone jumped out from their cover with a war cry, startling the poor girl.

"There, that will teach you to creep up on men," he said.

"I do not need to be taught a lesson by one such as you," she said. "Husband, why have you been avoiding me?" she asked Beckwourth.

"I do not avoid you, Little Wife. I wish only to hunt with my friend."

"Of course, husband," she said. "But I do not speak of just today. I am sad that you do not come to see me at my tipi."

"Go back to the village, youngster," said Hunts Alone. "We have no need for a woman here, and less need for a girl."

Little Wife's eyes flashed. "Husband, are you going to allow this one to speak to your wife so?"

Beckwourth admired her spunk. "Hunts Alone," he said, "you must not speak so to my cherished wife," he said in jest.

Hunts Alone stiffened.

"It was not my intent to offend you, my friend," he said.

"And no offense is taken, my brother," said Beckwourth.

"But perhaps it would be best that I leave you with your precious second wife," said Hunts Alone.

Beckwourth had thought it was impossible to offend his friend, but now he saw otherwise. "Come, friend," he said, "show me how to hunt antelope."

"You will find it no great task for a great warrior like yourself," said Hunts Alone. And without another word he mounted his horse and headed home.

Beckwourth watched his friend disappear across the plain.

"I know the ways of the antelope," said Little Wife.

"Be quiet, girl."

"I will be your companion now. And I can butcher your kill and carry it back. Let that one turn his rear to you if he wishes."

Beckwourth weighed following his friend. Better to let him cool down, he decided.

"Very well, child," said Beckwourth. "Follow me."

The antelope herd was grazing not far off now, moving slowly in their direction. Beckwourth and Little Wife dismounted and approached using brush cover.

"Let them see us a little," said Little Wife.

"Why do this?"

"Antelope are curious and approach what they cannot see."

Sure enough, the antelope approached. "They sense us, husband," said Little Wife. "Get ready."

Beckwourth nocked an arrow, rose swiftly, and let the arrow fly. His startled prey fell, and the rest of the herd skittered away in an instant. Little Wife ran to the antelope and ended its suffering. Together they skinned and butchered it.

Now that she had her betrothed's undivided attention, Little Wife was of very sunny disposition. As they crossed the meadows on their way home, she asked an incessant string of questions about his past life and the ways of white people. He obliged, telling her of the great cities of huge, wooden huts, and grander ones made of stone; of land canoes on hoops drawn by teams of horses lashed together, and of larger ones drawn by animals like hairless buffalo. He told her of the great canoes on the water that swam upstream, belching smoke. All this fascinated Little Wife greatly.

"Are the white women as pretty as Indian women?" she asked.

"White women are very pretty," he said, "but much more frail than Indian women."

"Did you have a wife in the white man's country?"

"I was courting a woman."

"Was she beautiful?"

"Of course she was beautiful."

"As beautiful as I am?"

"Do not ask such foolish questions, youngster."

"She must be very beautiful," said Little Wife. "To be worthy of a warrior such as yourself. Does she wait for you?"

"I do not know, young one. She may think that I am dead."

"I would wait for you," she said solemnly.

That night they camped in the open and roasted antelope steaks. Not as good as buffalo, but entirely satisfactory. When it came time to sleep, Little Wife carefully made a place for herself across the fire from Beckwourth. When her breathing became deep and rhythmic, he crept to her and, for a moment, gazed upon her tenderly and laid a blanket on her.

When Little Wife wakened, she was pleased to find his blanket over her. She restarted the fire from embers and cooked the antelope. When Beckwourth stirred, she spoke to him. "Many women must offer themselves to you."

"I do my best to ignore them."

"I see that you guard your *maxpe* from women, my husband. That is why I asked to be your wife. I am chaste as well."

"I see that," he said.

"There is a Crow ceremony to honor the chaste woman. I intend to be that woman."

"None would honor you more than I for that, Little Wife," said Beckwourth.

"What was the name of your white woman?" asked Little Wife.

"She is not a white woman. She is darker than me."

"Is she a slave?"

"What do you know of slaves?"

"I have heard of this."

"She is not a slave. She was freed like me."

"You were a slave to the white man?"

"I was born a slave, but my father, who was white, freed me."

"The Crow do not take slaves. Other tribes take slaves, but the Crow take captives as their own children and their own wives. As with me."

"I have been told that," he said. "I am lucky to have been adopted as a Crow."

"Myself as well," she said. "Do you wish to return to the whites?"

"Someday." He did not want to tell her that 'someday' might be soon.

They finished their meal, packed, and mounted their horses.

"Eliza," he said.

"Yes, Husband?"

"You asked me her name. Her name is Eliza."

❊ 17 ❊

Beckwourth felt the warmth of Crow esteem along all the paths he walked. But as the weeks progressed into the Yellow Grass season, the specter of another winter away from home did not appeal. Perhaps Eliza did wait for him, perhaps she did not, but in any case, the lure of family and the riches his pelts would bring back home beckoned. This had been an unparalleled adventure, but it was time to go home.

Ever since the tiff over Little Wife, Hunts Alone had avoided him. Finally, Beckwourth went to his friend's tipi, since by Crow tradition he could not be refused as a guest. Hunts Alone sulked. His wife offered Beckwourth a meal.

"Brother," Beckwourth said. "You must not be angry with me. You know that I do not know Crow ways. I could not know that you would be so offended for favoring my wife over you."

"Is that how a white man speaks to his brother in front of his wife?" Hunts Alone huffed.

"I do not know what sort of spirit induced me to act so," said Beckwourth.

"You should have asked me before you took that

child for a wife. I would have told you to keep only one wife. There is always trouble with more than one." His own wife smiled a knowing smile.

"I should always listen to your advice, my brother. That is why I come to you now."

"I am still your brother," said Hunts Alone.

"I long for my home in St. Louis."

Hunts Alone's face showed no response. "Join me in a smoke," he said. With great deliberation he produced his pipe, and lit tobacco. He puffed on it and handed it to Beckwourth.

"I wish to first trade furs with Kipp," Beckwourth said. "From there I will take a canoe to St. Louis. Will you come with me to trade with Kipp?"

"If you wish it, I can do no other," said Hunts Alone. "We are still as one person and will always be so."

"Let us gather up our beaver pelts, then," Beckwourth said, "and see who else wishes to go with us."

"What of your wives? Have you told them that you will return to the whites?"

"No. They will come with us. I will trade some of my pelts for such goods as to make them the envy of all the other women, and so their hearts will not be so heavy when I leave."

The trip was uneventful, and they arrived in good time. The trading post consisted of a few ramshackle cabins surrounded by a tall palisade fence, but to Beckwourth it seemed positively cosmopolitan after two winters in the wild. Kipp greeted them in sign language and passable Crow. But who was this at his elbow but his old foe Davis? So, Davis had survived on his own after all. He did not seem to recognize Beckwourth, who decided to not declare his identity.

The pipe was passed, and speeches were made on

both sides, declaring the history of friendly relations between the Crow and the whites and of their mutual hope that this encounter would be fruitful. Beckwourth savored his first taste of real tobacco in months, inhaling it slowly and blowing it out of his nostrils. Kipp gave gifts to the Crow and promised that he had much finer goods to trade if their pelts were of good quality. He inquired of the conditions the Crow had met on the trail, while his Arikara wife padded around with offerings of food. On hearing that it had been an easy journey, Kipp was pleased. He expressed his hope that the Crow would therefore continue to frequent his fine post, and again he enumerated the many valuable articles he had for trade. He told the Crow what he knew of the activities of the surrounding tribes, and he bade them return the next day to trade. They retired to pass the night outside of the palisade with Beckwourth's identity still hidden.

The next day, bargaining began in earnest. Kipp examined the furs one by one, praising some, but overall declaring them to be of poor quality, though Beckwourth knew them to be quite the opposite. Davis affirmed Kipp's opinion, examining furs and finding imaginary flaws. Beckwourth bit his tongue while the other warriors traded, for to have intervened would have implied that he thought them to be weak. Hunts Alone was next. The same charade unfolded, and Beckwourth fumed silently. Midway through this, Hunts Alone sought a certain article in trade. Over and over again, he asked Kipp for a 'be-has-I-pe-hish-a', showing with his arms the size of a large item.

"Have you any idea what he wants?" Kipp asked Davis.

"Mangy savage," Davis spat. "Tell him to take

what we're offering and be happy about it."

"Gentlemen," said Beckwourth in English. "That 'mangy savage' as you call him, wants scarlet cloth."

If a bombshell had exploded that moment in the fort, Kipp could not have been more astonished.

"You speak English!" he said. "Where did you learn it?"

"With the white man," Beckwourth replied.

"How long were you with the whites?"

"More than twenty years."

"Where did you live with them?"

"St. Louis, mostly."

"In St. Louis! In St. Louis! You have lived twenty years in St. Louis?" asked Kipp. "You are barely that old yourself. I swear, you are no Crow."

"No, I am not."

"Then what may be your name?" asked Kipp.

"Ask him," said Beckwourth, motioning to Davis.

Davis approached Beckwourth much as a dog might approach a porcupine and scanned him knees to nose. "Well, I'll be," he finally said.

"Goddamn right," said Beckwourth.

Davis let out a whoop. "This here," he said to Kipp, "is James Beckwourth, the meanest, orneriest naggur you will ever meet."

"You take your life in your hands when you call me that," said Beckwourth.

"All right, you mulatto bastard," said Davis. "I got a right to call you names anyhow. I near got killed when you forced me out."

"I did not force you out. You left against the urging of the entire party."

"Ah," said Kipp. "This solves the mystery of the 'JB' initials. We thought they must be Jim Bridger's. Anyway, we heard you were dead."

Ah, thought Beckwourth, *so Ashley did report me*

dead. "Well, as you can see," he said, "news of my demise was somewhat premature."

"Indeed," Kipp laughed. "Well then, what have you for trade today, Mr. Beckwourth, you strange mortal?"

Beckwourth looked to Hunts Alone and the rest to see how they were reacting to all this. Pride was evident in Hunt's Alone's face. Pride that one of their own could talk the white man's language, and deal with them as an equal.

"You will see that I bring only superior pelts for trade today, gentlemen," said Beckwourth. "I have watched you transact your business without interposing a word. You have cleared two or three thousand percent on your investment, I'll wager. Now, finish with my friend in a more generous manner. And then I will get the full value of mine, or you will not see the Crow again for a very long time."

Thus, Beckwourth obtained a good deal for his friend and sold his pelts for more goods than the rest of the Crow obtained for all of theirs together, including a fine gun to replace the one he had traded to Traps Alone. The Crow were wide-eyed at his apparent good fortune, and admired him for it without a trace of envy.

"You drive a hard bargain," said Kipp. "How about the rest?" He motioned to pelts that Beckwourth still had bundled up.

"Those I'm taking to St. Louis with the next boats."

"Hmm. You know," said Kipp, "we don't get but a fraction of the skins we should get from the Crow. Why don't they bring us more?"

"The Crow value bravery in battle first and foremost. Stealing horses comes next; that is their sport. Trading in furs is at best a poor third."

"How anxious are you to get back to St. Louis?"

"Quite."

"Hmm. This is something," he motioned to Beckwourth's pelts, "but I could make you so much richer."

"How would you propose to do that?"

There's some real money in it for you if you could get the Crow to adjust their priorities, if you know what I mean," said Kipp.

"No one could change that. War is bred in them. It is inculcated in them every day of their childhood. Their very mothers scorn them for cowardice if they do not prove themselves at every opportunity."

"I am prepared to offer you a healthy salary if you will help us," said Kipp.

"What exactly do you consider healthy?"

"Say, twenty-five hundred dollars a year."

"That is tempting," said Beckwourth. "Things must be pretty bad for you."

"Well, it is not only that the Crow don't bring us much. But on top of that, the Blackfeet, the Gros Ventres, the Assiniboine; my in-laws, the Arikara, they don't bring us much, either. They complain to us that they don't have any time to trap, 'cause they have to spend all their time recapturing their horses that the Crow stole."

"The way the Crow see it, they are the victims," said Beckwourth.

"Revenge and retribution, revenge and retribution," said Kipp. "It's a constant cycle among the lot of them. Maybe you could break that cycle. Consider my offer."

Beckwourth considered. If he returned to St. Louis now with what furs he had, it would be enough to get him a good start on a new life there. But most likely it would be a life without Eliza.

"Four thousand," said Beckwourth.

Kipp grinned. "Three thousand."

"I will give it some thought."

That night, Beckwourth was quiet around the fire as the Crow told stories of their exploits and boasted of victories to come. The Crow treated him with more deference than even before. They had known him as a warrior, then as a leader; now he as well had been their advocate with the whites. Beckwourth slept poorly that night. The next morning, he went to the post alone. Davis lounged at the trade counter.

"He's out riding with his woman," said Davis.

Beckwourth nodded.

"Arikara squaw," said Davis. "I got me one, too."

"A squaw man? You?"

"Why not me?"

"You don't seem the domestic type," said Beckwourth.

"Never would have thought so myself," said Davis, "'til last month."

"Newlywed, eh? Well, be careful, she might take the disagreeable streak right out of you," said Beckwourth. "And if she does, I don't know what would be left of you. You aren't really anything but disagreeable."

"Doubt any one woman could do that," Davis grinned.

Kipp returned, and he and Beckwourth shook on the salary. Their business finished, the Bckwourth and the Crow headed home. At the crest of the hill overlooking the post, he turned around to take one last look at that furthest outpost of white civilization. He pulled out his necklace and looked at the silver dollar, the date worn off from years of rubbing against his chest. He kissed it and followed the Crow.

❧ 18 ❧

On the trip back, Beckwourth ruminated over how he might bend the Crow to more peaceful ways. When the men spoke of their deeds around the campfire at night, he was silent, but when there was a pause, he told of how they and their families would want for nothing if they concentrated on trading with the whites. Blank stares were what he got in return, but no matter; he knew this would take time.

Big Bowl was delighted to see that his son had returned, but he was agitated, or as the Crow would say, his *maxpe* was up. Horses had been stolen by the Blackfeet, some of them Big Bowl's, and he was making preparations to catch the thieves. But he had raised only a pitiful, few warriors.

"Father," said Beckwourth, "I fear for your life if you go on this raid."

"Do not fear for my life, for I do not," said Big Bowl. "Our enemies have stolen my horses; I will have my revenge."

"But your enemies are many and you are but few. I fear you will all be rubbed out. Let me get your horses, father. I have never lost a man on a raid. If you go, yes, you do not care if you die. But what of the others who would go with you? What of Ishkali, who would be left all alone? Let me get your horses."

"Then you lead, my son, and I will follow."

"No, father. I will go, and I promise that I will return with your horses, or ones better than those you lost. But I go only if you promise to stay."

So, although Beckwourth had returned from Kipp's with full intention of using his influence to dissuade the Crow from such activities, the first thing he did was to organize a raiding party. This for his father, who was so wealthy that he still had more horses than he knew what to do with.

The raid was a success, and Beckwourth returned with dozens of horses. Again, through a combination of caution and good fortune, he suffered no losses among his men. But, he found on his return that his main objective had not been achieved. Despite his promise to the contrary, Big Bowl's *maxpe* had overcome him soon after Beckwourth's departure and he had gone off on a raid in another direction. Beckwourth anxiously awaited his return and was relieved when the old man sauntered into camp, successful.

"Father," said Beckwourth, "I am pleased to see you safe."

"That is as it is," said Big Bowl. "I have my horses now."

"Why did you go, father? You promised to stay."

"I meant that promise when I said it," said Big Bowl. "Never let it be said that Big Bowl does not speak from his heart."

"What is gained for the Crow by this constant warfare, father? There is more wealth to be had in trade with the whites."

"The whites do not have horses for trade."

Beckwourth persisted, knowing that what was

163

done was done, but wanting to practice his arguments. "The Crow have more horses than they need," he said. "The Crow could lose half of their horses and still have too many. It takes all the time of the young men to take them out to pasture and guard them, and many Crow warriors lose their scalps when they go out to recover them. They could all hunt and trap instead, and trade for guns and bullets enough to hunt and protect the women and children. The Crow are a small tribe that strikes fear in the hearts of their enemies, but they could be even stronger if they hunted more and traded with the whites and grew to be a larger tribe because their warriors would not be killed so."

"I went because I am an old man."

"What do you mean?"

Big Bowl broke into song. "Sun and earth are everlasting. / Men must die. / Old age is a thing of evil. / Charge and die."

There was no way to answer that.

Hunts Alone was not an old man. Beckwourth tried the same arguments on his friend.

"I would do this for you, because we are brothers," said Hunts Alone after hearing Beckwourth's plea, "so that what you want is what I want also. But the Crow will never turn from war."

"Why not?" asked Beckwourth.

"A boy aches to be a man. What is a man to the Crow except what he is as a warrior? Any woman can trade beaver pelts with the whites."

Beckwourth was at a loss for an answer to this. He sincerely believed that peaceful trade was the best path for the Crow, but how could he convince them? When opportunity presented, he continued to present his case. But blank stares began to turn to looks of derision. His words fell on ears that were stopped up, and away from his hearing he was mocked, particularly among the Fox.

As Beckwourth knew, the Crow were taught from the earliest age to bear any injury without complaint, thereby diminishing the power any foe might have over them. Some wore their injuries with pride, but for others, their injuries were like embers placed in a horn when the village moved, ready to be taken out and fanned into fire. So it was for Crooked Smile.

Wife stealing was a common mischief in the rivalry between societies, especially in a certain season. Crooked Smile, who had only recently restored his household after his punishment from Rotten Belly, returned from a hunt one day to find his wife gone. It did not take long for him to determine that the Dog Soldiers had stolen her, and now she was the wife of one of their own. Crooked Smile's concealed his anger, but it gnawed at his insides. He could not take revenge against his wife's new husband, as that would have been a sign of weakness. This had been the action of the Dog Soldiers, not just one man among them. Who among them would he most like to hurt but Beckwourth? And well he knew that the greater injury could be inflicted by attacking his closest friend, rather than the man himself.

So, day after day, Crooked Smile took every opportunity to insult Hunts Alone with vile obscenities and insults to his bravery, never mentioning Beckwourth, but always implying that all Dog Soldiers were cowards and women who wanted to avoid the warpath and just trade with the whites. At first, Hunts Alone was content to fling obscenities back, and describe in detail to Crooked Smile how his former wife was now so much more pleased sexually with her new husband. But as Crooked Smile became more threatening, Hunts Alone took to carrying his war club with him at all times. Beckwourth saw this and worried for his friend, but to have intervened would have been a mortal blow to Hunts Alone's pride. Finally, one day, gentle Hunts Alone snapped at Crooked Smile's insults and took a swing at his tormentor. Pipe carriers, the Crow equivalent of police, had been alert for this and immediately stepped between them, thrusting their peace pipes between the two and demanding the violence cease. To have continued fighting would have meant banishment or even execution for either, so they stopped, but both vowed revenge when next they met. The Dog Soldiers rallied around Hunts Alone, and the Foxes rallied around Crooked Smile. There was a real risk of widespread bloodshed between them, so the pipe carriers took the matter to Rotten Belly.

The great chief sat in his tipi with the most trusted of his lesser chiefs at his side. They passed the pipe and listened to the Fox and Dog Soldiers each insult the other as they recounted the thread of conflict between them. Rotten Belly wanted to deliver a fair decision, for if he came up with one that one side thought was unfair, they would of course carry that injury into a future conflict between them.

"Enough!" he finally said. "I have heard from your own mouths all I need to know. You persist in calling each other cowards, day and night, night and day. Enough! This is what you must do: eighteen warriors of the Fox and eighteen warriors of the Dog Soldiers must go out against an enemy. Whoever returns with the most scalps is the victor, and there is not to be any more mention of this, not ever."

"This is good," said Crooked Smile. "Let us go against the Gros Ventres, I say. But I do not need eighteen Fox warriors. I will take only twelve, and still return with more scalps than eighteen of the Dog Soldiers."

Thus it was that Hunts Alone came to Beckwourth one day, with the proposition that his friend come with him and lead the Dog Soldiers against the Gros Ventres. Beckwourth pointed out that he was trying to promote peace. He also pointed out to his friend that as brothers they were not to fight in the same battles, but his friend's *maxpe* had been raised to a boiling point, and these words had no effect.

"No, brother, I want you to go with me and die with me," said Hunts Alone. "We will enter the Other Side Camp together, where the inhabitants are all brave. There are better hunting grounds in the country of the One Above Person than even in Crow country, which are the best on earth. Come!"

"I would rather not go on such an errand," said Beckwourth. "I am happy among the Crow on earth, with my wives and my family."

"Ah," said Hunts Alone, "so the real reason that you, the bravest of the Dog Soldiers, will not go is your love for women! Leave them and come join us. There are prettier women in the land of the One Above Person than any here, and your beloved beaver are there in much greater abundance. You must go with me. Perhaps your *maxpe* will save not only yourself, but all of us. If so, it will be so much the better."

Beckwourth could see that his friend would go alone if he would not go. It seemed he would never be able to change the way of the Crow. "I must speak with someone before I decide," he said. "Come with me, and we will find this person."

So, Beckwourth led Hunts Alone through the village. The first day he had been brought to the Crow, it had looked like a chaotic jumble. Now he knew its order and who lived where, and he could read what the markings on the tipis meant about its owner. He knew the ways of these people.

"Crooked Smile," Beckwourth said, "may we have some of your smoke?"

"I will share my pipe with you," said Crooked Smile, honored at this visit by his rivals.

They sat cross-legged across from each other and passed the pipe between them, Beckwourth and Hunts Alone, Crooked Smile and the Fox men called for this parley.

"You are about to enter a contest of scalps," said Beckwourth to his host. "A contest with the Dog Soldiers."

"This is so," said Crooked Smile. "We will show the Dog Soldiers that they are but women compared to us. And after this, I have agreed that there will be peace between the Fox and the Dog Soldiers, even between me and this one," he motioned to Hunts Alone with scorn.

"Your face is twisted when you scorn others," said Beckwourth. "It is ugly and not fitting for a great warrior. Not a Crow warrior."

"What do you know of what fits a great Crow?" spat Crooked Smile.

"I know well enough," said Beckwourth. "I have been asked to carry the pipe for my Dog Soldiers."

"I am pleased with this." said Crooked Smile. Now we will now see who is the greater warrior, you or me,"

"I have not yet accepted this," said Beckwourth.

"How can you not?" asked Crooked Smile.

"I have tried to set the Crow on a path of wealth, not war," said Beckwourth. "I grieve every time a

Crow warrior is killed, and the bloodshed of the grieving makes my heart even heavier."

"You want us to spend our days trapping beaver and trading with the whites," said Crooked Smile. "That is not our way. If you do not come with us, your own Dog Soldiers will call you a coward, and they will laugh at you behind your back."

"I might lead the Dog Soldiers," said Beckwourth, "but only if you agree to one thing: you and I will ride into battle, side by side at the same moment. Let us no more trade words about who is the bravest. Let us go as quickly as possible to the battlefield, and let our weapons talk for us. And when it is over, may be obvious who is the bravest. Let that settle any difficulty between us. I will agree to lead the Dog Soldiers against the Gros Ventres, with whom I have no quarrel, if you agree to this."

"I agree to this," said Crooked Smile.

The two parties set out, war horses with notched ears and cropped tails trailing behind each mounted warrior. Their faces were daubed with red ochre, their horses painted and decked out in beaded finery. Carefully packed away were their eagle-feather war bonnets and their medicine bundles. Soft buffalo robes fell about their waists, quivers, and shields over their backs, war clubs on their pommels. It was Yellow Grass season now, and the sun beat hard on the men as they trotted out of their territory and into that of the Gros Ventres.

At a stream where they stopped to water their horses, Beckwourth pulled his horse alongside Crooked Smile, who merely scowled.

"What is so sacred about being a Crow that no matter what I do, in your eyes I cannot be one?" asked Beckwourth.

"I will tell you a tale now of my youth," said Crooked Smile, "while my horse waters, so it will be short. I was on a raid against the hated Sioux, and my father's brother was captured. It was night, and I was in hiding and could not move or hardly breathe or I would have been detected. The enemy held my uncle, who defied them with his silence. The Sioux took out their knives. First, they cut off his fingers, one by one, all ten of them. My father's brother did not make a sound, for he was a Crow, and his *maxpe* was strong. Then the Sioux cut off his hands. Still, the air was so quiet that I could hear the wind in the grass, for my uncle was a true Crow warrior. In the moonlight, I was so close that I could see that my father's brother only stared them in the face while they did this. The Sioux argued among themselves. Some wanted to start a fire and burn my uncle, but their chief respected his bravery and cut his throat. When I came home, I told my father how his brother had died. He said it was good, that his brother had shown the Sioux what it meant to be a Crow warrior. I was sixteen winters old."

If that is what it takes to be a Crow, you are right, my friend, I will never be one, thought Beckwourth. But he thought he saw in Crooked Smile's face similar doubts.

Later that day, scouts told of a small Gros Ventre war party breaking camp ahead. The Crow put their travel ponies in the care of the boys, mounted their war horses, and donned their eagle feather bonnets. They grouped on a hilltop in sight of the enemy, who were thrown into hectic activity upon seeing them. Their chief gathered them for a fight. Beckwourth pulled up alongside Crooked Smile.

"See their chief?" said Beckwourth.

"The one loading his gun," Crooked Smile said.

"Let you and I go against him together."

"He is the one," said Crooked Smile. But his words lacked enthusiasm. His *maxpe* waned just when it should have filled his heart.

"Dog Soldiers!" cried Beckwourth. "Follow me!"

Beckwourth spurred his horse forward with a whoop. The battle was on. At full gallop he charged, racing Crooked Smile. They spanned the distance quickly, but not before the chief could raise his weapon. It seemed that either Crooked Smile or Beckwourth must die, for they were equal targets. To be the faster of the two would be the only target. In the electricity of the moment, Beckwourth saw that this was what Still Water had dreamt of. He spurred his horse ahead of Crooked Smile. The chief levelled his fusee and cocked its mechanism as Beckwourth came a horse length away. Beckwourth grabbed the barrel of the gun with his left hand and struck with his war club at the same moment that the gun fired. He was stunned by the blast and felt a searing heat on the left side of his face. He wrestled the gun away from his foe and struck him repeatedly until he fell from his horse. Outnumbered and leaderless, the rest of the Gros Ventres turned to flight. The Crow chased them, all but Beckwourth and Crooked Smile. Beckwourth wiped his cheek with his palm. No blood, just gunpowder. He dismounted clumsily, his ear ringing, his eye watering.

Crooked Smile looked at him impassively. "You have bested me. You are in my eyes, now and forevermore, a Crow."

"Chose a difficult way to blacken my face, though," Beckwourth muttered in English.

Both societies tallied their losses and their scalps. The Dog Soldiers came out the victors in number of scalps, and the Fox had lost a man, so the Dog Soldiers were the clear winners of the contest. On return to the village, they all blackened their faces and paraded their scalps, and Beckwourth painted the faces of Still Water and Little Wife.

That night, Beckwourth came to Still Water in the darkness of their tipi, upon the floor of which she had placed a half-dozen buffalo hides, the ones taken in the winter, with thick, soft wool.

"I wish to thank you, my love. Your dream saved me."

"Did you hesitate?" she asked.

"Only until I remembered your words, my wife," he said, his words slurred by his swollen cheek. "I will always have this tattoo on my face to remind me to listen to you."

Still Water cradled his cheek and kissed him tenderly. Beckwourth slipped his hand under her breast and down to her thigh. She responded with a gentle sway and brought him next to her on the soft pile of buffalo robes.

G ame in the area became scarce, and the carcasses of what they had killed were beginning to stink. A lesser chief by the name of Big Rain determined that the next day they would move camp. Heralds announced it, and the following morning the women began packing before dawn. Wizened old wives directed the younger women as in teams they folded the tipi hides, lashed the long poles to their horses, and secured the tipis to those. As always, the very frail, the elderly, and toddlers were placed in these travois as well, the toddlers with safety cages of willow constructed over them. Excited children mounted ponies in twos and threes, eager to ride to a place they had never seen before. Babies less than six months were carried in the arms of their mothers, who were tied securely to their horses. Older infants were swaddled in cradle boards, faces shielded from the son by willow and hide awnings, lashed to the pommels of their mothers' saddles. Every dog carried a pack or pulled a travois. The men watched all this activity and went about their usual routine. When all was packed, Big Rain gave the word, and the whole village went on the move; hundreds of people, more horses than people, and nearly as many dogs. They headed over the gentle hills in search of buffalo, Big Rain in the lead, followed by the rest of the chiefs and warriors, scouts on all sides, women and children following in a long, dusty line stretching as far as the eye could see.

The first day of the trip, scouts came upon a white man. It was Davis, who was brought to Beckwourth.

"What can I do for you, my friend?" asked Beckwourth, with a smile twisted by his still-swollen cheek.

"Kipp sent me," said Davis. "What happened to you?"

"I was involved in a test of nerves with another of our warriors. As you can see, I won."

"If you are what the winner looks like, I pity the loser."

"That Arikara wife of yours must be a wondrous creature to have introduced you to such a new emotion as pity."

"I ain't so evil as all that, Beckwourth. Anyhow, Kipp wants me to see how well the bargain goes," said Davis.

"Well, I am sorry to report that although I have tried my best to convince the Crow to trap, there have been some distractions, let's say, and I have met with no real success."

"Too bad," said Davis. "We could all be rich."

"My view, as well," said Beckwourth.

"Where we goin' now?" asked Davis.

"We?" asked Beckwourth. "You wish to accompany us?"

"Don't see why not."

When among the Crow, Beckwourth was as stone-faced as the best of them. But among white mountaineers, he reverted a bit to their ways and patterns of speech. He cocked his head and screwed up his face. "You got a lot of nerve," he said.

"Oh, come on," said Davis.

"No, really. You got a lot of nerve. I still have your teeth marks on me. And you know what you called me. I should send you packing right now."

"Wagh. But you won't. We are of a brotherhood. We's mountaineers, and mountaineers is like family."

"Family!" said Beckwourth. "You and I are family?"

"Nobody in your family never called you a name?" Davis asked. "Nobody in your family never beat the tar out of you?"

No, Beckwourth thought. *No, no one in my family ever beat the tar out of me. And that they did that to you explains a lot.* "Wagh!" he exclaimed. "I am worried about you, though."

"Pray tell," said Davis.

"I told you that Ree wife of yours might just take the disagreeable streak right out of you."

"So?"

"Like I said, won't hardly be nothing left of you if she does."

"You should talk."

"So here you are, willing to let yourself be led across the wilds by a bunch of savages and a mulatto bastard, with no regard for your higher station in life."

"Mock me all you want. But I need action. Got tired of the trading post life."

"No shortage of action when you cast your lot with the Crow," said Beckwourth. "Come on along, then."

The next morning, the camp awoke to a beautiful, late summer day in foothills studded with rock outcroppings. A surround was organized to raise game. While the men hunted, Beckwourth took Still Water and Little Wife on a little horseback excursion. Halfway up a hill, Beckwourth stopped and raised his hand for the other two to be quiet. A faint shout came to his ears. A war whoop? He galloped ahead to the crest of the hill, and then returned.

"Return to the camp, both of you," he said. "There will be a battle."

"I will follow you, husband," said Still Water.

"And I, as well," said Little Wife.

"Very well then, come," he said, and they sped off. Over the hill, fifty Crow were gathered within arrow shot of a rocky natural fortress, which varied in height from six feet at one end to an imposing twenty feet at the other. The elements had cut a deep groove into the wall that ran its full length of fifty yards, and in that groove the enemy had taken refuge, out of sight except when they popped up to fire their weapons. Some Crow had tried a frontal assault and now lay wounded and dying. Others had had better success and now sheltered at the base of the wall. More Crow streamed in, and soon they would vastly outnumber their foe.

Beckwourth rode up to Crooked Smile. "Which enemy is this?" he asked.

"Sioux dogs."

The Sioux. Beckwourth turned to Still Water. "Woman, get my war instruments. Both of you." This was no sooner said than he saw the backs of his wives as they sped away. The Crow milled about before the enemy, signing insults and letting loose war whoops. As more and more Crow streamed in, there were those who sought to prove their bravery and rush the fort, with no better results than before; another fell, mortally wounded. Rotten Belly arrived and took counsel from his lesser chiefs. Little Wife returned, not with his weapons, but with Davis, who had intercepted her.

"Watch and learn how the Crow fight, Mr. Davis," said Beckwourth. "Here is the excitement you sought."

"I brought my rifle and hatchet, and the will to use them."

"This is not your battle. The Crow will think no less of you if you only watch."

"I want my part of the fun," said Davis, hefting his hatchet.

Still Water arrived, dismounted, and presented Beckwourth his war club.

"I must tell you something, husband," she said.

But just then Rotten Belly spoke to all. "Warriors, listen! See those who have fallen already. Our marrow bones are broken. The enemy has chosen a strong fort. We cannot drive them from it without sacrificing too many men. Warriors, retreat!"

Beckwourth looked at Stillwater, still holding his war club up for him to grasp. The dying words of Water Carrier reverberated in his ears. "Warriors, hold!" he said. "Listen to my words. If these old men cannot fight, let them retire with the women and children. We can kill every one of these Sioux. Let us do it. If we attempt to run from here, we shall be shot in the back, and lose more warriors than if we stand and fight here and now. If we get killed, our friends who love us will mourn our loss, while those in the spirit land will sing and rejoice to welcome us there, if we ascend to them dying like braves."

The men wavered. Beckwourth knew he must convince them in the manner of their own thought. "The One Above Person has sent these enemies here for us to slay. If we do not slay them, he will be angry with us, and will never let us conquer our enemies again. He will drive off all our buffalo and will wither the grass on the prairies. No, warriors! We must fight as long as one of us survives. Let us fight like Crow!"

"Shoots Good in the Dark!" shouted Crooked Smile, raising his lance. "Lead us, and we will follow you to the spirit land."

Hundreds of warriors shouted their agreement. The air was so charged with excitement that Beckwourth felt invincible.

Rotten Belly called a council. "Shoots Good in the Dark, the people have spoken," he said. "Tell us your plan."

"Hunts Alone will lead our best bowmen," said Beckwourth, "and on my word they will fire as one to keep the Sioux from showing their faces. At that moment, the rest of us will run like antelope to the base of the enemy wall. "Once there, let the Fox warriors harass the enemy with their lances. My Dog soldiers will circle around to the back of the fort where it is tallest, and the enemy will not expect us. My men will climb on the shoulders of the strongest of our number and scale the wall. From the top, we will fire our arrows and guns down on the Sioux from behind, before they know we are even there. Not a man of the Crow need have a hair out of place on his head before every Sioux is dead."

"I believe this is a foolish battle," said Rotten Belly. "But I have said what I have to say, and the Crow have decided to fight. It is good. I will lead the charge against this wall. I will be at the forefront of my warriors."

The council dispersed.

"What about me?" Davis asked Beckwourth.

"Take your rifle and hang back with the bow-men." He gave Davis to the care of Hunts Alone.

Beckwourth divided his Dog Soldiers into two groups and instructed them in his plan. When all was ready, he gave the signal, and with a great whoop the Crow rushed the wall at the same moment that the archers let their arrows fly. But Beckwourth felt him-self restrained, as if his clothing were stuck on a branch. He turned around to see Little Wife holding him back by his horsehair belt.

"Child, there is no time for this." he said.

"I cannot bear to lose you," she said.

"You will not, unless you make me a straggler." He cut the belt with his knife and zig-zagged to the base of the fort, leaving a tearful Little Wife holding his belt in her hands.

Beckwourth zig-zagged to his men and led them around the back. They took their places in pre-arranged pairs. All in place, Beckwourth was about to give his men the signal when he heard a great commotion coming from inside. He hesitated but gave the signal and climbed the shoulder of his part-ner, pulling himself up on the top of the stone for-mation. He looked down on a scene of carnage and confusion, where Sioux and Crow engaged in close-quarter combat. The Fox had not heeded his orders. His Dog Soldiers called to him for directions. There was no way to fire anywhere without hitting a Crow as easily as a Sioux.

"Leave your guns and bows behind!" shouted Beckwourth, as he leapt into the fray, knife at the ready in his left hand, club in his right. An enemy lunged at him. A short swing of his club stunned the man, and his knife finished him. Crow now poured into the fort, Dog Soldiers and Fox. The Sioux knew they were doomed but fought all the harder. Beckwourth heard cursing in English. Turning to the sound, he saw Davis lunge at a Sioux with his hatchet, but the warrior twisted and inflicted a knife wound deep in Davis' thigh. Screaming in pain, Davis grappled with his foe on the ground. Slippery with blood, the two lost their grips on each other. As they separated, Beckwourth stunned the Sioux with his club, allowing Davis to finish him off. Every surviving Sioux faced multiple Crow now, and in a minute the battle was over.

"I owe you," Davis said, panting and wincing.

"You would have done the same for me," said Beckwourth, inspecting the nasty gash on Davis' thigh.

"Looks like I will be out of action for a time."

"I told you to stay with the bowmen."

"You told me to hang back. I'm not a 'hang back' kinda fellow," grinned Davis, covered head to toe with blood.

Still panting, Beckwourth assessed the aftermath of battle. The moans of the dying Crow and Sioux mingled and reverberated within the walls of the enclosure. The smell of blood was nauseating. But they had won, and he had survived once more. The Crow finished off the dying Sioux and ministered to their own. Their own dead numbered some twenty. The Sioux were annihilated.

Beckwourth helped Davis over the wall and climbed out himself. Here lay Rotten Belly, surrounded by his chiefs, with hundreds of warriors milling about at a distance. An arrow had run through him shoulder to hip, and those who surrounded him knew his time on this earth was short. Still Water cradled his head.

"Warriors," said Rotten Belly, "I will lead you no more. My home will soon be in the Other Side

Camp. Oh, One Above Person, my people would not listen to my counsel. I am no longer of use to them, so now you take me home to you. Do not be angry with them. Shoots Good in the Dark, come to me."

"I am here, Great Chief."

"You must now take my place. You are brave, and the people listen to you above all others. Your *maxpe* is powerful. You are cautious and cunning; you wait to act until the right time. You do not lash out at the first enemy you see like a wounded badger. My eyes grow dim. Shoots Good in the Dark, are you listening? I cannot see."

"I am listening to all you say," Beckwourth replied.

"It is good. Then take this shield and this medal; they both belong to you. The medal is from your chief by the salt water where the sun rises. It was given to me many winters ago by the red-haired chief. It belongs to you, and then to him who succeeds you." He turned to Crooked Smile. "Listen. Tell my most beloved wife that if our unborn child is a son, she must tell him who his father was."

"I will tell her," said Crooked Smile.

"Is Big Bowl here?" Rotten Belly asked.

"I am here, my friend," said Big Bowl.

"Many have been our battles together, my friend. Wrap my body in my robe and let it be buried under this spot. Allow no warrior to set foot on this ground for one season. Then come and seek my bones, and I will have something good for you. I can hear the voice of the One Above Person. It sounds like the moaning of a mighty wind through a dark and gloomy forest. He calls for me to come to the Other Side Camp. I must go." His voice faded. "Do not forget my words."

Big Bowl rose. "He breathes no more."

A most dismal howling went heavenward from all. Still Water sobbed and held his body close. Warriors cut themselves, spilling more blood than had been lost in the battle. *These are now my men*, thought Beckwourth. The mantle of leadership had been thrust upon him. He examined the medal. The worn visage of President Jefferson stared back at him. He placed the medal around his neck, where it rested next to the coin from his mother.

Beckwourth dispatched a messenger to inform the village of the deaths of Rotten Belly and the others. He bade Little Wife to take care of Davis' wound, and forbade that she mutilate herself. Still Water rose from her father's side and came to him.

"You will need strength, now," she said.

"You are my strength."

"I am pregnant," she said. "I tried to tell you."

Beckwourth drew close to her. "My heart is glad, my wife. It is unfortunate that your father could not know."

"I whispered it to him. He heard."

Beckwourth mounted and led the multitude back to the village, dreading what he knew he must find. On an overlook, he paused to survey the scene. The tipis had all been struck and lay in heaps on the ground, and the dogs ran about, barking in confusion. The wind carried the doleful shrieks of an entire people. Crooked Smile rode up next to Beckwourth.

"You attacked when I said to wait," Beckwourth said.

"Ha! The man of caution speaks. You cannot know the anger we felt when Rotten Belly fell. Yes, you are a Crow now; I agreed to that. But you were not with us when Rotten Belly was in his prime, when he saved our entire people from being rubbed out by these very Sioux. You are but a sapling to the mighty tree that was Rotten Belly." He rode away.

Indeed, thought Beckwourth. *How on Earth am I to lead such a people?* He entered the chaotic village. Piercing shrieks punctuated a background chorus of wailed lamentation. Warriors sang their death songs, and every individual old enough to comprehend the meaning of the loss of Rotten Belly cut themselves. Beckwourth watched helplessly as Hunts Alone cut two long parallel lines on his arm a half inch apart and pulled a ribbon of skin from his body without flinching. It sickened him, but he dared not intercede.

Only Beckwourth's wives did not cut themselves. Still Water wailed mightily for her father, but in her wailing, she explained to the One Above Person that she kept all the blood inside her body to honor her husband, who had taken revenge on the Sioux. Davis limped to Beckwourth.

"I seen him put that medal on you. So, are you the big chief now?"

"It would seem so."

"You don't seem so happy about it."

"Look about you," said Beckwourth. "I should have listened to Rotten Belly when he called for retreat. But I let my thirst for vengeance overcome me. I caused the chief's death, and by doing so caused all of the grieving and disgusting self-mutilation you see."

"Wouldn't beat yourself up so much about it. They are savages, you know," said Davis.

"What makes you sure we are better?" Beckwourth asked. "Who are we to call them savages?"

"'We'?" asked Davis.

For a moment, Beckwourth thought Davis was rejecting the notion that he and a mulatto could be part of a 'we.' But Davis grinned and shrugged.

"We mountain men, when one of us dies," said Davis, "the others tell stories to each other about what a great man he was. I seen it, too many times. They forget all his bad parts and just talk about the good. Hell, they would even have good things to say about me. That's what we do. Far as I'm concerned, that's better than skinning yerself by degrees."

Beckwourth contemplated a clump of bloody hair at his feet. "If it be in my power, I will put an end to this dreadful mourning without the need for an enemy scalp," he said.

At dawn the next day, Beckwourth, now Chief Medicine Calf, ordered that the village move a short distance, looking for a fresh wind, and hoping that busy hands would not be looking to mutilate. Once there, he commanded that a great lodge be erected for a council of all the medicine men and chiefs. At the appointed time, the elite of the village assembled, and a great ceremony unfolded. The Crow national history was recited with great gravity by elders, starting as always with the split from the Hidatsa, through the acquisition of horses and guns, and all of the great battles with surrounding tribes. Rotten Belly's deeds were emphasized. Beckwourth watched the next generation of warriors absorb the tales like sponges. The recitation of history came to the most recent battle, as told by Crooked Smile, who repeated the dying words of Rotten Belly.

"Stop!" said Beckwourth. "Rotten Belly is no more. By now he has met his fathers and kindred who preceded him to the Other Side Camp. He has told them of your deeds of bravery, and in that they rejoice. The One Above Person wishes the Crow to be the greatest among nations. He has given you a victory against your greatest enemy, the Sioux. Let it be as if all of us blacken our faces now in victory, and let the fire of revenge in our hearts go out. I wish to help the One Above Person make the Crow to be the greatest among nations. If you blacken out your fire for revenge now, I say, you can be that and more.

"Brothers, do not make war on your enemies for the sake of old grievances. Should they attack us and kill our people, then we must attack them, or if they steal our horses, then we must punish the ones who did this, but not ride forth with blind vengeance in our hearts against whichever of our enemies we happen to meet first.

"I want all my warriors to lay aside their war clubs and lances for a season and turn their attention to hunting and trapping. Let us keep our women busy dressing buffalo robes and beaver, and not keep them as mere playthings for ourselves. We must also not send out small parties to hunt that are vulnerable to attack, but only large ones. And if our enemies do attack us, we will be strong then in numbers and can kill ten of them for every one of us, so my *maxpe* tells me. I am not willing to see the consequences if you disobey me, not willing to see the Crow nation become weak, flying before our enemies, and our women and children carried off into captivity. Obey and assist me, then, and I will do my best in your behalf. Warriors, I have done."

This speech was received with grunts of approval. Word was sent to the Mountain Crow that Rotten Belly was no more, and Medicine Calf, the one they had known as Shoots Good in the Dark, now led the River Crow.

❧ 20 ❧

Beckwourth's speech dampened the mourning to some degree. He congratulated himself for having so deftly played on the superstitions of his people, implying to them that the One Above Person was the one who wished they rein in their warlike ways. It was by now his habit to play on them like this for both matters of importance and also for trivial matters for his own convenience. Such a trivial lie was that he said he could not eat buffalo tongue, because to do so would hurt his *maxpe*. Really, he just did not like it as it was customarily served: raw and the texture of India rubber.

One day, Beckwourth went to Hunts Alone's tipi and found his friend absent, soon to return. So, he waited. Hunts Alone's wife politely offered him a meal from the stew pot. He found the stew to be perfectly delightful and ate heartily. On Hunts Alone's return, Beckwourth complimented the meal and asked the wife what it was.

"Tongue stew," she beamed.

Hunts Alone jumped up in horror. "Tongue! Tongue! You have ruined his *maxpe*. Should Medicine Calf be slain in battle, you are a lost woman."

Beckwourth could only take pity on the poor woman, her face reflecting abject terror. He felt that he must remedy her plight. He ran out of the tipi roaring like a bull buffalo, with his tongue protruding in the most grotesque manner he could manage, pawing at the ground. Frantically he ran in circles, frothing at the mouth, all of which attracted a large crowd of sympathizers. Finally exhausted, he lay on the ground limp. A minute of that, and he rose with the dignity of a great chief. "I am well," he said. "My *maxpe* is restored." He strode to his tipi.

The impetus behind the mourning was powerful, such had been Rotten Belly's *maxpe*, and the self -mutilation began to grow again. Still Water saw his distress at this and came to him.

"Husband," she said, "the people suffer, and I see in your face that you suffer."

"I know not what to do, my wife," he said.

"You wish them to all blacken their faces for good," she said. "If you truly wish this, you know what you must do."

She was right. He knew the most expeditious way to end this. So, even though he preached peace, among his first acts as great chief was to organize a raiding party. He chose carefully from among his warriors for men who would obey and not thirst for their own glory, nor be overpowered by their own desire for vengeance at the moment of battle. He chose from both the Fox and the Dog Soldiers, for their rivalry needed to be dampened as well. They set out, with his intention being to take only one scalp. Due to his caution, and the discipline of his men, they succeeded in stealing a herd of horses with no harm to themselves. There had been two teenagers watching the herd, and it was their scalps that ended the mourning; not one, but two. Beckwourth was not proud of this, but horses alone would not have ended the mourning. On return, he obliged his wives by painting their faces. The victory celebration lasted for three long days, but Beck-wourth did not dance around the scalp pole himself. Little Wife noticed this and came to him as he sat with Davis, watching, Davis with his wounded leg propped up.

"Husband," Little Wife said, "you do not dance, and you barely speak. Are you angry?"

"This will pass, young one."

"Should I tell Still Water to stop her dancing, husband?"

"She should do what is in her heart, as I do as in mine."

"Why is it not in your heart to dance?' she asked.

Davis did not know the Crow language or sign very well, so Beckwourth communicated to Little Wife in sign, and spoke English.

"I do not kill for revenge, nor do I kill children. These boys whose scalps hang on the pole that the Crow dance around now were your age, young one. A part of my heart mourns for those boys."

"But they were enemy," she said.

"Yes, they were enemy, my wife. I will tell you a story of my childhood, and you will understand my heart better. Please sit."

She sat on her heels, knees on the ground, in the fashion of all modest Crow women. Beckwourth told of his playmate, Amanda, and how he had come upon her and her family that day, and how he still carried this with him. He paused. He had seen much killing since then, but describing it still brought a tightness in his throat. "My friend was the first I saw, lying on the ground, a grimace on her face in death, her bloody skull flecked with flies where her beautiful blond hair had been. The rest of her family lay about in the same manner."

"Your eyes were not used to such things," said Little Wife.

"No one's eyes should be used to such things," he said. "She was so young. A man can be brought to do such a thing when he allows revenge to overpower him. This is not good. He is to be scorned who carries the scalp of a child as a trophy."

"I understand, husband," she said. "I wish to tell you a story of when the Crow captured me from my people. This may help you."

"Please tell me, child, and I will tell the white trader."

"I do not recall how my parents were killed, though I know they were. What I remember is the ride to the Crow village, me behind a warrior on his horse, my older brother seated behind another warrior on his horse ahead of me. My brother waited until a time when he could look me in the eyes, to say goodbye. Then, he grabbed the Crow's knife and plunged it into his captor's kidney. The Crow killed him immediately. That is how my brother died. My brother was ten winters old. The boys whose scalps you see here, they were older than ten winters. Yes, my husband?"

Beckwourth translated this for Davis and responded, "yes, my child."

"Do not tell what I say next to the white trapper, husband."

"Of course, my Little Wife."

"It is for the memory of my brother that I am chaste. I do not wish to lie with Crow men. I have been treated well, I am a Crow and proud of it. But I choose thus to honor the memory of my brother. Unlike men, I have no medicine bundle to hang in the back of my tipi to signify this. Instead, once a year, the Crow have a ceremony for the chaste woman. It is to the shame of the Crow that such women are so rare. At the next ceremony, I will present myself to be honored as a chaste woman. For you it is different. I see the eyes of many women on you. Perhaps you will take even more wives. Others will want just to lie with you when their husbands are away. You are a powerful warrior, and I am pleased to be your wife, to have you paint my face when you return from the warpath. This is enough for me. I am done speaking of this."

Little Wife left them.

"What was that all about?" asked Davis.

Beckwourth shook his head and pursed his lips. "She promised me that things will be the same between us now, even if I am the big chief."

21

Fewer war parties went forth. Not none, but fewer. The men hunted for furs and there was for a time no mourning over fallen warriors. Autumn came, and Davis' leg healed sufficiently for travel, so he and a Crow escort headed back to Kipp's with a load of pelts and buffalo hides.

The men occupied their idle hours as they always had: in contests with bow and gun, wrestling matches, and a game similar to Lacrosse; always betting, always laughing, bragging, and challenging one another. But there was more of this idle time now, and a restlessness. Also, power corrupts. From this, and from the idleness, Beckwourth would soon subvert his own best intentions.

Among the Crow women, there was one whose beauty stood out above all others. Slender and proud, with a piercing gaze, she knew that the eyes of all the men took her in. Her name was Red Cherry, and she was the wife of Big Rain, the chief who organized hunts and led migrations. He had achieved his station by his actions as a younger man, but had not recently gone on raiding parties, let alone war parties. The young warriors scorned him for this, and it seemed to them that such a man did not deserve the most beautiful woman around. So, in these idle times, talk among them often drifted to schemes of who might kidnap her and how. Crooked Smile's wife had been stolen in a certain season that allowed for such thievery, but this was no longer that season. Stealing the wife of this chief would carry a severe penalty. But the men made light of the beatings they would receive by Crow law from the husband, and of their horses that would be confiscated, for this would be a good way to show their bravery when there was little other way to do so. And it would be worth it if they could have such a beauty for their wife. Beckwourth shared their admiration for Red Cherry. He had himself approached her more than once with the ceremonious obeisance due a woman of her beauty and station. She had not encouraged him, but neither had she discouraged him.

As the weeks of Still Water's pregnancy progressed, she had a morning sickness such that she returned to the tipi of her mother. Little Wife moved in with Beckwourth, in order to cook and sew for him and comb his hair in the morning, but only that. Beckwourth was at loose ends and pent-up desires. The days dragged on with his Dog Soldiers, always smoking, bragging of great deeds, and plotting new ones. When his men plotted raids, he steered them away from that, but when the conversation turned to kidnapping Mrs. Big Rain, he was loath to quash their fun. As they plotted and boasted, he listened.

A Dog Soldier named Sees the Clouds was one who lazed and plotted her kidnapping incessantly. This man was not the most handsome specimen of the Crow race, and he was just a hanger-on among the Dog Soldiers, never going on war parties or horse raids. There were among the Crow a few like this —

men who had only one coup to their credit. For if they performed that one coup, they were allowed to marry young, whereas otherwise they had to wait until they were twenty-five. This one had done nothing since his one coup. Though such an individual was following the path of peace that Beckwourth now advocated, still he held Sees the Clouds in contempt for his lack of past deeds. Beckwourth knew that he was himself a walking contradiction in this, but still, the man's bragging was offensive to his ears.

"How is it that you think Red Cherry would have anything to do with you if you did take her?" Beckwourth said to him one day. "You are lazy and as ugly as a dog butt."

The men laughed. 'Dog butt' was an insult that the Crow usually reserved for bearded white men, for they themselves did not grow beards, and considered the mountain men that did unsightly.

"I am not as handsome as you, oh Bloody Arm Shoots Good in the Dark Medicine Calf, great warrior from the land of the dog butts. But I have what you do not. I have a potion that makes women fall in love with me. And I use it on the wives of the Fox women when their husbands go on the warpath."

"All the potions from all the lands of all the tribes and then also from the lands of the whites, this would not make such a beautiful woman fall in love with you," said Beckwourth.

"Oh, but there is such a potion, James Beckwourth," said Sees the Clouds. The men fell silent. None of them had ever called him by his white man's name before. "I have a potion from the one who saved you; Red Blanket who ran a lance through a Sioux while you were trying so hard not to fall off your horse." Sees The Clouds flailed his arms around as if falling, to restrained snickers. "Such half-men, half-women, they know of potions that we warriors know not."

Beckwourth seethed at this challenge in front of all the others. But it would have been a sign of weakness to show his anger at this one who was of no note except for his lack of notability. He knew how to counter this insult.

The next day, Beckwourth went to Red Cherry's brother, whom he knew greatly admired him, and who was a neighbor of Big Rain. Beckwourth let the brother know that his heart burned for a female relative of his, though without divulging whom exactly. He calculated that this warrior would be happy to be related to Beckwourth by marriage, if such should be the outcome.

Beckwourth had gauged the brother's admiration properly, for he replied, "Your enemies call you Bloody Arm, and fear you like none other. It is only right that your desires should be gratified. If it is in my power, Medicine Calf, I will assist you."

"Thank you, honored warrior," said Beckwourth. He gave this fellow a large plug of white man's tobacco, a rare treat among the Crow. "Please accept this small gift in thanks for your friendship. Now, I want you to invite into your tipi tonight all of your neighbors for a smoke. I know you are an experienced warrior, and I am sure you have enough tales of your exploits to last until all this tobacco is smoke and ashes. In the meantime, while you and your neighbors smoke, I will be busy."

Beckwourth next went to Hunts Alone and acquainted him with his plan, enlisting him as a sentry to watch the comings and goings at the brother's tipi during the smoke. Hunts Alone was quite amused and more than willing to be an accessory to the crime.

On the appointed night, Beckwourth put on his finest clothes, and gave Little Wife the impression that he was going out to plan a raid. Her innocent joy at this news gave him a pang of conscience, which he only made worse by telling her that she might someday soon have the honor of carrying his shield on a raid. But he put his conscience behind him and skulked off to meet Hunts Alone. Near the tipi of Red Cherry's brother, they watched until Big Rain himself arrived to smoke the white man's tobacco. With all the stealth he could muster, Beckwourth entered Big Rain's tipi and found Red Cherry asleep, along with others of Big Rain's family. He touched her brow, and she sat up.

"Who is here?" she asked.

"Hush," he replied. "It is I."

"You!" she whispered. "What do you want?"

"I have come to see you, because I love you."

"How dare you! I am Big Rain's wife," she whispered.

"Yes, I know that," said Beckwourth. "But he does not love you like I do."

"Your love is foolish, like a boy's," she said.

"I am a great warrior, and your man is not. It is said among the Crow that it is good to die young, and he says this also, but it is only from his lips, not his heart. He has become like an old woman, the big chief of the tasks of women."

"Think this if you wish, but you can be certain he will kill you if you take me away."

"If he kills me, then it will be good for you, for the Crow will talk of you for many winters, and say that the great brave, Medicine Calf, died in honor of your beauty."

"If you are successful in stealing me away," said Red Cherry, "your father will lose all his horses, and all his other property, and will become poor in his old age. I respect your father and all your relatives, and my heart would cry to see them poor."

"Big Bowl would be proud to lose his horses if his son could win a wife as handsome as you. Come with me, and you can go to war with me, and carry my shield. With you by my side, I could kill a great many enemies, and bring home many scalps. Then we could often dance, and our hearts would be made merry and glad."

"Go now," she said, "for if my husband should return and find you here, he would be very angry, and it would crush my heart to see him kill you. And worse yet, I would not be allowed to grieve for you. Go now at once!"

Beckwourth's heart gladdened at this. She would grieve for him, were he killed.

"No," said Beckwourth. "I will not go until you give me your word that you will be mine when an opportunity comes."

Hunts Alone called the signal. The smoke was at an end.

"That is the signal for me," said Beckwourth. "I will not risk this twice. You must decide now, and quickly."

Red Cherry slipped a copper ring off her finger and placed it on Beckwourth's little finger, where it fit only to the first knuckle. She held his hand in hers for a moment. "Go," she said.

Beckwourth fled the tipi and padded to the side of Hunts Alone.

"Where is she?" his friend asked.

"Her heart is mine," said Beckwourth. He showed his friend the ring.

"Her heart is her own, and she is not here with you," said Hunts Alone. "For all this trouble, you should have brought her here."

"I have my ways," said Beckwourth. "You will see."

The following day, Beckwourth returned to Big Rain's lodge with a half dozen Dog Soldiers, their horses bedecked in beaded finery. Red Cherry averted her eyes and attended to her work.

"Medicine Calf," said Big Rain, "where are you going, my friend?"

"We go to steal horses from the Arikara, Big Rain."

"This is good," said Big Rain. "The blood of the young men clots in their veins of late. But you are the one who tells your men to attend to hunting and trapping, not war and stealing horses. Has your heart changed?"

Beckwourth's thoughts stumbled, due to his own duplicity being called out so. "I have advised the Crow to push vengeance from their hearts. This is not for vengeance; this is like a hunt. The Arikara have more horses than they can use, and their horses paw at the ground in dismay, for they wish to graze in the lush meadows of our land."

"May you return with many fine horses," said Big Rain.

"Yes," Beckwourth answered. "But I need to know your plans for moving the village, so that we can find you when we return, and also that if we encounter a large force, we can return to warn you."

"That is wise," said Big Rain. "Many have been those who skulked away at night and not shown such concern for their families. We will stay until you return. Go, and may the One Above Person protect you."

Either the One Above Person or lady luck smiled upon Beckwourth, for he happened upon a circumstance that was ideal for his plan. On their second day out, they spied in the distance a party of two dozen Blackfeet in full war gear just emerging from a pass in the hills. Their only object could have been to attack the Crow. Quickly, Beckwourth's men retraced their steps, riding day and night nonstop. When within sight of the village they signaled with a mirror that an enemy was approaching. When a great stir was seen in the village and they knew the message had been received they proceeded. Beckwourth told Big Rain of the Blackfoot approach, and preparations were made to go forth with an overwhelming force the day following. Beckwourth returned to his tipi, where Little Wife was pleased to see him. But his conscience nagged at him for what he was about to do. He was aloof and cold.

"Husband, what is wrong?" she asked in a low voice.

"Nothing is wrong, my child," he said. "I go tomorrow to exterminate an enemy."

Red Cherry approached, leading a powerful war horse. "My husband sends this horse to Medicine Calf, whom our enemies call Bloody Arm," Red Cherry said. "Chief Big Rain wishes him great success against the Blackfoot dogs."

Little Wife saw that there was something unspoken between the two. After Red Cherry left, she retrieved his shield and presented it to him. "Husband, you know that I have never before made demands of you but to have my face painted on your return from the warpath. Still Water should be the one to carry this shield to the battle but is not able. Therefore, I ask this one time that I may have the honor instead."

"Child, the danger is too great," said Beckwourth. The entire village was aroused to cut to pieces a handful of an enemy. Never would there be less danger in such a situation, but to honor her so would only heighten the dishonor that he contemplated. "Do not be sad, my cherished one. You may carry my shield at the victory dance."

"I am saddened more that you hide your heart from me, husband, than I am that you keep your shield to yourself."

Big Rain doubled the village guard, and all slept fitfully that night, in eager anticipation of the surprise in store for their enemy. At first light, Beckwourth sent scouting parties out and waited. It was not twenty minutes before a gunshot in the direction of the river signaled that the enemy had been found, and every warrior in the village sped in that direction, with the women and children close behind. The river was seasonally low, and the Blackfeet had retreated to an island and thrown up a driftwood fort. Beckwourth arrived to a chaotic mob scene. Crow warriors shouted to each other and sang their war songs, while the women yelled encouragement and dogs howled. Young warriors used this rare opportunity to show off for their girlfriends, charging the fort just to challenge the Blackfeet or to send an arrow flying, then retreating. Beckwourth had lost control of his people. Unless he could get them to act of a single mind, over time Crow warriors would be picked off by the Blackfeet, one by one.

Big Bowl and another old warrior had already charged the Blackfoot position and reached an embankment just below the driftwood fort. Here they spoke almost casually to one another. Beckwourth dismounted and zig-zagged to their side, carrying only his lance.

"My son, why are you here?" Big Bowl asked.

"I put the same question to you."

"We are old warriors, and do not wish to become so much older that we should become objects of pity," said the other.

Beckwourth inspected the driftwood wall above them. They were close enough to hear the murmurings inside, and through a small aperture he could see the shadows of the enemy as they moved about. A shadow paused, and Beckwourth thrust his lance upward. There was a momentary cry, and when Beckwourth pulled back, his lance was covered with blood.

"There, you old warriors," said Beckwourth, "stay here and look for your own opportunity, but I must return to the young warriors, or too many will die."

Beckwourth zig-zagged back to the Crow, whooping and thrusting his lance in the air for all to see that he had drawn first blood. He gathered the warriors to his side.

"Lead us, Medicine Calf," said one, and a chorus called out his name. Beckwourth organized a single charge, and in minutes the Black Feet were finished.

The Crow returned to the village in a jubilant mood. But two Crow warriors had fallen in the final assault, and Beckwourth dreaded what was to come.

"Do not mourn our fallen warriors by cutting off fingers and painting yourselves with your own blood," he said to the crowd. "Let us instead heap riches upon them and place them high with greatest honor. Let that be enough."

The next day, the fallen were both dressed in finely decorated robes. With arms folded they were gently placed in the best scarlet blankets, in which were strewn the most costly trinkets, and they were lain over the backs of their favorite horses. With the whole village following, they were taken to waiting platforms, their wives following, singing mournful songs. There, just out of sight of the village, they were placed on their platforms. The warriors' horses and a faithful dog were sacrificed beneath them. The entire village painted themselves in mourning colors and joined in mourning so. And it was enough; for once even the closest family mourned without bloodshed.

The victory celebration started at sunset. Warriors paraded through the village, led by a herald and trailed by Beckwourth who cradled his pipe in his arm. The entire village danced that night around the pole as the *berdache* Red Blanket beat a rhythm on it. The women danced with their men's medicine bundles and their shields, and the whole village joined in their chant. Little Wife danced with Beckwourth's shield, treading softly and with no enthusiasm.

The drums reached a crescendo, then ceased. Red Blanket shouted, "Untie your horses and take them away, for the lodge striking is now!" The people obeyed with a collective laugh, and young boys took up willow branches that had been set aside for this. On cue from Red Blanket, the boys struck Beckwourth's tipi in one motion, making a tremendous booming sound that startled the horses, even though they had been taken distant. The people laughed and clapped and resumed their chanting and dancing. The men sang the traditional song, "I went away; I have returned; kiss me!"

Beckwourth drew Little Wife to him and kissed her lightly, but she did not smile, and instead danced away.

Beckwourth approached Never Wavers. "I have a request of you, my sister."

"Anything for my brother, the great warrior," she replied.

"Tomorrow I go again on a raid. I will send you some gifts that I wish you to bring to Red Cherry."

"Why do this, brother?"

"Tell her to send me her extra moccasins in return. She will know what I mean.

Never Wavers examined his face. "Brother, I fear what you plan."

"It is nothing. I am gathering another raiding party." He saw how appalled she was, so he added in an offhand manner, "I wish her to accompany me and carry my shield."

"Brother, do not do this," said Never Wavers. "You who argued with all the Crow for peace, now wage war merely for the affection of a woman."

"It is not war," said Beckwourth, "only an excursion for horses. The Arikara have more than they can use, and poor land to feed them. I pity their horses."

"Brother," said Never Wavers, "your father and your mother and I shall all become poor if you do this. We shall none of us have a single horse to ride."

"It will not be so," said Beckwourth. "Look now at how I am the greatest among warriors. All will look at this and say it is good, for such a man deserves the most beautiful woman. Now go, and have her also tell you where I should meet her tomorrow, when the evening star first shows itself."

"Brother, I will do this if you say. I will go as you command to the wife of Big Rain and make your offer to her. If she be so faithless to her husband, then so be it. But I will not cry for the consequences you must surely suffer. I am done dancing and celebrating. If this is what is in your heart, I will go to her now."

Never Waver's rebuke stung, but Beckwourth was

intoxicated by the thought of Red Cherry. The next day, at the appointed time and place, Red Cherry was waiting. Beckwourth spurred his horse to her. "My heart is glad to see you, Red Cherry," he said.

"I go with you as your wife."

"My beauty, I will protect you and provide for you." He handed her his shield.

The warriors set out, some with their women, plus eager boys and moccasin dogs. They travelled for several days into Arikara territory. It was nightfall when they arrived within sight of the enemy village on a shallow river and fell back to make their camp. Success came easily again. The Crow stole nearly a hundred horses and were far ahead of their pursuers by the time they were discovered. There was no need to take scalps and not even a scratch was suffered among them. Jubilation was theirs on return. But Beckwourth knew to brace for punishment at the hands of an offended husband.

Big Rain was in the crowd that met the returning heroes, though he was in no mood himself to welcome them. He and his women relatives surrounded Beckwourth and Red Cherry.

"Strip," he said and pointed to a place for Beckwourth to lie down. He ignored Red Cherry but for a threatening glance.

Beckwourth obeyed. By Crow law, if he resisted by word or action, Big Rain would be entitled to kill him on the spot. Deliberately he stripped and handed his clothes to Hunts Alone. He sang a sea chanty learned from his brother, except that the chorus was, "Watch closely Red Cherry, and see how much your Medicine Calf endures for you." With all the majesty he could muster, he lay face down in the dirt. Big Rain and his womenfolk beat Beckwourth with sticks, with every stroke intoning, "This is for stealing Red Cherry," while Beckwourth continued his song, though it was marred by a reflexive gasp now and then. He kept this up until they beat parts of his body twice.

"Beat me more!" he said, "but harder so that you draw blood." If they had, by Crow law he would be justified to kill them himself. The beating stopped. Beckwourth rose from the ground, hiding as best he could the pain of his every movement. He faced Big Rain with head held high.

"Your horses are now mine," said Big Rain, "all of them, and your father's as well. These, your buffalo hides, and anything else of yours that I desire. Wife, come with me now."

Beckwourth could see fear in her eyes, for some husbands abused their wives for infidelity. But he knew she had no choice. "Are we finished?" he asked Big Rain.

Big Rain scowled. "We are finished," he said.

"You will not treat Red Cherry badly, for every warrior would then see you as a coward. For my part, though I have no horses, I will dance the victory dance tonight, and I invite you and your very fearsome womenfolk to my tipi to dance as well, if you have not exhausted yourselves from beating me. I am a great warrior and returned today with many Arikara horses that now are yours, and you should dance in celebration, since it is so long since you have danced over horses you yourself have stolen that only the medicine men can recall this."

Beckwourth hobbled home with Big Bowl at his side.

"My apologies, father," said Beckwourth, "for the loss of your horses."

"Your sister warned me, and I gave many horses to relatives," said Big Bowl.

"Still, I wish to bring a quick end to this. I will again go on a horse stealing raid tomorrow and bring you home more than you have lost."

"Will you take the woman with you again?"

"Yes, if she can bear to see me beaten again."

"Then those horses also will go to Big Rain."

At his tipi, Beckwourth endured the silent treatment from Little Wife as she attended to his wounds. He offered no apology. When done, Little Wife spoke.

"Why did you do this, husband?"

"Still Water is with her family, and you are a chaste woman," he said.

"Perhaps you wish that I give myself to you."

"No! I have no such desire for you. I wish that you are only as you are."

"All I ever asked was for you to paint my face when you return from stealing horses, and once, only once did I ask to carry your shield."

"You are too young to carry my shield, child," he said.

"Do not call me 'child' anymore!" she said. "I am your wife, not your daughter."

"Certainly, my wife," he said.

Beckwourth sent Hunts Alone around to find warriors for another raid. He selected from them the most stealthy and sent his friend to ask Red Cherry to carry his shield once more, and to prepare to see him beaten again.

"Did she agree?" he asked his friend on his return.

"She did not say, brother," Hunts Alone answered.

Beckwourth met his warriors at the appointed place, his every move an act of will. But his bruises were forgotten when Red Cherry arrived and took his shield.

"You have not been mistreated?" he asked.

"I am well," she demurred.

The raiding party was gone four days and returned with three scalps, as they had met a party of nine enemy, and six managed to outrun them. Beckwourth again submitted to a flogging as vigorous as the first, and Big Rain took the horses that were Beckwourth's portion. When he limped back to his lodge, Beckwourth found Still Water waiting for him. Her pregnancy was beginning to show.

"I see that you persist after this woman, husband," she said.

"It is good to see you well, Still Water," he said.

"Was she worth the beating?"

"I did not do this to anger you."

"Have I not been a good wife to you?"

"Yes, you have, Still Water."

"Did I not sew the moccasins you wore on this raid? Did I not carefully, lovingly pound berries into pemmican, then stuff that into intestines that you carried to sustain you? Did I not spend my days pounding brain into buffalo hides that are now taken by this woman's husband?"

"I did not know they would take the fruit of your labor, my wife," he said.

"Ha! You are at least enough a Crow to know this," she said. "The One Above Person has blessed you in your days among us. If you keep this woman, he will turn his face away from you."

"I am the greatest of warriors," Beckwourth said. "A great warrior deserves many wives."

"Many wives, yes. But you who could have chosen any maiden in the village instead chose to steal a married woman, and for this, we are to be impoverished, and your father as well. Perhaps she is more beautiful than I," said Still Water. "But tell me, husband, is she that much more beautiful?"

"I will replace all the horses before the next moon," he said.

Still Water shook her head and sighed. "I went to the spring where women go when they are with child, and I left a toy bow and arrow and a toy hoop."

Beckwourth was impassive, not knowing the significance of this.

"You should know, my husband, that the spirit of the spring took the toy bow and arrow."

He still gave her a blank stare.

"You are going to have a son," she said.

❧ 22 ❧

Beckwourth sat cross-legged on the ground in a circle with others of his Dog Soldiers, plotting their next raid. Beckwourth shifted uncomfortably from one buttock to the other, to the amusement of Sees the Clouds.

"Perhaps," said Sees the Clouds, "perhaps we should wait for your poor suffering buttocks to heal before we go on this raid."

"We will go on this raid when the time is right with no regard for my buttocks," said Beckwourth, "Soon all my bruises will heal and nothing more will distract me from nights of passion with Red Cherry. Meanwhile, you will still be plotting to steal the wives of others, but only those who can tolerate the looks of such a one as yourself."

The Dog Soldiers snickered, but before Sees the Clouds could answer, there was a single gunshot in the distance. All rose to look in that direction. It was a party of white trappers, announcing their presence. Beckwourth sent runners to bring them to him. Their leader was his old acquaintance, Bracken; he who had given him the swayback horse the day he had held Ashley at gunpoint. The usual pleasantries were exchanged, and inquiries made of their journey and its purpose. The trappers related that they were on their way to trade with neighboring tribes.

"Davis told us that you are the big chief now," said Bracken, cocking his head to look at Beckwourth's face. "And 'bout that powder burn."

"This?" Beckwourth pointed. "I have not had an opportunity to look in a mirror. Do you think it improves my looks?"

"Looks like a lopsided beard," said Bracken. "You should get the same treatment on the other side."

"I will take that under advisement," said Beckwourth. He informed them that he was about to leave on a raid, and of how he expected to receive another beating on his return, and the cause for this. Putting them in the care of Big Bowl, he left with his warriors. Red Cherry again proudly carried his shield, and they had great success. Their triumphant return was spoiled, however, when they met Bracken's party, afoot and much dejected.

"Where are your horses?" asked Beckwourth.

"Some of them Crow," Bracken spat, "seems to have forgotten they are friends of the white man." He related how a cadre of the Crow had confiscated all their horses and their trade goods at gunpoint. Beckwourth could not tell from their description who had instigated this outrage.

"I will not allow this," he said. "Come with me, and I will have your things returned to you."

Bracken hesitated. "The one that did this said we was dead men if they caught sight of us again."

"I am chief," said Beckwourth. "Come with me now and I will punish those responsible."

"You seem damn sure you can do that," said

Bracken. He looked to his men and got doubting glances and shaking heads. "More sure than me."

Beckwourth explained the situation to the Crow. It was Red Cherry who responded.

"Let them go, then, and wear out their white man's boots as they trudge back to their lodge on the river, defeat and disgrace hanging over their heads. They do not deserve to follow the great Medicine Calf."

"What did she say, Beckwourth?" Bracken inquired.

"She casts doubt on your bravery, I'm afraid." Beckwourtth said. "You boys, look at the faces of my warriors. These are the bravest of the Crow. They go into battle and dare the enemy to kill them. If I say that they should cut those who stole from you to pieces, they will do it in a moment."

Bracken consulted with his men. "All right," he said, "I'll give you a chance. Chief."

At the village, Beckwourth went straight to his father. He apprised his father of the situation, but it was Never Wavers who spoke.

"I told you to keep your manhood in your breechclout."

Ah, thought Beckwourth, *Big Rain*. He had thought the old man to be too timid to have done this, but no, it was him. Beating Beckwourth with sticks had apparently invigorated the old man's *maxpe*. He returned to Bracken.

"I have a plan," Beckwourth said, "But this will take more finesse than if it had been any other who had stolen your goods and horses."

"Maybe we should head back to Kipp's," Bracken said. "Lick our wounds and start all over."

"No," said Beckwourth. "I will get you your horses and goods. Come with me."

Beckwourth proceeded to the abode of Hunts Alone, who of course had not gone on the raid, and told him of his predicament.

"It would have been better if you had let the white men go on their way," Hunts Alone said. "But come, I will help you get their horses back."

They gathered the Dog Soldiers and the whites. It did not take long to find Big Rain, planted at the village center, surrounded by his supporters.

"Are you here to return my wife?" asked Big Rain.

"Your wife detests you," said Beckwourth. "She knows you are a fool to steal from these whites who have only been good to the Crow. These whites who have fought against your enemies with you, and provided you with weapons so that your enemies, who are all greater in number than you, that they do not exterminate you."

"What you think my wife knows or does not know is of no concern to me," said Big Rain. "Lie down here, in front of all your men and the whites, Medicine Calf, and take your beating like a Crow, even though you are not one."

"I will give you that satisfaction, as I respect Crow law," said Beckwourth. "But first you must return to these men their horses and trade goods."

"No. First take your beating," said Big Rain. "Then we will talk."

The beating would this time be administered by warriors, not by women with sticks. This was not what he had meant by 'finesse.' Beckwourth took a step toward where Big Rain pointed.

"Stop," said Hunts Alone. "You have whipped Medicine Calf twice, and you shall whip him no more, nor shall you do him any more harm. Red Cherry loves him, and she does not love you. She will always go with him. You might as well try to turn the river back to its mountain sources as to attempt to separate them, unless you kill them. And so that you would not contemplate that, I tell you this: if you were to spill the blood of the beautiful Red Cherry, you would be branded a coward and cast out from our people. Fight Medicine Calf man to man, if you wish, but if you do so, you know he will kill you. And know that if you let him go now, but then assassinate him later, we would avenge his death. No, no! Big Rain must not hurt our chief."

Big Rain read the faces of friend and foe about him and stalked off in defiant capitulation. Beckwourth seized the moment and ordered his Dog Soldiers to search every tipi for the trade goods, while at the same time others recovered Bracken's horses. All the goods that could be found were returned, and guards were placed on Bracken's horses. All this did not placate Bracken, however. In fact, he upbraided Beckwourth in the most vile and racially insulting terms. It seemed he was still missing his own horse and thought that Beckwourth was holding back that and the goods that could not be found. Beckwourth stared at Bracken impassively until the man had exhausted his vocabulary of insults.

"Are you through?" he asked.

"Through? No, I'm not through with you, you thieving, red bastard."

"So, to you, if I am not one color of bastard, then I am another, eh?" Beckwourth paused for an answer, but he could see that his meaning was lost on Bracken. "Well, say what you will, but be careful what you do. My men understand none of your invective, which is fortunate for you. But please be aware that if you were to touch a hair on my head, I could not prevent them from tearing you to shreds."

"Yes, yes. But if you have such power over them, why then didn't you keep them from stealing from us in the first place?"

"Horse thievery is the chief sport of the Crow, so what happened is not surprising."

"You had damn well better return my horse, or I swear, some day you will pay."

Beckwourth took a description of Bracken's horse and sent his men scurrying to find its whereabouts. They returned. It seemed that Big Rain had it picketed outside his tipi, and he had declared that he would under no circumstance give up this horse.

"Mr. Bracken," said Beckwourth, "my powers as chief do not allow me to merely confiscate your horse as I have done with your other possessions, as the one who has it is a chief in his own right. Besides this, he is the one you have just seen, whose wife I have been pursuing. This adds some delicacy to the situation. Still, I will try to help you."

Beckwourth called a boy to him, one of Big Rain's relatives.

"My most capable fellow," he said, "please go to your uncle and say that Medicine Calf respectfully asks that he return the white man's horse. Be sure to say 'respectfully'."

While he waited, Beckwourth tamped a pipe and shared it with his men. He offered a smoke to Bracken, who refused. Soon the boy returned.

"He says 'no'," the boy reported, "But also that he will tell you so himself."

Judging by the boy's manner, Beckwourth could see that Big Rain had said 'no' rather emphatically. Hearing this news, Bracken became visibly agitated, but then sulked silently. Beckwourth waited serenely. Soon, Big Rain rode in on Bracken's horse.

"Medicine Calf," he challenged, "did you call for this horse?"

"I did," said Beckwourth.

"Well, here he is," said Big Rain. All Crow could see the implication: *and try to take him.*

"Take him back," said Beckwourth, "and keep him safe until I call for him."

Big Rain sauntered away, with a parting sneer for Bracken.

"What the devil are you doing?" Bracken asked.

Beckwourth puffed on his pipe. "Do you remember my little tiff with Ashley? The episode with the swayback horse you gave me?"

"Of course."

"I might get your horse back if I held Big Rain at gunpoint. But I have learned much since then," said Beckwourth. "There are better ways."

"If I could get my hands on that horse, your whole passle of savages could not take him away from me," said Bracken.

Beckwourth was greatly annoyed by this hollow bravado, but he remained outwardly impassive. "Mr. Bracken, please be my guest for breakfast tomorrow."

The next morning, Little Wife served a sumptuous breakfast, though she fumed silently as she did this.

"Coffee is a special treat around here," said Beckwourth as he handed Bracken a horn of it. "White man's soup, you know."

Big Rain rode up to them. "Here is the white man's horse," he said. He let loose of the reins and stalked away.

Beckwourth motioned a boy to hand the reins to Bracken, exuding the attitude that this was the only possible outcome of this entire episode. "Mr. Bracken, I hope you are pleased at this outcome, but I suspect that Mr. Big Rain only gave your horse up so easily because he intends to take him from you again; this time as a matter of his offended honor, rather than just out of greed as before. I think it best that you leave immediately and travel for three days and nights without stopping any more than to water your horses, which by now are well rested and fat on the sweet grass around here. I will detain Mr. Big Rain for as long as I can, but I assure you, he will follow."

Beckwourth was quite happy to see Bracken go, for the great lack of gratitude that the man had shown. He managed to detain Big Rain for two days by having others entertain him with feasts and speeches, but then, one night, Big Rain slipped away with a few warriors. When they returned, he had some of Bracken's horses. Beckwourth figured he had done the best he could for the man, and he was relieved that he saw no white scalps.

This matter finished, his final beating averted, and with no affairs of state before him, so to speak, Beckwourth turned his attention to his beautiful new wife. He took Red Cherry to his tipi. Just as they were about to enter, the flap was thrown in his face by Little Wife. Startled momentarily, she glared at him through tears and hurried away.

"She is a child," he said to Red Cherry.

"And I am not," she replied.

The first snow fell, and the Crow settled into their winter routines of legends and stories told in the sweat lodge. Winter calm fell over the village, though they were more watchful so as to not be caught un-

awares again as they had been by the Sioux. Red
Cherry and Medicine Calf used this time to their advantage on luxurious heaps of buffalo robes, their
bodies tangling and untangling, blissfully ignoring
the outside world.

Beckwourth still kept track of the white man's
calendar, and when this, his third Christmas away
from family came around, he felt that familiar melancholy again. He went down by the river alone on that
cold winter day, and sat down, wrapped in his buffalo
robe. The air was calm and crisp, and the river bab-
bled beneath its frozen surface. He lashed together a
cross, stuck it upright in the snow and sang songs
from his youth. What would he find now if he returned home? When he tired of song, he pulled the
cross out of the snow and threw it into the middle of
the stream, where it would have the best chance of
making the journey back to St. Louis, without him.

The winter passed uneventfully, and when grass first
appeared in patches hemmed with snow, the village
moved in search of buffalo. Where they found them
there was also an abundance of beaver, and Beckwourth encouraged his men to trap the streams.

One day, a woman he did not know approached
Beckwourth with a bundle in her arms.

"Still Water rests," she said. "See here, I bring
you something that will gladden your heart." She
showed him a sleeping baby. "He will make as great
a brave as his father. His name is Black Panther.
Here, look at your son."

Beckwourth was overjoyed. He showered his
wife's entire family with gifts and gave a horse to a
poor man in honor of this great event, as was tradition. These things he had the village crier announce,

and that Hunts Alone would have the honor of piercing the child's ears when he was of that age. Beckwourth had such wealth now that each of his wives had her own tipi. But still they squabbled, and there was tension when they tired of squabbling.

One morning, some few horses were discovered to have been stolen. It would usually have been beneath a great chief to bother with retaliation for this, but Beckwourth wished to escape his domestic life for a bit, and so he led the foray. It was a disastrous outing, with several men killed, and the lamentations and cutting began anew. Desire for revenge led to a retaliatory raid which fared as badly as the first. Beckwourth forbade any more parties from going forth, but this only made things worse, as the ones that snuck out were small and also fared poorly. Then it happened that the buffalo disappeared. Things were bad, and cross looks from Never Wavers told him that she blamed him for taking up with Red Cherry. Things were so bad that there were rumors that Crooked Smile might split his Fox warriors off into a separate band. A distraught people cried out for guidance from above.

And none were more distraught than Little Wife. "Husband," she asked him one day, "why has the One Above Person abandoned us?"

"I do not believe that the One Above Person has abandoned us, my flower."

"It is obvious that the One Above Person is angry with the Crow," she said. "And the women suffer more than the men. The men die happily because they go to the Other Side Camp and hunt and make war the same as on this side. But his widow must care for the children and still haul wood and work the hides as before, but now with no husband. No, the One Above Person is more angry with the women."

It was impossible to argue with this reasoning. Beckwourth waited for her to finish.

"The wife of a Crow warrior sleeps with any man she wishes when her husband is away. This is shameful and not the way of the other tribes. The One Above Person is angry with the Crow women for this. I will atone for the Crow women, and the buffalo will come back. The Green Grass Ceremony is to be soon," she said. "I wish to undergo the purity ordeal for the benefit of all the Crow. Only this way will the One Above Person forgive his people."

Beckwourth had never seen such intensity in Little Wife. He did not want to risk her ire, nor show his ignorance of this ceremony. "Great will be my honor if you do so, my child," he said.

"I am not a child," she hissed. "I am your faithful wife, while you cavort with your plaything. Your plaything, who has eyes for others while you are away. Husband, from now on I ask that you call me only by my Crow name. Call me One Who Strikes Three."

Beckwourth approached Hunts Alone, as he always did when his understanding of Crow ways was incomplete.

"My friend, I have a problem."

"I wish only to help," said Hunts Alone.

"I have been told that Red Cherry has eyes for others. I am concerned that it may be even more than that."

Hunts alone paused. "She is a beautiful woman."

"So, it was as I suspected! And you did not tell me. I thought we were as one. You said that there would be no secrets between us."

"There is no secret. If you do not see this, you are blind."

"When I am away, you remain. You see things I cannot."

"The one you wounded still has a hard heart for you."

Crooked Smile. Ever the thorn in his side.

"Who knows this?"

"Not everyone."

"What am I to do now?"

"You may cast her out. You may beat her, though I know you will not. Or you may pretend you do not know."

"Which is it that you think I should do?"

Hunts Alone considered. "She is a beautiful woman."

Beckwourth put off his decision. "Here is another thing," he said. "What is the Green Grass Ceremony?"

"Ah," said Hunts Alone. "It is to show the One Above Person that we are a humble people who only wish to do as he wants. There is fasting by all. Men drag buffalo skulls on thongs that pierce their flesh, until the thongs pull through their skin. And for the women, one is chosen who is said to be chaste. She will fast for four days and is then taken to the men to prove her virtue. The highest ideal of the Crow is that a woman be chaste, and all the higher for the rarity of it."

"How can such a thing be proven?" asked Beckwourth.

"If a man knows otherwise, he will say."

"And what happens if a man says this?" asked Beckwourth.

"More than once I have seen with my own eyes a woman hacked to pieces."

❊ 23 ❊

Beckwourth applied red ochre to Little Wife's face, then framed it with white chalk, the same that she used to soften buffalo robes. Hunts Alone watched nearby.

"Such is your beauty, One Who Strikes Three," Beckwourth said, "that the flowers will bow down to you when you pass."

"When I was a child and we played grown up, I was different," she said. "The other girls would let a boy kiss them when he brought them a coyote skin, pretending it was a scalp. No boy ever kissed me. So has it been since I became a woman."

"You bring honor to Crow women, One Who Strikes Three," he said.

She rose, her soft elk skin dress resplendent with geometric patterns made of colored porcupine quills and glass beads. She swayed for a moment, weakened by her fast.

"Go, my husband, make a place for yourself. Sit with the men and watch your devoted wife."

Beckwourth and Hunts Alone proceeded to the place of ceremony. A large crowd surrounded a domed frame structure with a hundred buffalo hides lain over its top. A double line of warriors snaked from outside to the interior, each man with weapons at his belt, chanting to a somber drumbeat. Beckwourth had confidence that Little Wife would pass this test. In the days prior, to be sure of this, he had sent Hunts Alone around to all the medicine men. These of course took the report from every raid, where the men confessed their dalliances while they pinched buffalo intestines. No one had ever reported an affair with her, as far as Hunts Alone had been able to discover. Surely, One Who Strikes Three would be greatly honored today, which would only add to the glory of Medicine Calf.

Hunts Alone nudged Beckwourth. "See him?" he asked.

"See who?" Beckwourth asked.

"Him. Big Rain."

Red Cherry's ex- shuffled into the line of warriors.

"He does not go on raids," said Hunts Alone.

So, we will have no intelligence on him, thought Beckwourth. "My wife would have nothing to do with such an ugly pile of dog droppings," he said,

"But what if he speaks lies of her to get back at you?" asked Hunts Alone.

"He would not dare," said Beckwourth, but he had his doubts. How deep ran Big Rain's wounded pride?

Big Rain scowled at Beckwourth, and smirked.

A herald held up his arms. The drums stopped and silence fell over the crowd. "Listen, Absaroka people!" he said, "One Who Strikes Three, wife of Chief Medicine Calf, offers herself for election as a woman of purity."

The drums resumed, and the men chanted her name to their rhythm as One Who Strikes Three approached the line. She paused to let an old woman present her with a bundle of sage to carry. The herald again called for silence. The drums stopped.

"I am One Who Strikes Three," said she. "The Crow people cry to the One Above Person and ask why he has turned his face from us. His anger has caused the slaughter of too many of our warriors. Their scalps at this moment flutter in the wind at the doorways of our enemies' tipis. And this was not enough to quench his anger, for now he has caused the buffalo to leave us. I do not know why the One Above Person has turned his face from us, but I can tell you that he has reason enough to do so solely because of the evil practices of the faithless women of the Crow. Are there no virtuous women among the Crow? Worse will come of this yet, I say. Our prairies will become wastes like you, wasted women, producing no good thing.

"Warriors!" she continued. "I have this day volunteered to submit to judgment. You are brave warriors, and I can only hope your tongues are not crooked."

Beckwourth watched Big Rain for a reaction but saw none.

One Who Strikes Three continued. "I have seen other women attempt this and be cut down. Such is the reward for deceit. I will now attempt it myself. Be it known that if there is one among you who will accuse me, I am ready to go to the Other Side Camp, for there the One Above Person knows me to be innocent of the bad deeds that disgrace the women of our people. I am finished with talk. Now I will walk between these noble warriors with this sage, the symbol of the toil of Crow womanhood."

The drums resumed, and the men again chanted her name. One That Strikes Three took firm steps and passed between the first men untouched. Chin up, she continued at a measured pace, her hunger out of her mind, looking each man in the eye as she passed between them, one side and then the other, showing no sign of fear.

Beckwourth kept a stony face, though turmoil roiled within him as his wife gradually drew nearer to Big Rain. Hunts Alone took the action his friend could not. Without a word, he jostled into line next to Big Rain, who gave him a scowl and placed his hand on the haft of his knife. Hunts Alone addressed the assemblage.

"Stop, for I wish to speak!"

One Who Strikes Three stopped, fearful at first, then puzzled when she saw it was her husband's friend. The drums and the chanting stopped.

"The One Above Person watches us, oh brave warriors!" he said. "And I say that He would punish us all if we kill this woman, though she be innocent. For this, our buffalo would never return, and instead stay in the country of a more virtuous people. We must not listen to one who would lie for his own purposes."

"Fool," said Big Rain under his breath, "be careful of your words."

"I accuse no one," Hunts Alone continued loudly. "But anything I say of my deeds, a dozen men can say, 'yes, this is true, I was there'. If this woman be accused, I will be the first to strike, but only if there is one other who says, 'yes, I know of this'."

The drums resumed. Little Wife, trembling from hunger and thirst, tread lightly to their rhythm as she made her way forward. She came to Big Rain and for a moment looked him in the eye.

"I am the chaste wife of a great chief," she said. "Everyone knows this."

Whatever Big Rain might have intended when he stepped in line, he said nothing and did nothing, but his face showed the bitterness of his heart. Little Wife passed him, and her steps turned to a dance. The crowd joined in the chanting of her name as she passed the last pair of men, where a bowl of water waited to slake her thirst. The crowd cried out as one, and women pushed forward to pass their hands over her, head to toe. Ishkali presented Beckwourth with a bowl of morsels. The women ululated as Beckwourth took the bowl and tenderly fed his wife.

❧ 24 ❧

The Green Grass ceremony put an end to the general mourning, and there was great celebration when the buffalo did indeed return. Beckwourth found himself unsettled, however. It did not sit well with him that the life of such an innocent as Little Wife could have been threatened so.

One night, an enemy made off with Crow horses. The alarm was given while they were still in the act, and the Crow chased them away with wild gunfire and arrows. The next morning, they found a Blackfoot who had been unable to flee, his leg shattered by a bullet. This warrior was very young, but he faced his fate with trembling voice and nocked arrow, hurling insults at them in his own language. Soon, the entire village was at the scene. Among the Crow was one who had been captured from the Blackfeet as a boy. He translated the Blackfoot's insults.

"He says, 'yes, you Crow dogs, dance away from me. My leg is broken, and soon I will be in the Other Side Camp, but my arm is strong, and first I will take more of you with me.'"

The crowd jeered, and a rivalry developed

among the warriors as to who could have first coup on this live enemy, in sight of the entire village. One by one, they rushed closer and closer, managing to dodge the arrows sent their way. Beckwourth stood uneasily with Crooked Smile and others of his chiefs as men, women, and children cheered on their favorites in this deadly bit of theater.

The Blackfoot faced his doom with valor, and the Crow/Blackfoot translated his invective: "He says, 'If you are going to dance like that, dance downwind of me; your stench is overpowering. The Crow roll in dog droppings every morning to cover the smell of their fear, but still the smell of it is too strong. All the tribes know this.'"

The crowd shouted back their own insults.

"Come then," said the Blackfoot. "This is my last arrow. Let me see how well you dance one more time."

The warriors argued among themselves as to who next deserved to show his bravery. Among them was Stands Again, the young 'son' of Big Bowl whom Beckwourth had taken on the raid against the Arapaho. Stands Again longed to impress his sweetheart who watched in the crowd. His friends knew this and argued successfully with the others that he should be next to attempt coup. Stands Again grasped his coup stick, crouched, and sprinted toward the Blackfoot with a war whoop. But that whoop cracked in his throat due to his age, and some women giggled. His youthful *maxpe* wavered. He zigged, he zagged, but when he planted to zig again, he slipped. The Blackfoot took that opportunity to let fly an arrow, which found its mark in the young man's torso. The crowd was momentarily stunned as he fell, then all howled in anger and dismay. The Blackfoot began his death song as the enraged Crow rushed him. The crowd dragged him to Beckwourth and his chiefs. The prisoner stopped his death song only long enough to shout more insults.

"He says all Crow women sleep with their brothers," the translator shouted, "but only when their fathers won't have them."

The crowd roared as one. Children pelted him with dog dung.

"This is a brave man," said Beckwourth. "Let us treat him as a brave man."

"Yes," said Big Bowl. "The one the Blackfoot killed was my son, and I deserve vengeance as much as any. Let me slit his throat."

"This will not be enough," said Crooked Smile. "The people cry for revenge."

"He is young," said Beckwourth. "Let him be nursed to health and given the chance to join the Crow."

"He does not wish to join the Crow," Crooked Smile said. "He is a warrior. He does not wish to trap beaver with you and have no stories to tell. I say we send his opinion of us up to the skies in smoke."

The rest agreed with this. A fire was built, and many hands tossed fuel on it as the Blackfoot continued his death song. Beckwourth watched his continued defiance with a mixture of admiration and dread. Even as he was lifted above the flames, the Blackfoot sang. A toss, and he was screaming in the fire. Men held him down with tipi poles for agonizing minutes until the writhing stopped. When his body was pulled from the fire, one of Stands Again's friends claimed his singed scalp and presented it to his friend's sweetheart.

Beckwourth was nauseated by the smell of burned flesh and numbed by the celebration before him. Hours before, he had felt himself to be the master of an admirable people. Now who was this he led? He trudged to his tipi and pulled out his book from its rawhide case. But his mind was too disturbed to read; he only turned the pages. Big Bowl called at the door.

"May I enter, my son?"

"Certainly, Father."

"I see your heart is heavy, my son."

"It is so."

Big Bowl's searched for his son's face in the darkness. "It is not the Crow way to do this," he said.

"Do not apologize for the whole nation of the Crow," Beckwourth said. "It was my words that were not strong enough."

Beckwourth saw his people through different eyes in the following days. The men he understood perhaps. The women who had danced while the Blackfoot writhed, and the children who had pelted him with dog dung, these he now saw in a different light. He withdrew from sight for days. Finally, he decided. It was time to say goodbye to his beloved Crow.

He went to Still Water first, for it was best she not follow him to Kipp's with a babe in arms. She shed tears on hearing his plans.

"When will you return?" she asked.

"I do not know," he said. "You have been a good wife. Raise Black Panther to be a powerful warrior, but also raise him to be a friend of the white man."

"I am proud to be your wife," she said, "And I will keep the fire of that pride burning for as long as I live. I will tell your son of your exploits, and he will live to be a glory to your name."

He next went to Never Wavers. "My sister," he said, "I have decided that I will leave for the land of the whites. Before I go, I wished to tell you that you were right. I was foolish to let my manhood dictate my actions."

"You are fortunate to have a wife who was able to set things right," she scowled. Her manner softened. "I will miss you, my brother. Do not worry for the Crow, we are a strong people. Nor should you worry for me, for I am as strong as any of them."

Saying goodbye to Red Cherry was easier. "If I do not return by Yellow Grass," he told her, "do not let the beauty of your youth go to waste."

"I will heed your advice, husband," she said. He knew she meant it.

One Who Strikes Three, Red Cherry, Hunts Alone, and Big Bowl each wished their Medicine Calf to stay, but if he had to go, they would accompany him to Kipp's. That left one important goodbye to be said. He sang his death song as he approached Big Bowl's tipi, followed by his Dog Soldiers, who beat drums as they all danced, two hops on one foot, then two hops on the other. He carried his gift aloft. With a gentle pounce, he stopped before his mother and presented to her his shield.

"Keep this safe for me, my Crow mother," he said. "For if I come back, it will be to protect the Crow people, and I will need it." Tears streamed down her face, and she kissed her son one last time.

Their path took them near Rotten Belly's burial place, and it was time to collect his bones as promised. Big Bowl gathered up his friend's bones with great solemnity and painted them with red ochre, telling of his deeds as he did so.

"Oh, Great Chief, my good friend, judge that we have followed your wishes. See how carefully we have painted your bones, showing that we cherish them for you. We wait for the day that you return from the ever-flowering spirit land and demand your bones from us. When you do so, we will obey." They packed the bones along, to be placed later in a burial cave.

On arrival at the post, Beckwourth was greeted warmly by Davis and Kipp. To his delight, his old friend Pappen was there as well. He told them of his plans and was informed that boats were soon expected which could take him home. News was swapped, and Beckwourth renewed his friendship with Pappen, regaling him with tales of life with the Crow.

The Mackinaw boats came, poled up-river to the rhythmic chants of their French crews. Beckwourth oversaw the trade of pelts and furs for baubles and necessities. The pelts were then flattened with wooden presses into dense bales to keep the center of balance as low as possible in the shallow-drafting Mackinaws.

Beckwourth called Big Bowl and Hunts Alone to him for a big talk. They smoked a long time, and he recounted to them how they had met, and of their many adventures together. They did not press him for his reason to return now, but he felt he owed them some sort of explanation, even if it was only a partial truth. "Both of you know that when you die, you will rejoice to go to the Other Side Camp, where you will be greeted by those of your family who have gone before you. It is so for me also. When I die, I expect to be with my family and my white friends. So, you can understand, that if I want that for when I die, I also wish to be with them now."

"If this is what you wish, it must be so, my son," said Big Bowl.

"Here," Beckwourth handed the Lewis and Clark

friendship medal to them, the one given him by Rotten Belly. "Hold a council to choose a new chief."

Beckwourth went to One Who Strikes Three.

"Cherished one," he said. "You who carry the virtue of all Crow women in your bosom. Your entire life lies before you. If I do not return by Yellow Grass, you must find a man worthy of you in every way, a man to whom you can give your love freely, and he to you only." Beckwourth was not at all certain that she could find such a man in her world, but he meant what he said.

"Do not speak so," she said, eyes glistening. "I know in my heart you will return for me."

The morning came for the Mackinaw boats' departure, and the Crow gathered at the river's edge to say goodbye. Beckwourth shook hands with Kipp and with Pappen, who chose to stay and seek his fortune in the wilderness. Davis had decided to return to St. Louis. Beckwourth climbed up on the platform at the stern of a Mackinaw.

"My people," he said, "I leave you now for the land of the white man, to return to you I know not when. I want you to remember the words of counsel I have spoken many times to you. I wish you to send out no war parties, because you want for nothing, and your nation is feared by all the neighboring tribes. Keep a good look out for your horses day and night, that your enemies cannot steal them. It is only from carelessness that your horses are ever stolen. If you would do this, you would have no cause for raiding the enemy yourself. It is better to not have your horses stolen in the first place than to risk the lives of your men getting them back."

"I commend to your care Mr. Kipp, whom you know as Slender Crane. Visit him and his wife and the other whites often, and see that they are not besieged or starved out by their enemies, who are your enemies as well. Do not let the Blackfeet or any other bad Indians harm them. Behave yourselves as befits a noble people such as you are. Goodbye to you all. I have finished."

Beckwourth made a grand arc with his arm and held it outstretched for a moment as the pole men pushed off, then stood still as a statue. The Crow climbed a small rise and watched silently until Beckwourth saluted them again. The Crow let out a mighty yell and fired their guns in the air until their Medicine Calf rounded a bend and was out of sight.

❧ 25 ❧

"Here, Chief," said Davis, offering Beckwourth a plug of tobacco as the boat surged forward under the force of the pole men's efforts.

"I'm no chief here."

"You got family in St. Louis?"

Beckwourth nodded as he prepared his pipe. "Near to it. My father's home is in St. Charles. Sisters are there, too." He envisioned life in St. Louis as a man of wealth and substance, attending to business by day, saloons by night. They glided past familiar terrain, past the rolling hills that now felt like home. The rhythm of the Frenchmen's chants soothed him and hinted of home. Beckwourth passed the time by swapping tales with Davis, day after lazy day. Every evening they pulled out and camped, ever alert for danger. Days passed into weeks, and the terrain beyond the tree-lined river changed from rolling hills to grassy plains. Beckwourth longed for home now, even taking up a pole now and then to push the boat forward.

One late afternoon, as they headed to shore to make camp, there was a sudden thud, and Beckwourth's boat lurched and swung sideways against the current. The pole men shouted directions at each other and furiously attempted to right the listing craft. Water poured over the gunwales, and their precious cargo was all pitched out, a third of an entire season's labor. Beckwourth jumped into the water. He swam to the nearest bale of pelts and managed to wrestle it to the shore. Seeing Davis similarly engaged, he ran downstream and charged into the water for another. Only with great effort was he able to grab that and make it to shore against the deceptively strong current, gasping with every breath. With no pause, he swam out again for another. Ultimately, he and Davis managed to retrieve every bale but one, which they watched wistfully as it was carried out of sight. They made camp in good spirits, shivering as they built their fire.

A single gunshot split the air. Beckwourth reflexively reached for his rifle, though it was wet and useless. But it was soon apparent that the shot was a signal from a U.S. Army detachment that had heard their shouting and commotion. Their commander was none other than General Atkinson, of the eponymous fort. He gave Beckwourth a suspicious look, soaking wet in his Crow buckskin, matted hair halfway to his waist.

"You boys on to St. Louis?" he asked Davis.

"Yep. What are y'all doing here?"

"We are in talks with the Cheyenne," said Atkinson. "Trying to make them see the wisdom of working with the Great Father in Washington."

"How is that going?"

"Tolerably well. Of what tribe is the Indian in your party?"

"Him?" said Davis. "Ain't no Injun. That there is James P. Beckwourth. Mulatto got hisself adopted into the Crow. Damned if he didn't become their top war chief."

"Don't say?" said Atkinson. "What's he doing with you?"

"Going home to his family in St. Louis."

"He must have stories to tell."

Davis and Beckwourth spent the next few days in cheerful revelry with the troops. They borrowed horses to hunt buffalo and told their stories around the campfire at night. Beckwourth made acquaintance with the Cheyenne, who were honored to include such a well-known warrior as Bloody Arm in their convocations with Atkinson. He knew that in other circumstances they would have been just as happy to take his scalp, but here their pleasure in his company was genuine.

One day, Atkinson and his interpreter entertained the Cheyenne chiefs and Beckwourth, all sitting cross-legged on the ground, passing the pipe among them. Within their sight, Davis was teaching the soldiers how to hunt buffalo. Buffalo bulls were commonly cast out from the herd when they became old and cranky, and the soldiers had one such old bull as their prey. Due to their inexperience and inaccurate fire, however, all that Davis' students managed to do was to enrage the massive animal. Beckwourth watched them chase the wily bull while Atkinson expounded upon the wisdom and power of the Great White Father in Washington. The bull at this moment decided that the best way to rid himself of his tormentors was to make a beeline for the river. Unfortunately, the camp lay in his way. He tore into tents, sent flying the guns that had been so neatly placed in tripods, and leapt over piles of baggage. Troops scattered in all directions. Reaching the river embankment, the old bull turned to survey the destruction he had wreaked. Seemingly satisfied, he trotted down the bank and into the stream. The soldiers regained their weapons and hurriedly fired at the half-submerged animal, to no effect. The bull hauled out of the river on the other side, shook off the water like a giant dog, gave his tormentors one more look of contempt and ambled away.

The Cheyenne watched in disbelief at the chaos that one elderly buffalo visited upon these emissaries of the Great White Father. Their chief tried very hard to suppress laughter at these antics, which itself caused Beckwourth to laugh. That cued the others to join in. Atkinson was not so very amused.

The time came for Beckwourth's group to continue their journey. They said goodbye to the soldiers and loaded the boats. A relatively uneventful remaining passage was their good fortune, the only notable occurrence being that they met up with another, larger group of trappers returning to St. Louis. Soon enough, their flotilla arrived close enough to St. Louis to send a courier ahead by land to alert the populace of their impending return.

What awaited him after all this time? Beckwourth climbed up on the back of the Mackinaw and craned his neck for his first view. They rounded a bend, and the city came into view. A puff of smoke from shore was followed by the faint boom of a canon. Slowly, the vague mass of the city separated into distinct buildings, and as they drew closer and closer, the murmur of the throng at water's edge grew gradually louder until they disembarked to the deafening shouts of friends and family struggling to be heard; a cheering mass of a thousand citizens. When the boats finally touched shore, there was laughter and tears; pushing, pulling, hugging, back slapping, and kissing in a scene like Beckwourth had never before witnessed. He searched awkwardly for familiar faces, buffeted but ignored by the crowd. He finally recognized an old friend from St. Charles and learned that his sisters had moved to St. Louis, and now boarded with his old landlady, Mrs. LeFevre. For Davis it was much the same hollow welcome. With a grunt and a nod, the two parted, venturing into a city that was more a sprawling metropolis than the village they had left.

Beckwourth made arrangements at the fur company office to settle accounts the next day. Without change of attire, he headed to Mrs. LeFevre's and knocked on the same door he had passed through in such great haste three years prior. Mrs. LeFevre answered and raised an eyebrow in recognition.

"Miss Lou, you ought to come here," she said.

Sister Lou came to the door. Her momentary caution gave way to joy. "My God, it is my brother!" she said, and flew into his arms. Tears and sobs gave way to giddy laughter. "We thought you were dead," she finally managed.

"Could easily have been, many times," said Beckwourth.

Lou laughed and pulled him inside. "Mattie!" she called upstairs. "Brother James is here!"

"Lou, you should be ashamed of yourself for joking so," came the reply.

"Come see for yourself," said Lou.

Silence followed. No movement from upstairs. Mrs. LeFevre called up.

"If this is not he, then come, Mattie, and help us identify this specimen, and say of what form of man or beast he may be."

A shadow tread down the stairs, and Matilda peered around a corner.

"Mattie!" called Beckwourth, with open arms.

"James!" she finally exclaimed and flung herself into his arms. When released, Beckwourth wiped away his own tears. Mattie examined him closely, still not willing to believe her eyes.

"The voice is yours, but my, how you have changed. What happened to the side of your face?"

"Powder burn courtesy of the Gros Ventres. Where is father?"

"Oh, James, he took a wasting disease. Went back to Virginia a year ago," said Lou. "He wanted to see his brothers and sisters one last time."

Beckwourth hung his head for a moment. "Too bad. I did so want to trade war stories with the old man. And what of the homestead? Why are you here?" Sale of that should have put his sisters in good circumstances, but their tattered clothes told of a marginal existence.

"Father had signed a surety for some friends," said Mattie. "When their business failed, he lost... everything, really."

"What about Quincy?"

"Your childhood friend. I'm sorry, James. It was awful. He was sold for the debt. Taken to New Orleans. In chains. Broke my heart."

Beckwourth smothered a moment of anger. Chin up, he asked the one last question that had haunted him so for long. "My Eliza?" he asked.

"Oh, James," said Lou. "I'm sorry. She got married. Nice, hardworking fellow. You know, we were told you were dead."

"Nice fellow, eh? That's good, she deserves that."

Other names were tossed back and forth over LeFevre's coffee, until they could dredge up no more friends or acquaintances to memory. Beckwourth tactfully inquired of his sister's circumstances.

"We do laundry," Mattie said, burying her

chapped hands in her dress. "There are worse things."

They seemed to have fallen out of their prior social life, as well. When asked of potential suitors, their answers were vague and evasive. The girls inquired of Beckwourth's good fortune with a certain wistfulness. The tales he told left them dumbfounded, even as he glossed over things he thought they might have trouble believing. Their eyes widened when he told of his wives, and of his infant son, Black Panther.

"Wait," said Lou. "You mean, I'm an aunt?"

"Well," Beckwourth pondered, "I guess I never thought of it that way. But yes, you are an aunt."

"Is there more than one?" asked Mattie.

"Not when I left."

"Do you plan to go back?" asked Mattie, ever the planner; the older sister that had had to take over when mother died.

"No plans. But some day, yes."

The next day, Beckwourth settled his account with the American Fur Company, and was given access to his funds in the bank. There was also the matter of the money owed him by Ashley, but he felt uneasy about calling on the general, so he put it off.

Still looking like a Crow chief, but now flush with cash, Beckwourth made a tour of the grog shops down by the river, where he met old acquaintances and regaled them with stories of his exploits. He swaggered about, buying rounds for the house and toasting new friends and old for much of the day and into the evening, enjoying himself immensely, as only someone who had cheated death so many times could. As he left the last of these establishments one evening, he heard a familiar voice.

"Beckwourth, watch your back."

"Davis, you devil's spawn," said Beckwourth. "Come join me for a drink."

"Some other day, chief. But I mean it, your life is in danger."

"I have heard rumors. What is afoot?" Beckwourth asked.

"There is a price on your head. They offered it to me."

"Really? How much?"

"Never mind that. Not enough to tempt me to betray a friend. But enough for your ordinary scoundrel."

"I always knew that you were no ordinary scoundrel," said Beckwourth. "Who is it that offers this reward?"

"This fellow led me to believe that he was an associate of Bracken."

"Bracken!" he said. "I rescued the poor bastard."

"He doesn't seem to see it that way," said Davis.

"Very well then. Thank you for the warning." They parted.

The next day, Beckwourth accessorized his outfit with a knife, mindful of the irony. So, this was home, he thought. He could forever wander a camp of so-called savages with no weapon but his sharp tongue. But here, back in civilization, he needed to arm himself. Thus attired, he made his way to the office of his father's lawyer, the one who kept his emancipation papers. He inquired of properties available for purchase, and of any partnership opportunities in the Indian trade, as it was called locally.

St. Louis had aspirations of gentility now, and the pinnacle of that was a new theater. Beckwourth could hardly neglect such a chance to elevate his standing in the community, so he bought a fine suit set out for an evening of elevated distraction among the better class of the new metropolis. Thinking that such company would frown on him being armed, he left his knife behind. The play was indeed lively and entertaining, and he thoroughly enjoyed himself. At intermission, he adjourned to an adjacent saloon. And there he came upon Bracken, in the company of two rough looking characters.

"There's the Crow," said Bracken, pointing to Beckwourth.

One of the others drew his knife. "Then we are Blackfeet, out for a scalp."

Beckwourth hopped behind the bar and kept his assailants at bay by throwing glass tumblers at them. They dodged and jeered and waited for him to run out of ammunition. Beckwourth was preparing to use the last of the tumblers as a cudgel when he felt a slap on his back.

"Looks like you could use this," said Davis, handing him a huge Bowie knife.

"Davis! I apologize for every foul name I ever called you."

"And this is my way of doing the same, chief."

"Join me?"

"I only got one knife, but I will do what I can."

Beckwourth leapt over the bar. "Come on, Bracken," he said. "If you let them kill me, you have to pay them that reward." He stepped toward Bracken but retreated again as the others edged closer.

"Bracken, you are a coward and an ingrate," said Beckwourth. "I'm going to show you the inside of your scalp while you still breathe and rub it in the face of your friends."

Beckwourth felt a hand on his shoulder.

"That will be enough, Beckwourth." It was Buzby, the lawman he had held at gunpoint three years ago. Buzby turned to Beckwourth's attackers. "Y'all go home. Show's over for you."

Knives were sheathed, and Bracken and his friends backed out of the door, muttering threats on their way.

"Welcome back, Beckwourth," said Buzby.

"No hard feelings, Constable?"

"Sheriff now," Buzby smiled. "Chief."

A property came to Beckwourth's attention, one that was within his means and that he thought would suit his needs. On inquiry, he found that the current proprietor was none other than General Ashley. Beckwourth decided it was high time to pay his former boss a visit. He was directed to an imposing home in a quiet neighborhood, far from the bustle of the city. A knock on the door summoned a black servant woman, who informed Beckwourth that the general was not home. Turning to leave, he was stopped by a sweet voice from within.

"Beckwourth, you say? My husband will soon be back," the lady said, "and he will be doubtless pleased to see you."

Mrs. Ashley was every bit the angelic presence that the general had described to him, that day in the mountains when the poor man seemed on death's doorstep. Beckwourth swiped his hat off his head.

"It's just a business matter, ma'am."

"If I mistake not," she said, "you are a mountaineer."

"I am that, indeed," he said with a slight bow. He was aware that he was acting like a shy schoolboy;

Bloody Arm, whose very name struck fear in the heart of his enemies, with three wives of his own. "I was with the general on his first overland trip to the mountains."

"Oh, do tell!" she said. "Come wait in the parlor."

"Well…"

"You must." She led him by the hand. Fine drapery and upholstered furniture of distant import bespoke the general's good fortune.

"The general is so modest that I feel that I know nothing of that adventure," said the lady. "You must tell me *something* of it."

There must be some story to tell that would show neither him nor the good general in a bad light, one with no bloodshed or such that might offend this delicate creature. As he sat in the most comfortable chair his bottom had ever known, Beckwourth wracked his brain for such an episode.

"Your name is Eliza, I presume?" he asked. She affirmed. "I cannot forget that name, because when the general first told me of you, he didn't know if he would live to see the next sunrise. I tell you, though, you were foremost in his mind at that moment. His undying love for you made an indelible impression on me."

"Oh, my," said Lady Ashley. "Tell me!"

"Well," said Beckwourth, "I am sure he told you of his pneumonia in the mountains."

"He never told me of this. He was near death, you say?"

Now Beckwourth felt foolish, for having revealed something that the general perhaps had wanted to keep private. He stammered forward anyway. "Well, maybe it wasn't all that bad, but the point is, I was going to tell you a story about… Well, the thing was that he is such a gallant gentleman that he insisted that we leave him there..."

"Leave him?"

"Well, yes, the boys were making him a shelter, and they were going to come back."

"Come back for him? When?"

"Well, the next day, I suppose, but the thing was..."

"The next day? What about wolves?"

"Well, there are always wolves in the mountains, ma'am. What you really have to watch out for is bears."

"Bears? My husband could have been eaten by bears? We had only been married a few months then."

"Well, yes, he told me that..."

"And you were going to leave him there?"

"Well, no, not me..."

"Beckwourth saved my hide that day, my dear." The general had slipped in unnoticed. "And that was not the only time."

"General!" Beckwourth stood awkwardly and was relieved when Ashley extended his hand and shook his firmly.

"Dearest," said the general, "I see you have made the acquaintance of James P. Beckwourth, the finest mountaineer I have ever known."

"We were just getting started," she said.

"So Beckwourth rigged a drag for me, and he and another two men dragged me to catch up with the rest of our party. Had he not, it is very likely that I would not be standing here today."

"General, sir..."

"Jim," said he, "I heard you were back in town. Why did you not come by sooner?"

"We had our disagreements, and I was not so sure of the welcome I might receive, sir."

"Well, strong-willed men at times disagree, Beckwourth. But now, I owe you money."

"Is it true you have several Indian wives?" Lady Ashley asked.

"Well, I don't know what folks might mean by 'several'," said Beckwourth.

"And what is this I hear of difficulty between you and Bracken?" asked Ashley.

"Difficulty indeed. He seems to have taken a dislike to me, to such a degree that he put a price on my head."

"And why would he do that?" the general asked.

"Damned if I know," said Beckwourth. "I did my best to get him out of a tight situation. Excuse me, ma'am. Darned if I know."

"No apology needed," the lady said. "But perhaps it is best that I leave you men to discuss business." Her skirt made a fine ruffling noise as she left the room.

The general explained that he had sold out of the fur business. It was obvious, though, that he missed the excitement of exploring, of seeing sights none other than the natives had ever seen. He inquired of Beckwourth's sojourn as a Crow and listened intently to every word. Beckwourth ended with the story of how he had interceded with Big Rain on behalf of Bracken.

"And nothing else transpired to cause animosity between you two?" the general asked.

"Never saw him after, until St. Louis," said Beckwourth. "Like I said, anyone who knows Indian ways would know I saved his scalp."

Beckwourth mentioned the property he was interested in.

"Come back on Tuesday," the general said. "I will have your pay, and I'm sure we can come to terms on the property."

Tuesday came, and Beckwourth found himself waiting for the general in his parlor again, but across from him was Bracken, glaring at him, feet under his chair like he was ready to spring on his enemy. Mrs. Ashley set coffee before the two in delicate cups.

"Thank you, my dear woman," Beckwourth said. He held his cup up to Bracken. "White man's soup," he said. "To our continued good health."

Bracken picked up his cup and slurped.

Beckwourth smirked. "Bracken, Bracken, my good man. Like this." He sipped daintily with his pinkie in the air.

"You're a fine one to speak of manners," said Bracken.

"Gentlemen!" Ashley swept into the room. "I am so pleased to see you both enjoying each other's company."

"Oh, we were just getting reacquainted, General," said Beckwourth. "I am doing my best to teach old Bracken here how to not make horse noises when he pours coffee down his gullet."

"That is so thoughtful of you, Beckwourth," said the general. "I'm sure that Mr. Bracken appreciates your efforts."

Beckwourth lifted his cup to Bracken and got a glare in return.

"Oh, if you men are going to be so…like boys," said Lady Ashley, "I suppose I must leave you to your business." She huffed out of the room.

"For my part," said Bracken, "it is only out of respect for you, General, your dear wife, and this expensive carpet that I don't spill Beckwourth's guts here and now."

"I assure you, my good sir," said Beckwourth, "that I would unburden your shoulders of your head before you could rise from your chair to attempt such a thing."

"Well, now that we have the formalities out of the way, gentlemen," said Ashley. "Let us get down to business. I brought you here to mediate the difficulty that has arisen between you two men, whom I respect greatly."

"I have no quarrel with the likes of him," said Beckwourth. "But for reasons unclear to me he seems to feel justified in attacking my person."

"And so, I have heard the same," said the general. "What is behind this, Mr. Bracken?"

"He knows."

"The last I saw you in the wilds, I had just restored to you your prize horse and all of your belongings," said Beckwourth.

"Is that true?" Ashley asked Bracken.

"Yes, but then not a week out we was attacked by the damned Crow again. It was all a ruse, what he did."

"Did you ride for three days straight, like I said?" Beckwourth asked.

There was a pause. "I don't take orders from the likes of you," said Bracken.

"What part of the likes of me is it that you find offensive?" Beckwourth asked, tensing.

"Let's not get into that," said Ashley.

"No, let's get into that," said Beckwourth. "What part of the likes of me offends you, Bracken, you mangy dog butt?"

Bracken looked uneasy but did not answer.

"You don't take orders from a Crow, or you don't

take orders from a half-naggur bastard?" asked Beckwourth.

Bracken still had no answer.

"If you can't answer that, Bracken," said Ashley, "Answer this: how do you know Beckwourth had a hand in the attack on you?"

"He was their chief, goddammit," said Bracken. "We all saw it. You could see all them damn savages taking orders from him like he was the lord a'mighty. He had to have ordered it. Or at least he knew and didn't stop it."

"A chief doesn't control his braves much," said the general. "Not in any tribe. You should know that."

"And Big Rain was a chief in his own right," said Beckwourth.

"I know what I know," said Bracken.

"That's all you can say?" asked Ashley. "You know what you know?" The general proceeded to his cabinet and produced a flask of brandy. He poured both men a glass and spoke in glowing terms of the fellowship of men who had endured hardship, and faced death together, pointing out to both of them instances of their own bravery and self-sacrifice. He detailed their individual acts of gallantry. Then he had them go over the entire episode with Big Rain again in the minutest detail. Finally, he ended by saying that he could not believe that Beckwourth would be guilty of the charges leveled at him and re-iterated that it pained him to see two men he so respected as enemies of one another. The brandy and Ashley's rhetoric gradually softened Bracken's face. He shifted uneasily in his chair.

"I ain't the villain here," he finally said.

"Beckwourth," said Ashley, "I regret that I did not at first give you the same chance I gave the others. Despite that slight on my part, you acted with the greatest of integrity, perhaps one would say, punctuated by fits of anger, but still, I know no man I would rather have on such an adventure as we had." He turned to Bracken.

"Beckwourth," Bracken said. "I see now I fell into bad company that influenced my judgment. I swear by God now I don't now believe a word of their nonsense, and I won't ever be so persuaded again."

"Not about the likes of me?"

"And maybe I was too easily swayed by what I thought of the likes of you, before I ever met you."

"For my part," said Beckwourth, "I acknowledge that you are a man of integrity as well, and I accept your apology."

There we go!" said the general. "Shake hands the two of you then."

And they did.

Beckwourth walked the streets easier after that meeting, and even more so when he heard that Bracken's cohorts, those faux Blackfeet, had headed upriver themselves. He met a lovely lady named Eustice, with whom he enjoyed his evenings. She was as beautiful as Red Cherry, and as strong-willed as Little Wife, and he lavished her with his attention. His time with her was blissful, and as spring approached, they discussed marriage.

There was also the matter of that property. He and Ashley came to an agreement, money changed hands and Beckwourth brought his sisters to see the house he had bought.

"How do you like it, girls?" he grinned.

"Oh, solid brick," said Lou. "Suits a solid citizen like you."

"Oh, now, here's the thing about that," said Beckwourth, with an impish look. "You know, I am not entirely comfortable in St. Louis society. It would grate on me if I stayed, you know, having to drag out my emancipation papers every time I wanted to buy a damn horse. So, that is the long way of telling you that this house is not for me." He let his smile broaden.

"You mean..." said Mattie.

"Yes," he said. "This is for you girls."

His sisters squealed with joy and hugged him over and over with tears in their eyes.

"But what about you, James? Does this mean you are leaving?" asked Mattie.

"St. Louis is fine for now, but I can't say where I will be in a year," he said. "There's a giant wilderness out there that beckons."

That business done, he spent his time with Eustice, and in saloons, where he gambled and bought round after round 'for the house.' The fall and winter went by pleasantly, and the spring as well. At the theater one day in late March, with Eustice on his arm, Beckwourth was approached by a gaunt, exhausted man whom he at first did not recognize. "Jim," said this veritable scarecrow, "you must go to Kipp's."

Only then did Beckwourth recognize him. "Pappen!" He embraced his good friend. "What happened to you?"

"Don't worry about me. Everyone in the fort is in grave danger. You have got to leave now and go as fast as humanly possible back to Kipp's."

Pappen told his tale. All had been well at the trading post after Beckwourth left, until one day the

Crow were seen gathering outside, without communicating what this was about. They wondered and watched. That night, Never Wavers came secretly to tell Kipp that the Crow intended to attack them. It seemed that Bracken's friends, the faux Blackfeet, had encountered some wandering Crow and told them that Beckwourth was dead. Not only dead, but that he had been executed for the crimes of making the wicked Crow rich and fighting with them against the whites. The entire nation was greatly angered at Beckwourth's supposed execution, and by the lie that they would have even thought of fighting against the whites. They grieved for days. Crooked Smile, appointed chief soon after Beckwourth had left, had channeled the Crow energy into an attack on Kipp's trading post. After hearing all this from Never Wavers, Kipp had assured her that all of this was foolish nonsense.

"I mourned my brother's death for three suns," said Never Wavers. "Myself and the entire nation, though I would not cut myself, because I knew that my brother would not want this if he were alive. I come now because I know that he would not want harm to come to you whites in the fort and your Arikara wife. Now you tell me that he is alive. What proof have you?"

"There is no proof that I can offer now. But what the white men told the Crow cannot be true, Never Wavers," said Kipp. "The whites would never execute one of their own for what you say."

"But Medicine Calf is not really a white man," said Never Wavers. "I know this. Some white men hate him because he is not a slave."

"The Medicine Calf has a paper," said Kipp. "That paper says he is free like a white man. That paper means that if a bad man were to harm him, the chiefs of the whites would take vengeance on that man. The Medicine Calf is alive and well, I guarantee you."

"Yes, he told me of this paper. But paper makes a poor shield from bullets and knives. I do not know if I believe you, though I want to with all my heart."

"Have I ever lied to the Crow?" asked Kipp.

"No, you have not."

"Go then," said Kipp. "Go to your people and soften their hearts. Tell Crooked Smile what I have told you, and that I love Medicine Calf as much as all of the Crow people do, and ask why then do they want to kill me? Ask Crooked Smile to grant me time to send for Medicine Calf where he is in the country of white men, and if what you have been told is true, I will lay down my head, and he may cut it off, and the warriors may kill us all, for we will not fight against our beloved Crow. Go and tell Crooked Smile that he must grant what I have said to you for your people's sake, for if he does not, Medicine Calf, when he returns, his anger will be without bounds. Go."

So Never Wavers went to Crooked Smile. "Oh, Great Chief," she said. "I come to you with a request. You do not know me well, but I am Medicine Calf's sister. I want you to know that I grieve for my brother like none other, and I ask that you would grant me one wish.

"I see that you have held all of your blood inside you, which must make your grief greater," said Crooked Smile. He surmised that she would ask for the manner of death of one of the whites, or for a scalp. "I will grant your request."

The next morning, Crooked Smile rode to the fort with Hunts Alone and his chiefs. "Slender Crane," he called, "what is the matter? Why are your gates closed against us?"

"I had a dream last night," said Kipp, "and it told me I would have to fight the Crow today, even though I love the Crow as much as I do my own people."

"I have heard from whites that Medicine Calf was executed in St Louis. Tell me what you have to say of this," said Crooked Smile.

"Medicine Calf is not dead. He is safe in St. Louis."

"Two whites told us that he was killed because he made the Crow rich, which is true, and because they said he fought at our sides against them, which is a lie," said Crooked Smile.

"These whites lie," said Kipp. "The whites love Medicine Calf."

"I do not know if the whites love Medicine Calf or hate him. But I know what these whites said."

"Where are these whites now who told you these bad things?" asked Kipp. "I wish to speak to them."

"Enough!" said Crooked Smile. "You should not try to escape by saying he is not dead, for we will not believe your words. You can neither dig into the ground nor fly into the air. If you attempt to run, I will put ten times one hundred warriors on your trail. They will follow you, and even if it takes them to the lodge of Clark; they will kill you there. We have loved the whites, but now we hate them, and we are all angry. All this I say from my own heart. But I have made a promise to the sister of Medicine Calf. I shall hold my revenge. You may send a messenger to Medicine Calf, if he is indeed alive. Tell him to show his face here before the cherries turn red. If he does not, you will die."

. . .

"James," said Pappen, "I was there when he said this. You must hurry."

Pappen presented a letter from Kipp to the American Fur Company office which confirmed what he said. The company stood to lose a hundred thousand dollars in goods, the lives of good men, and likely would never be able to set foot in Crow territory again if Beckwourth did not get to the fort in time. They gave him *cart blanche* for supplies and five thousand dollars to pay however many men were needed. Beckwourth chose to just enlist the services of Davis and Pappen. Sometimes a small group can accomplish such a thing easier that a large one, it being possible to conceal themselves better.

Beckwourth bid his sisters goodbye and promised to return soon.

"James," said Mattie. "You know who you should say goodbye to. It would be a good thing."

So Beckwourth knocked on the door of a humble home. A man came to the door. There was a flash of recognition.

"Eliza," the man said.

His first love came to the door, her gentle movements so familiar. A lump formed in his throat.

"Jim," she said. "It is good to see you."

"Couldn't leave for Crow country again without saying goodbye," he said.

Across the room, a baby squalled.

"I have heard such stories about you," said Eliza.

"I have lived a strange life."

"You were really the big war chief?"

"One thing led to another, really."

"I can well imagine, knowing you."

"Who is the little one?"

"Her name is Cleo."

"I will say one thing. One could disparage many

of the habits of the Crow, but in child rearing we should follow their lead. I never saw a hand raised, nor a sharp word, and still the children leap to their tasks."

The husband gave Beckwourth a look that said to mind his own business.

"I had to come," he said.

"I am glad you did."

"You said you were proud of me, when last we parted. Proud that I stood up for myself. That kept me going." *That and the memory of your kiss*, he thought. "Fare thee well, my dear."

❧ 27 ❧

The trek through hostile country went as well as it could have; nearly two anxious months of nonstop travel. When they arrived in Crow country, the cherry trees in the river bottoms bore ripening fruit. They pressed on. Would they find the post a smoking ruin, the bodies of their friends like pincushions for arrows? The post came into view. The walls were intact, the gate closed. All was well; they had made it in time.

Beckwourth galloped into the Crow village. "I have returned," he called. "I am angry." He paraded through the village like a herald, calling this out over and over, with Pappen and Davis in tow. Every ear was turned to him, every gaze averted. No pot was stirred; the fashioning of weapons ceased. Women seized children who were too young to recognize the gravity of the situation and spirited them inside. Beckwourth did not speak to any man individually, or even acknowledge his own wives. Once satisfied that the whole village had felt his presence, he wheeled his horse toward the fort and galloped away. He banged his war club against the gate.

"Halloo, boys," he cried cheerfully. "Open up. I made it."

The gate opened just a crack to admit them, then closed. Beckwourth was pleased to see that all confined therein appeared anxious, but well. The Crow had not tried to starve them out while they waited. He spent some minutes apprising Kipp of his journey, while at the same time he turned over in his mind how to deal with his people, the Crow. There must have been factions that had pushed for war on the whites, and those opposed. If he went first to Hunts Alone or Big Bowl for council, he would appear weak. And should he go now, or wait here at the fort, reinforcing his affiliation with the whites in the minds of the Crow? He decided that it was best to confront the Crow while they were still thunderstruck that he lived. He rode his horse out of the fort, advising Kipp to keep the gates closed in case things did not go well. Kipp sent his Arikara wife with Beckwourth, so that he might have an independent report of the proceedings, and Davis, ever in search of action, tagged along.

Beckwourth dismounted short of the village and sat on the ground cross-legged, his buffalo robe over his shoulders; hunched, chin on his chest. The village gathered. No one spoke. Birds far away at the river's edge could be heard twittering. Beckwourth did not move. His Dog Soldiers slowly formed a circle around him at a respectful distance, and the rest surrounded them. One Who Strikes Three broke through the circle of men, followed by Still Water and Red Cherry. With heads bowed and eyes averted they circled their husband. As each passed behind him, she placed her hand on the back of his neck. Still, not a word had been spoken by the entire village.

Finally, Crooked Smile approached. "The people tremble before the anger of Medicine Calf. Tell us, who is to blame for your anger?"

"Did I not tell you," Beckwourth said, raising his chin off his chest, "that the Crow were to protect Slender Crane and the other whites during my absence? And what do I behold on my return?"

"Yes," said Crooked Smile, "we told you that we would take care of Slender Crane and these other whites while you were gone, and we have done so. Our warriors have killed buffalo for them to eat, and our women have brought them wood and water, and they are all alive. Look! Yonder is the Crane. His white people are all with him. Are they dead?"

"No, they are not dead, but you might have killed them, had I been delayed two suns on my journey. Had one accident befallen me on my journey from the white man's country, I might have arrived to find a river of blood pouring from the gates of the post."

"Yes, it is true, Medicine Calf," said Crooked Smile. "If you had not returned before the cherries ripened, we would have killed them all, and we would have taken all their weapons and like a grass fire spread outward from our lands and killed all the whites we could have found. This we would have done, and I would have been the one to lead our warriors. Now, hear what I have to say:

"Suppose now that I am you and you are me. I go to war against a powerful foe, and I am killed. You and I were not friends, but neither were we enemies. One of my wives comes to you because you are now chief, her hair pulled out, and her scalp bloody. She cries mournfully and paints your chest with the bloody stump of her freshly cut finger. Your heart pities her, this wife you know to be of great virtue. You have seen her triumphant at the Green Grass

ceremony; a blessing to all her people. She is the virtuous widow of you, the most esteemed warrior
among us, beloved and respected by the whole nation. She asks you to avenge her loss, the loss that has
deprived her of her husband. In such a case, what
would you do? Speak!"

Beckwourth's heart sank with the realization that
it had been Little Wife who had agitated the Crow to
kill every soul in the trading post.

Beckwourth slowly rose to his feet. "Crow people,
I am no longer angry with you. You have your ways,
and I can no more change them than to make the
rivers run back up into the mountains." He didn't
know what else to say to the assembled multitude, so
he was grateful for the distraction when Mrs. Kipp,
the Arikara, burst into the ring of warriors and
started berating them.

"I have lived the past three moons listening to
Crow warriors taunt me, telling me day after day in
what manner they intended to kill me. The gates are
wide open now. Here we are," she mocked them,
"and yet you sit on your butts here. You yearned for
the kill. Why don't you quench your thirst for blood
now? What is wrong? Has a dead man come to life
and frightened you so?"

The braves pretended to neither see nor hear her,
but Beckwourth was fearful that if they heard much
more like this, they might silence her for good, and
then there would be no telling what would be next.
Fortunately, One Who Strikes Three interrupted her
tirade.

"Quit yapping, Arikara dog," she said. "If any
woman has something to say here, it is me. Yes, husband, I came to your father, and to Crooked Smile,
and to anyone who would listen, covered in blood
and grieving with all my heart. I wiped blood from

the stump of my finger on their bare chests and pleaded with them, and it is all my fault that my people were set against the whites in the post." She kneeled before Beckwourth arms upraised. "Husband, I beg your forgiveness. I have finished."

"Rise, woman," said Beckwourth. "I forgive you. I forgive you, and I will always have tenderness in my heart for you." He addressed the assemblage. "I am no longer your leader. I love you all, but I must still leave you. I wish now to smoke and tell stories with my friends. I am finished."

Beckwourth had his smokes and the telling of tales with his Dog Soldiers, and he was sad to think that this would be no more a part of his life. He had a smoke with Crooked Smile, wily fellow.

"Crooked Smile, great chief of the most feared people of all the tribes," he said. "Do you remember when I came to you while you fashioned an arrow?"

"This I remember."

"You told me that alone among the Crow, you could see through the lies of white men."

"This I told you. And I was right. You were not born a Crow; you have said so yourself."

"This is true. I tell you now, the day will come when it will be good that you do not believe everything the white man says, and good that it is you who leads the Crow."

Next, he went to Big Bowl.

"I have lived a thousand lives with the Crow and would have it no other way. But now it is my wish now to have a peaceful life, once I return to the whites," Beckwourth said. "I have a new woman, and I will settle with her and trade with the tribes up the Missouri."

"I only wish to help you choose the path that is

best for you, my son," said Big Bowl. He and Beck-wourth embraced arms.

Beckwourth next went to Hunts Alone and told him also of his intent to settle down.

"I do not see you as one who could live so," Hunts Alone said. "Your blood will clot in your veins if you are no longer a warrior. You should be a warrior with the whites."

"You know my heart as well as any, my friend. But war among the whites, it is a terrible thing. Huge guns shoot balls larger than your fist and kill dozens of men at a time from inside forts that make ours look like anthills. And no one counts coup, they only kill to rub out their enemy." He told his friend of how much St. Louis had expanded in the years he had been gone, hinting at the nation's inevitable westward expansion.

"Then you must come back some day," said Hunts Alone. "Your people, the Crow, will need you more tomorrow than they need you today, if all these things you say are true."

The next day, Still Water made her way to Beck-wourth, and showed him that Black Panther had just learned to walk. It made Beckwourth's heart glad to see this, and heavy at the same time.

"I come to you as your wife and the mother of your son," Still Water said, "who will one day be a great chief. You have made the Crow strong, and your desire is to keep us strong. You left us once, and the One Above Person has sent you back to us. Do not offend him; make your home with us now and forever. I know you not like war, though you are the greatest of warriors. Stay with us, and do not go to war unless it is to protect us. Stay with me in our lodge. It will be a happy place, and we will raise our son to be a great warrior together. Stay with us, now and forever, and when we depart to the Other Side Camp, we will be there together."

"My wife, the mother of this fine boy," Beckwourth said. "You are very wise, and you care for me deeply, as I care for you. But if I were to stay but not be a warrior, what would I be? Even if I become a pipe carrier and keep peace in the village, I will be an object of pity among the warriors, or worse, their scorn, the same as I scorned Big Rain, who was once a warrior, but no more. My place in the world is not at your side, even if I wish that it were so with all my heart."

Still Water hid her sorrow and left with her child clutched tightly.

Red Cherry did not seek him out, nor did he seek her. She had taken up with Crooked Smile, so it was just as well. She did not bind him to the Crow.

Beckwourth sought out One Who Strikes Three and took her hands in his. She pulled away, hiding her amputation.

"I see now," she said. "You think I am foolish."

"No, no, Little Wife."

"Your eyes have seen distant things. You have a woman in St. Louis, one who would never spoil her beauty so."

"I see now that I will never have a woman who could cherish me more than you. I did not value as I should have."

"It would please me if you stayed."

"I am not sure of what lays before me in life, but my time with the Crow has come to an end," he said.

She looked into his eyes. "Then you must go," she said.

. . .

The Mackinaw boats arrived. All that remained for Beckwourth was to say his final goodbyes.

The Dog Soldiers led their Medicine Calf away to the water's edge, where he climbed on the steering platform of a Mackinaw and addressed his people.

"I have lived a thousand lives with the Crow," he said. "And I wish that I could live a thousand more with my noble people. But the river of life pulls at me now; I must go. Everywhere, you will be in my heart, and I will always measure my deeds as they would stand in your eyes. Farewell, my people. I am finished."

The Frenchmen poled the boats away with Beckwourth standing wrapped in his buffalo robe, painted with his four deeds on it. Just before he went out of sight around the bend, Hunts Alone raised his weapon and shouted the charge to battle, and the Crow people echoed that cry.

HISTORICAL NOTES

A reader of this novel may well wonder where history ends and fiction begins. This section is meant to address that for the interested reader. Editors tell me that those will be a decided minority, so you should feel no obligation to read on.

The basis for my novel is "The Life and Adventures of James P. Beckwourth," written by Thomas Bonner after he spent the winter of 1854-1855 interviewing Beckwourth. That work is available online for free. For anyone who wants to learn more, the edition of Bonner edited by Oswald is excellent, as he cross-references Bonner with other sources in an extensive epilogue. Oswald details how Beckwourth's account, though rife with exaggeration, has been largely supported by other sources as they came to light over the years. Elinor Wilson's biography of Beckwourth also supports the general veracity of Bonner's account. "Raven Men of the Yellowstone" by Brian Keefe similarly affirms much of what is found in Bonner but shows up some of the exaggeration. In particular, Keefe's history tells us that it was not Beckwourth but someone else who was appointed chief when Rotten Belly was killed (page 343 of Keefe).

In contrast to my novel, where race and identity are central, Beckwourth makes no mention of his race in Bonner's account. From other sources we know that he was born a slave and that his father, who was white, signed emancipation papers for him three times. I draw inferences about Beckwourth's attitude about his race from two passages in Bonner. One is regarding his status on Ashley's expedition as an employee, not a partner like the others, which he alludes to on pages 370-371 of Bonner. My supposition is that Beckwourth was given this inferior status due to his race, and that this was part of the reason for the conflict with Ashley. The second inference comes from the episode where Beckwourth and Ashley hold each other at gunpoint (page 47 of Bonner). Beckwourth says that, "another volley of curses descended uninterruptedly upon my head," from Ashley who called him an "infernal scoundrel." A few lines later, Beckwourth replies, "General, you have addressed language to me which I allow no man to use, and, unless you retract that last epithet, you or I must surely die." I find it unlikely that anyone would draw a gun for being called an "infernal scoundrel." Such language is tame by any standard. It seems more likely to me that a racial epithet provoked Beckwourth.

My novel is essentially the Hollywood version of Beckwourth's life, compressing eighteen years into three. Though I use at most a third of what we are given in Bonner, I do attempt to accurately portray what Beckwourth relates of his motives and misgivings.

One of Beckwourth's motives was to return to his fiancé, a woman named Eliza. He describes a painful goodbye to her on pages 90-92 of Bonner, and his sadness on learning of her marriage to another on page 382. In the paragraphs just after his adoption into the family of Big Bowl, Beckwourth says, "There was but one recollection troubled me, and that was my lonely one in St. Louis. My thoughts were constantly filled with her."

Beckwourth admits in a few places that the pursuit of wealth was a big motivator. But he was also dismayed by the violence of Crow life. To clarify to us that his participation in their warfare was not purely in quest of wealth, Beckwourth gives us certain insights. On page 232 of Bonner, he says that by warring against enemy tribes he "...saved more life and property for the white man than a whole regiment of United States regulars could have done in the same time." He also says that the Crow never killed a white man (pages 198-199). But more than these rationalizations, he tells us how seeing his slaughtered playmates when he was a child of nine motivated him: "Impressed with the recollection of these early scenes, I hardly ever struck down an Indian but my mind reverted to the mangled bodies of my childish play-fellows..." On page 120 he adds, "...if a man has feeling, in a short time it becomes callous toward the relentless savage, who can mock the dying struggles of the white man, and indulge in inhuman joy as he sees his warm life-blood saturate the earth..." It is easy to see how with this view, killing (non-Crow) Indians did not bother him much.

As I show in my novel, Beckwourth did try to turn

the Crow away from warfare, as he relates on pages 220-221 of Bonner:

> "My intention was to induce the Crows to devote their undivided attention to trapping, not alone for their own benefit, but for the interest of the company in whose service I was engaged. I well knew that if I was with them they would capture five beavers to one if left to themselves. I had obtained great influence in the medicine lodge, and could often exert it to prevent a war-party from making a useless excursion against their enemies. I would tell them in their council that my medicine told me not to go to war; that it was to their interest to employ their warriors in trapping all the beavers possible, so that they might have the means of purchasing ammunition and weapons for themselves, as well as beads, scarlet cloth, and blankets for the women; that by-and-by we should be attacked by the enemy, and be unprovided with the means of defense; that they would then kill all our warriors, and make captives of our women and children, and the Cheyennes had captured my mother when I was an infant, many winters gone; that they should save all their warriors against a time of need, and only engage in war when the safety of the village was at stake."

On pages 268-269 of Bonner, Beckwourth relates his speech to the Crow following the death of Rotten Belly, where he goes over those same points, adding that he would advocate with the whites for them but

threatening to leave them if they did not turn
from war.

Over time, Beckwourth became disillusioned. In several places he laments the mutilation that mourners
inflicted upon themselves. But apparently it was not
the mourning or the danger to himself that dismayed
him most. On pages 198-199 of Bonner he says,
"(d)isgusted at the repeated acts of cruelty I witnessed, I often resolved to leave these wild children
of the forest and return to civilized life; but before I
could act upon my decision, another scene of strife
would occur and (I) was always the first sought for by
the tribe."

Finally, he decides to leave. His reflection upon his
time with the Crow on pages 370-371 of Bonner
shows his state of mind just before he left them. On
page 403, when he returns for the second time he
says, "I knew that, if I remained with them, it would
be war and carnage to the end…"

Most historical fiction fills imagined details into a
framework of known history. For those works, the author has little to go on for the details of daily interac-
tions. The background material for my novel is
different from this in that it is detailed down to the
dialogue. So, instead of sticking to the Historical
framework, I have picked and chosen the most important or most illustrative episodes in Beckwourth's
life and stitched them together into a cohesive story,
mostly in order. If any reader is interested in that
how close each chapter sticks to a particular episode,
what follows is the page numbers in Bonner that cor-
respond to each chapter in my novel, along with
some background references. Following that is an

epilogue with a summation of Beckwourth's life following the events of my novel.

Chapter One
1824 is the year Beckwourth left with Ashley's expedition. The episode with the blacksmith and the constable follows Bonner's account pretty closely, pages
18-19, but that occurred in 1817. There was a girl-
friend, then, but the Eliza he was engaged to is from
pages 91-92. Some published accounts of Beckwourth say he was illiterate, but on page 18 Beckwourth says he was sent to St. Louis at the age of ten
to attend school, and continued in school until 1812,
which would have been four years.

Chapter Two
Beckwourth departs his family on page 20 of Bonner,
though my novel skips several years of his travels before he signs on with Ashley on page 23. His account
of finding his neighbors slaughtered is found on
pages 15-16.

Chapter Three
Beckwourth's trip with Black Harris is based on Bonner's account, pages 24 -32, including that Beckwourth threatened to shoot Harris down if he left
him. I added the wrestling. A year is skipped, as
Beckwourth returned to St. Louis after his journey
with Harris, then returned to his party. The episode
with the teal duck is closely based on Pages 37-40 of
Bonner (Beckwourth says that remorse for that self-
ishness stuck with him the rest of his life). He kills a
buffalo he thought was a bear on pages 40-42 of
Bonner.

Chapter Four

Beckwourth and Ashley hold each other at gunpoint in an episode on pages 45-51 of Bonner, and many of the expedition side with him. Horses are stolen by what later turns out to be Crow. Ashley takes sick and it is Beckwourth who constructs a litter to drag him to the others, pages 52-54.

Chapter Five
Beckwourth's account of gathering four men to fire at raiding Indians in the night is on pages 76-77 of Bonner. The episode of Ashley's fortuitous misfire saving them from being wiped out by the Crow is on page 77. They are confronted with the Crow scalps on page 78. The parley with the chief is on page 79 and is combined with dialogue about Clark from an interaction with another party entirely, on page 84.

Chapter Six
On the way to the rendezvous on page 102 they did battle the Blackfeet, but I substitute the battle at the horseshoe bend from pages 127-128 of Bonner. As a prank, Greenwood tells Crow warriors that Beckwourth is a long-lost Crow on page 140.

Chapter Seven
A rendezvous is described on page 107 of Bonner. Readers are likely aware of Hugh Glass' ordeal from the movie "Revenant." From other sources we can determine that Jedediah Smith would have been recovering from his own ursine-inflicted injuries at this rendezvous, and Clyman was there to describe sewing his ear back on. Beckwourth tells the tale of the "stolen" beaver trap on page 143 and an unnamed trapper and he end up at gunpoint with each other. It was Bridger who advised Beckwourth to leave for a few days on page 144, but I substitute

Ashley's and parting words to Beckwourth from page 112. Beckwourth's capture by Crow herders is on page 145.

Chapter Eight
Beckwourth is declared to be a long-lost son by Ishkali on page 146, and he becomes familiar with his new family through page 148. What he learns of Crow life I take from various sources.

Chapter Nine
Beckwourth's first battle as a Crow is on page 153 of Bonner, and Big Bowl's resulting distribution of his belongings follows. Beckworth's bonding with Hunts Alone (whom he never names in Bonner, which would appear to be out of respect for Crow custom regarding deceased relatives) is on pages 155-156. The account of his friend's father dying of powder burns comes from "Two Leggings: the Making of a Crow Warrior," by Nabokov, page 1.

Chapter Ten
Beckwourth's initiation by buffalo intestine ceremony and the following raid is based on pages 156-158 of Bonner. In "The Crow Indians," page 49, Lowie confirms this tradition, and goes on to say that warriors would even admit (or brag?) that they had had sex with the wives of men present at this little ceremony. This was because they felt that success of the raid depended on their honesty. Only the women faced consequences; a double standard that is discussed by Lowie.

Chapter Eleven
This chapter starts with an imagined interaction with a berdache. Beckwourth does not mention *bate*, as

they were called by the Crow (page 47 of "The Crow" by Hoxie) in his narrative, but they are noted throughout sources on Native American culture of the time. The most complete sources for this I have found are "The Cheyennes: Indians of the Great Plains" by E. Adamson Hoebel, (page 77), and "Indians of the Great Plains" by Daniel J. Gelo, (pages 127-129).

My account of Beckwourth leading Big Bowl's "sons" in a raid is much as described on pages 159 to 161 of Bonner.

Chapter Twelve
Beckwourth celebrates Christmas down by the river on page 172 of Bonner. My story combines that with events on pages 148-149 where he acquires Still Water as his first wife, which actually occurred in his first few days with the Crow.

Chapter Thirteen
This chapter is largely from imagination. This is a good place to mention that Crooked Smile is the combination of three minor characters found in Bonner. We start with an unnamed warrior who was wounded by Beckwourth's crew when the horses were stolen, pages 76-77 of Bonner. This fellow and another were appeased by gifts from Ashley on page 79, and the chief commented that whites "shoot good in the dark." This fellow is combined with the unnamed warrior on page 175 who has a contest in battle with Beckwourth, and lastly combined with Yellow Belly, who in the last chapter lays siege to Kipp's post.
A couple sources describe the buffalo–rib sleds.

Chapter Fourteen

The Sioux attack on the village is in Bonner on pages 162-163. On page 166, Beckwourth describes how small war parties fared poorly when seeking revenge for this raid and tells of the women lifting the tipi off of him and showering him with gifts to convince him to lead a larger party against the Sioux.

Chapter Fifteen
Rather than a council choosing him to lead as in my story, Beckwourth says he was able to rally men around him due to his reputation. Also contrary to what I show, it appears that Beckwourth never told the Crow his real origins. His adopted father did get word of his real son, though. Sometime after Beckwourth's adoption, Big Bowl traveled to a Cheyenne village to try (unsuccessfully) to convince his now grown son to return to the Crow (pages 216-218 of "Raven Men of the Yellowstone," by Brian Keefe). The raid against the Cheyenne is much as described in Bonner (pages 167-169).

Chapter Sixteen
Beckwourth acquiesces to taking a little girl as a wife in name only on page 169 of Bonner. He says that he already had seven wives at this time, each with their own tipi. In my story, I keep the relationship non-sexual, but eventually, in reality it progressed, as it was Little Wife who was the mother of Black Panther, not Still Water. The antelope hunting episode comes from page 170 of Bonner (though it was sheep).

Chapter Seventeen
They go to see Kipp on page 177 of Bonner, and Beckwourth humorously plays with him as to his identity. This was the first time in three years he had seen whites. Beckwourth's pay arrangement with the

American Fur Company was $3k per year (page 272). He relates how the fur company berated him for letting the Crow impair the fur trade with other tribes by their warfare and horse-stealing, page 360.

Chapter Eighteen
Beckwourth goes on a horse raid in an unsuccessful attempt to prevent his father from doing the same on pages 180-181 of Bonner. The contest between the Dog Soldiers and the Fox is based events on pages 183 to 188, though the spark for the conflict was not wife stealing (more on wife stealing below). The contest between Beckwourth and Crooked Smile that results in the gunpowder blast to Beckwourth's face is based on page 175. How anyone could withstand torture as described by Crooked Smile is beyond my comprehension, and probably that of my readers. This episode is based on an even more severe torturing described in "Memoirs of a White Crow Indian" (LeForge, pages 51-52), in which the victim did indeed remain silent throughout. He further states that he never saw the Crow torture anyone (page 177). How are we to understand the silence of a victim of torture? In "A Journey to the Rocky Mountains 1839" by Wislizenus, page 156, the author explains: "An Indian will often endure, without the slightest manifestation of pain, the most torturing modes of death, simply to defy his enemy."

Chapter Nineteen
The attack on the Sioux in their natural fortress is based closely on an attack on the Blackfeet, pages 190 to 195 of Bonner. Davis is a combination of the unnamed trapper who ends up at gunpoint with Beckwourth on page 149 as mentioned above, and Mildrum (misspelling of Meldrum) a trapper who

fights with the Crow at this battle. Much of this
battle was confirmed by another trapper by the name
of Leonard, including that it was Beckwourth that
rallied the men (Wilson's "James Beckwourth" pages
62-63). The death of the great chief is from a separate battle starting on page 263. Beckwourth's eulogy
is from page 267.

Chapter Twenty
The episode of eating tongue is from pages 171-172
of Bonner. The story Little Wife relates of her
brother is based on a similar episode on page 284.

Chapter Twenty-One
Stealing Red Cherry follows Bonner pretty closely,
pages 238 to 247. Wife stealing was common among
the Sioux also (page 172 of "The Oregon Trail," by
Parkman). Among the Crow it was so common that
the children imitated it in their play villages (page 38
of "The Crow Indians" by Lowie). Lowie goes into
great detail on wife stealing from pages 186-189,
telling us that wife stealing occurred just 4 days in the
spring, and that a man was shamed if he took his
wife back, to the extent that he might be smeared
with dog droppings.

Chapter Twenty-Two
Completing the wife stealing episode, to page 247 of
Bonner. It was a former classmate of Beckwourth's
named Adams who had his goods stolen on page
248; that is a starting point from which I proceed to
the episode of Fitzpatrick's stolen goods on pages
274 to 283.
Beckwourth's infant son, who was named Black Panther, is brought to him on page 247 of Bonner. This
son, later known as Crazy Hair, was a noted warrior

as an adult according to Beckwourth and other
sources.

Chapter Twenty-Three
Little wife runs the gauntlet on pages 293-296 of
Bonner. I do not find confirmation of such a poten-
tially bloody ceremony anywhere, though there was a
reverence for women who remained virgins into late
life (page 47 of "The Crow Indians" by Lowie).

Chapter Twenty- Four
Beckwourth relates how sickened he was by the im-
molation of the injured Black Foot on page 323 of
Bonner, and at the same time says that some of the
very worst savages he knew in the mountains were
whites. I take a detail or two from a similar execu-
tion/torture by the Sioux in "The Oregon Trail" by
Parkman, page 255.
Beckwourth describes the wider world to Hunts
Alone on page 320 of Bonner. He describes the state
of mind that leads him to return home on pages 370-
371. His farewell and admonishments to the Crow
are on page 376-377.

Chapter Twenty-Five
The encounter with the soldiers is from a much ear-
lier trip home on page 226 of Bonner.
His homecoming with his sisters, who had previously
heard he was dead, is on page 379. The saloon fight
with Bracken and associates closely follows a fight
with Fitzpatrick on page 384.

Chapter Twenty-Six
The visit with General and Lady Ashley is on pages
389-390 of Bonner. It was actually prior to that
meeting, on page 388, that Captain Sublette, not

Ashley, made peace between Beckwourth and Fitzpatrick.

Chapter Twenty-Seven
Pappen tells of the Crow siege and they proceed to
Crow country, pages 390-403 of Bonner. I have given
Little Wife Pine Leaf's tirade against Kipp's Arikara
wife. As mentioned previously, Crooked Smile is
given the speech by Yellow Belly.

EPILOGUE

Beckwourth's party stopped downstream at Fort Union and tried to negotiate a deal there that would have allowed him to make that his base of operations. He was not successful, he told his biographer, due to the trapping business being "unusually dull" at that moment. Therefore, he proceeded to St. Louis intending to marry, but that engagement fell through, leaving him at loose ends.

The Seminole Indian war was on; a sorry episode in American history. A General Gaines came to St. Louis seeking men who would fight the Seminoles. Gaines raised sixty-four mountain men as a fighting force, of which Beckwourth was made the captain. When his days with the army in Florida came to an end, Beckwourth returned to the West to trade with the Cheyenne. Tiring of that, he roamed much of the West, fighting in the war with Mexico and the Bear Flag war in California. In Gold Rush times, he pioneered a route in California that still bears his name, where he built a way station for emigrants. It was there, one winter in the mid 1850's that he dictated his biography, which serves as the basis for this story. Later still, he was an unwilling participant in a shameful massacre of the Cheyenne by a General Carrington and testified in the court martial that followed. The quote at the beginning of my novel is from that trial. His last years were spent trading in Colorado where he was an advocate for the Cheyenne, and Montana, where he could have come in contact with a very young Calamity Jane, which is what piqued my interest. His end came in his midsixties, when the army sent him to parley with the Crow. The most reliable reports indicate that he developed a nosebleed, which may have been a sign of severe hypertension. At any rate, he died suddenly and is buried in a Crow cemetery.

Dear reader,

We hope you enjoyed reading *Absaroka War Chief*. Please take a moment to leave a review, even if it's a short one. Your opinion is important to us.

Discover more books by Bryan Ney at https://www. nextchapter.pub/authors/bryan-ney

Want to know when one of our books is free or discounted? Join the newsletter at http:// eepurl.com/bqqB3H

Best regards,

Bryan Ney and the Next Chapter Team

ABOUT THE AUTHOR

Bryan Ney is a semi-retired physician and a writer of historical fiction that is anchored in the truths of the time and place about which he writes. His first work, "Calamity Jane: How the West Began" was a finalist in several contests. He lives in Malibu, California, and when not writing or practicing the new art of telemedicine, he can be found on the tennis court, where win or lose, having is having fun.

Absaroka War Chief
ISBN: 978-4-86747-032-9
Mass Market

Published by
Next Chapter
1-60-20 Minami-Otsuka
170-0005 Toshima-Ku, Tokyo
+818035793528

13th May 2021